the SCENT of LILACS

With gratitude & Warm wishes

Giglio

ANTONIA GIGLIO

 FriesenPress

One Printers Way
Altona, MB R0G 0B0
Canada

www.friesenpress.com

Copyright © 2022 by Antonia Giglio
First Edition — 2022

All rights reserved.

No part of this publication may be reproduced in any form, or by any means, electronic or mechanical, including photocopying, recording, or any information browsing, storage, or retrieval system, without permission in writing from FriesenPress.

The Scent of Lilacs is a work of fiction. Content, names, characters, places, locales, incidents, events, protocols, assessments, businesses, companies, and depictions are the product of the author's imagination or are used fictitiously. Any resemblance to actual persons, living or dead, is entirely coincidental.

ISBN
978-1-03-914528-3 (Hardcover)
978-1-03-914527-6 (Paperback)
978-1-03-914529-0 (eBook)

Fiction, Thrillers, Domestic

Distributed to the trade by The Ingram Book Company

Acknowledgements

I am deeply grateful to Brian Henry whose class exercise gave rise to this novel and to Beverley Burgess Bell for her masterful, literary contributions.

Thank you to Maggie, Barb, Linda, Janis, and many others who helped along the way including: Dr. Maria Antoniou, Shilpa Mehta, Myles Anevich, and Andrea Spiteri-Giglio.

I dedicate The Scent of Lilacs to:
    My husband ………………………………………………my rock
    My children ………………………………… pillars of support
    My grandchildren…. that they may believe and never give up

Prologue

Marla pivoted, shifting her feet to study herself.

Ooh, not bad.

Becky stood back and gazed at her. "I can't believe your mother picked out this dress. It's so ... classy." Her hand flew to her mouth. "Sorry, Marla. I wasn't trying to be offensive." She glanced around. "Hope she didn't hear me."

"No need to apologize. The whole town fears the one and only Claire Slater. To be honest, I expected something bohemian. Thought I'd have to fight over it in the bridal salon. But the diviner nailed it."

Did her mother know her better than she knew herself?

Not only had Claire chosen her dress, she had also, in a way, selected Adam for her as well. 'Someday you'll thank me' echoed in Marla's head.

Today was that day. And so far, seamless. Her dress, a vision. The lilacs and magnolias, full and fragrant. Rhythmic, warm breezes rustled the tender foliage of the trees. Tulle and satin decorated the chairs and pergola. Claire had conspired with the gods for perfection.

The sound of heels clicked up the hall and came to a stop at her door. "Darling, you look exquisite. Adam's going to flip."

"Darling, sweetheart, baby..." Typical terms of endearment spoken by normal mothers—not hers. Yet they'd been spilling out all morning.

Professor Shapiro's lecture on narcissism sprang to mind. Marla thought she'd had her mother pegged according to the DSM checklist years ago. Had she been wrong?

"Honey, the photographer is here." The words trilled.

Marla waited until Becky had fastened the last pin to the coils of her hair. After giving her head a little shake to ensure the veil was snug, she twisted her neck around.

The doorway casing framed her mother like a Master's painting—Titian or Rembrandt. Bewitching eyes, playful dimples, flawless skin, and a massive crown of curly, brown hair that even today, she'd chosen not to tame. Her mother would have exuded beauty in burlap, but in silk palazzo pants and a backless, ivory halter with rows of ruffles and lace? Aphrodite herself, held no comparison.

"Wow! You look amazing, Mom!"

No, she hadn't been wrong.

Her mother couldn't even let her be the star on her own wedding day.

Marla swallowed the lump that had formed in her throat. Never mind, she was about to marry the man who loved her from the moment he saw her. The man who patiently waited for her to love him back.

A siren interrupted the clicking of the camera.

Marla hurried to the living room window. Was that Adam's old Mustang at the end of the motorcade? She thought he'd gotten rid of that car after high school. Bittersweet memories came crashing back. Why had he dredged up the past today? She shrugged. Adam would never hurt her on purpose.

The cruiser door opened. Her dad stepped out in his formal police uniform—minus the hat, of course. Years had faded the freckles and shock of red hair, giving Chief Bill Slater a softer, ginger look. But he was still Marla's handsome, distinguished dad.

Adam leaped out in tandem, wearing a light grey tuxedo with a sprig of white lilacs on his lapel. He pulled her heartstrings.

The two most important men in her life now stood side by side, their shoulders touching. Her dad's face beamed, but Adam looked as if he was about to face a firing squad. Something metallic caught her eye. Marla's stomach churned as the men strode forward and out of view. She rushed to the back window and caught sight of them approaching the pergola to the roar of laughter. If only she could have heard their remarks as her dad ceremoniously removed the shackles from their wrists. With a loud *whew,* Adam wiped his forehead and grinned at the cheering guests.

What a performance!

Zing—the violin.

One at a time, the bridesmaids filed out.

With Becky holding her train, Marla centred herself and followed on cue.

Her dad stood watching her, chest puffed, chin quivering.

But what was this, her mother, too?

Her whole life, she'd been hearing, "She's all yours, Bill." Now, here was Claire, owning up to her role as a mother. The role she'd rejected. The role that had led to the creation of the 'pinky promise'.

Her parents took their places on either side of her and began the march up the aisle.

Adam's eyes were fixed on her. She'd never seen him look so sweet and vulnerable. He was a man of many faces and she loved them all. No regrets.

Her mother squeezed Marla's gloved hand and stepped aside while her father lifted her veil and kissed her tenderly before moving into position beside Adam.

Reverend Vera Volk looked out at the guests with open arms. "Welcome. It is my honour to officiate at the wedding of Marla Beth Slater and Adam Gareth Mansfield."

Turning her eyes towards her and Adam, the reverend continued, "Marla and Adam, you have invited your friends and relatives to witness the affirmation of your love."

Good start. Secular and simple.

"Through the years, your relationship will change and grow. There will be good times, along with sadness, conflict, and challenge. Embracing all gives marriage meaning and richness. We are here today to share in the ceremony that marks the begin of your journey together as man and wife. Who stands with this couple in marriage?"

Her parents responded, "We do."

A hush fell over the garden.

"Marla and Adam, I invite you to speak your promises to one another," said the minister.

She met Adam's eyes as he pinned the lilacs from his lapel onto her dress, then held her hands. This was the magical moment she'd been waiting for. The moment no one existed but the two of them.

"Marla," said Adam, "these lilacs are a symbol of the day I fell in love with you. Their fragrance will always fill our home to remind us that we belong together. I love you. Put your trust in me. I will protect you, care for you, and treasure you."

Jeez, that sounded a little possessive. What happened to their discussion about respect? Did 'treasure' mean the same to Adam? Of course, it did.

A single, happy tear rolled down her cheek as she made her promise to him.

The exchange of rings was next, but not until the reverend had infused them with a litany of meanings that led to excerpts on marriage from Kahlil Gibran's The Prophet, passages she and Adam had seriously debated. Luckily none of their disagreements had amounted to deal breakers.

Marla glanced down at the precious golden band encircling her finger and was so deep in thought, she barely heard the pronunciation "... You are now husband and wife. You may now ..."

Still in the rapture of Adam's kiss, Claire's booming voice shattered the silence.

Light My Fire? No! They'd requested Johnny Mathis's *Chances Are* and had even provided the DJ with the CD.

Marla gave Adam a sheepish grin. There'd be no stopping Claire today. Or it seemed ... anyone.

A flurry of activity followed as Marla's dad loosened his tie and sprinted towards the pergola where his guitar had been conveniently leaning.

Reverend Volk shoved a pen and the marriage certificate in front of Marla and Adam, then tore off her robe and pulled a trumpet from a case beside the podium. Putting the horn to her lips, the silver-haired lady blew into it and yelled, "Let's get this party started!"

Marla had been so busy finishing university papers she'd left the ceremony details to her mother. It was clear now. Vera Volk was no traditional clergywoman. She had to be the legendary musician-turned-minister from her parents' commune days.

The minute they signed the certificate, Adam grabbed Marla's hand and steered her towards the makeshift dance floor. "Kick off your shoes, Red." He unbuttoned his tuxedo jacket and flung it onto … a *hedge*?

Who was this man? Hadn't she married a perfectionist?

By the time Marla removed her veil and heels, Adam had broken into a sexy solo-move. He beckoned her closer. "Come on, you heard the minister. Let's party."

"Yes, Master," she laughed.

Adam reached for her hand and with a snap, twirled her against him. "Woman," he whispered in her ear, "you're mine."

Chapter 1

After twelve years of marriage, Marla could predict her husband's every quirky habit and gesture. She heard his catlike feet approach and pictured him standing by the bedroom door, the thumb of one hand pressed on the metal latch while the other hand held his fine leather shoes. He'd no doubt glance down the long corridor towards the girls' rooms and grin with pride.

Three, two, one—the door opened. No matter how quiet he tried to be, his presence resonated. The lock clicked into place. Marla kept her body rigid under the covers, her mind alert to his every move. The thick pile of the carpet cushioned the sound of his shoes being lightly dropped in the corner. One piece at a time, his tailored suit and accessories fell to the floor. The small night-light by her bedside illuminated the haphazard trail. The designer belt, silk tie, and monogramed shirt falling willy-nilly, as if they didn't matter.

Out of character for a punctilious man defined by order and neatness. Had to be the champagne.

Through eyes narrowed to slits, she watched Adam sneak towards the bed. A momentary pretense of caution gave way to a carefree lunge as his strong, lean, naked body hit the mattress with a muffled thud. She flipped onto her side, hoping to deter his interest, but his arm still came to rest on her. He pulled her close, yawned, and settled into heavy breathing, the kind that signified comfort and, she hoped, a quick sinking into oblivion.

She softened her breath, tongue, and the backs of her eyes. Anything to conjure sleep. But her usual go-to gimmicks eluded her.

Just let him sleep.

Why provoke him?

Why?

Perfume. He reeked of the white floral scent. Orange blossom and jasmine. Faint, alluring, and powerful. Worn by a woman with the same qualities, a woman who knew what she wanted and how to get it.

Why couldn't she be that woman?

To hell with regret. She'd already put up with too much from him. "Adam," she hissed. "Get off me. Same perfume I smelled on you twelve years ago. Why'd you bother to come home at all?"

No answer.

Her annoyance grew. "How drunk are you? Don't you even remember Paris? You told me you'd been to a perfume factory as part of the art tour," she said, more or less talking to herself to make sense of things. "I even thought, 'We're newlyweds, and for God's sake, I'm pregnant'." She choked back a sob. "I trusted you, Adam."

Still nothing.

"Then I thought maybe having a cop father made me too suspicious or my hormones were out of whack. I made myself believe you." She let out another angry, "Hah! ... My instincts were right. You're a bastard." Tears stung as they rolled down her cheeks.

Adam gave a loud sigh, then tightened his hold before lifting his leg over her hips.

There, she'd done it again! She'd rattled his cage and unleashed the lion.

"Don't ever call me a bastard," he snarled. His voice was laced with acid as he grabbed a strand of her hair. "If you want to talk about loose mothers, you *do* remember how *you* came into this world?" He paused. "By the way, I don't appreciate you taking on your mother's bad habits. Cussing doesn't suit you."

Fear should have made Marla sensible, but her anger made that impossible. "I wish I'd picked up more from her. My mother would have kicked your ass out by now."

Adam let out a quiet chuckle. "I really don't understand why you're complaining about perfume on opening night of an art show. You know my patrons are sensual creatures and it's my job to schmooze. Just remember who keeps you in this house, the kids in private school, and you in runway style."

The next pull sent a sharp pain through her scalp. Marla tried to pry his hand away. "Stop it. That hurts. You know I never cared about material things. I'm from Stoneham. Department stores have always been good enough for me. You're the one who cares about image. And let's not forget who chased whom. Too bad I was dumb enough to fall for you. Why are you doing this to our marriage ... to me? You said you loved me."

Seconds ticked without a word, but she could feel the tremor in his chest grow.

"You're right, Marla. I did pick you." He flung her onto her back and straddled her, then grasped both her wrists and dug his nails in. Tucking one arm under her, he pressed his body down and raised her other arm above her head, his knuckles finding her forehead first.

She struggled and almost called out to Sarah and Susan, but the thought of the girls witnessing this scene made her clamp her jaws shut.

"I needed you. You were part of my plan." Adam spat the words into her face, then rubbed his chest against her breasts.

"No, Adam. Please," she groaned.

"Honey, you've been waiting all night for me. It would be rude of me to neglect you."

Marla's spine quivered.

With his free hand, he ran a finger down her face, outlining each feature, then smelled her neck and kissed her shoulders.

Why had she called him a bastard? Hadn't she learned her lesson?

Never, ever use the word 'bastard'. Never, ever reference his mother.

Adam's strength and size seemed to double as he reached for the straps of her nightgown.

She bit her tongue, closed her eyes, and drifted away—deeply, deeply, until the undulating rhythms of Chopin's *Nocturne* coursed through her like musical morphine. She phased in and out till the dullness took hold.

A breeze woke Marla. Adam must have opened the window a crack. How goddamned thoughtful. The air felt cool and soothing, but only temporarily.

Please, just let me die.

She opened her eyes and squinted as the sunlight streamed in. Her stomach flipped.

What was that smell?

She looked around and followed its trail to the night table beside her. Coffee and a croissant. Marla swallowed the bile. This was no act of contrition or a *mea culpa* from Adam. Simply a reminder that all was well in his world.

She massaged her temples, piecing together the events of the early hours. No wonder Adam had picked a house with the master in a separate wing. It had nothing to do with romance.

She felt a stab of pain from the bite marks and looked down at her naked body. Slowly, she used her elbows to shimmy herself up to a sitting position then glanced around. All traces of the torn nightgown had disappeared. Evidence gone.

Noise from the hall made her ears perk up. Could he still be home? She waited. A few more steps. No, just Pepper. Adam had left the bedroom door open enough for her dog to slip through.

You'd think he had a conscience.

The duvet rustled as Pepper brushed against it.

"Come here, boy." Marla winced as she pulled her black-spotted spaniel onto the bed. "You my friend, sport?" She scratched his neck.

It felt good to speak her secrets out loud, even to a dog. "Did Daddy take the girls to school? You bet he did. Wouldn't want to deal with nasty explanations. Such a perfect father figure."

Humiliation and anger bubbled up in her. Marla grabbed the nearby telephone, punched in 9-1, then dropped the phone back in its cradle and covered her face. "I can't, Pepper. Sarah and Susan need me. By God, we'll show him, though. We'll survive, won't we?"

As she dragged herself out of bed, her hand flew to her mouth remembering the dinner party she'd planned for that night. *Cancel?* No, too late. She couldn't disappoint the girls. Good thing she'd already prepped. "Come on, Pepper. I'll put the pot on simmer, then take you outside. You can chase squirrels while I pretend to make this bloody house look balanced and beautiful." She felt anything but.

After washing down a painkiller, Marla pulled her brimmed hat down over her forehead, adjusted the gardening gloves to cover the scratches on her wrist, and stepped into the sunlight.

The wheelbarrow, laden with dirt and plantings, looked heavy. Her mother had always tapped her chest whenever she felt weak. Could there be something scientific to it, a trigger for adrenaline? Hocus-pocus or not, today she'd welcome any relief.

Whether through renewed energy or resolve, Marla gripped the handles of the barrow, lifted, and pushed. Momentum helped glide it along the walkway towards the two enormous urns that flanked the entry. She set the wheelbarrow down close to them, filled the pots with dirt, and began arranging the begonias, coleus, and ivy in patterns of colour and height for best effect. As much as she tried to lose herself in the task, her demons surfaced. Why was she still in this house? Did she think she could salvage her marriage?

From the day she and Adam had met, Marla had questioned everything about him. His arrogance, his advances, and even why he'd come to Stoneham alone in the first place. Turned out he was an orphan. No one would make up a story like that. Sure, she'd empathized, but it had been Jimmy's idea to befriend him. "Adam's smart, worldly—someone to learn from."

Her mother had also been a fan. "New boy is hot—those high cheekbones, raven black hair, and rare blue eyes you could drown in. He belongs on a magazine cover, and ... he's so sophisticated, Marla. You should get to know him."

Where the heck had Claire even met him?

"Oh, I ran into him with Jimmy one day. I hear you have a lot in common. Art, music, books."

"So?"

"He's got a hell of a flashy car, too. That boy's in a class of his own. Grab his coattails, girl. I didn't give up my dreams for you to end up with that boring Snow kid."

Marla had fumed at her mother's insults. "Jimmy's not boring. Besides, Adam's not my type—too intense, too bossy, too shrewd. He makes me uncomfortable."

"Speaking of too much, what about you? You afraid you can't catch a prize like Adam?"

Guess what, Mom? I did catch him—or should I say, he caught me!

Marla rubbed the bruise on her forehead as a breeze swept across her face.

Prize, my ass!

She stopped digging and kicked the wheelbarrow.

She'd spent the rest of '89 and the greater part of first year of university avoiding Adam and thought she'd succeeded in making a full break. But like a viper, the guy had simply been waiting for Jimmy to be convicted and sentenced before he struck. Hell, Adam was even the one to break the news to her.

If only Marla hadn't been blinded by Adam's kind, caring ways after Jimmy was out of her life. If only Adam hadn't been so entertaining, so clever, and so sincere sounding. If only she hadn't embraced the new Adam and trusted him enough to marry him! The only good thing that had come out of it was their two beautiful children.

Their marriage had started so well. Why had Adam changed? Hadn't she been a good wife? She gave up a career in teaching to stay home with the twins. She'd done everything he'd asked.

Her mother's curse when she left Stoneham had always haunted her. "Let's see what you accomplish." Had it become a self-fulfilling prophesy?

Marla heard Pepper bark and looked up to see him stalking a bird on a low perch. *Was she that bird?* Her lip quivered as she picked up the trowel and stabbed the earth a few times. Tears cascaded down her face.

When had her marriage started falling apart? Was it in Paris? Or had Adam always been evil?

Answers, Marla ... you need answers.

Those early memories continued to filter back. Such a brilliant mind, you could rarely trip him up on anything. He'd gone to elitist schools and travelled the world, but instead of being grateful for the lavish lifestyle he'd been given, he showed nothing but disdain for his father and stepmother. "Winnie and Hunter," he'd called them, and he'd spit or do something crass after mentioning them.

Should she have tried to find out more about him in early days? Why? *Adam* wasn't her boyfriend. *Jimmy*, the sandy-haired boy with the baseball cap, was. Besides, her father, the chief of police, checked out the new boy in town and found no red flags.

Marla sighed. All those memories should have set off alarm bells.

Yes, Adam had been broken all along.

But then ... so had she.

She pressed the last seedling in place, folded her arms across her chest and stood back to examine the pots. "What do you think, Pepper?"

He yipped and circled her legs.

"Thank you. Guess I can be proud of something."

Adam had actually encouraged her to take the landscaping design course. Marla had been surprised and excited to think she could finally sink her teeth into a paying job while working from home. "As long as it doesn't interfere with us," he'd warned. She'd learned later that the 'hobby' was intended to keep her busy while he globetrotted with Miss Perfume Lady.

Hobby, my foot! She'd make landscaping her ticket to freedom!

Marla threw the trowel into the wheelbarrow and studied the pots one more time. Thoughts of Adam had taken the shine off them. She gave a shrill whistle, gathered the rest of her tools, and entered the house through the mud room. Pepper lumbered behind her.

The pungent smell of the earth was replaced with the fragrance of the slowly simmering cassoulet. Pepper's tongue lolled. "I'll feed you as soon as we clean up, sport. Then we're going to make this a night to remember."

As Pepper tucked into his bowl, Marla tied on an apron and stirred the pot. "This was the first meal I made for Daddy when we came back from Paris." She smacked the wooden spoon on the counter. "Hope he chokes on it."

"You know, it was a rascal puppy like you I wanted for my birthday, not cooking school. 'If you're a good girl' Daddy said. Well, I must have been damn good, eh, Pepper? As soon as we got back from Paris, there you were."

The timer pinged on the stove. After placing the pot on the warming tray and clearing away the dirty dishes, she scanned the kitchen and dining room. Perfect. She'd even hung the tea towel her friend Evelyn had given her as a joke. *Remember, as far as anyone knows, we're a nice normal family.*

The warm spray of water from the showerhead soothed her, but not for long. She wrapped a towel around herself then sank onto the chair in front of her dressing table and combed her hair back.

"Who are you?"

A blank face stared back.

"Why are you so weak? Stand up to that jerk." The longer Marla stared, the more visible the bruise became.

The woman in the mirror lowered her eyes.

Was the weakling asking herself why she'd instigated trouble and called Adam a bastard? Had she dared to accuse him of something she couldn't prove? Or had she blamed it on the booze again?

Huge tears flooded down the face in the mirror.

"You're a pathetic wimp!" shouted Marla. She wiped her eyes, opened her makeup case, and smeared on concealer. The bathroom door had been left open enough to catch a glimpse of the Polaroid camera on the wardrobe. It was a relic, but film could still be had for it.

Instead of capturing spontaneous shots of the girls, maybe it was time to highlight the resident artist's handiwork. But where would she hide the photos? Bathroom might be too obvious. She scooted to her closet. There, that old shoe box. Adam would never think to touch anything that grungy.

Had she replaced the last film she'd used? She opened the dresser drawer. *Yes.* She tore open a fresh roll and inserted it into the camera, then lifted the lid of the trash can to throw away the crumpled packaging. Something purple stuck out. She trembled as she pulled out her torn nightie and placed it in the shoe box—her new 'Memento Box'.

A chill went up her spine.

Trust? She didn't have much lately.

She locked the bedroom and bathroom doors and scrubbed off the concealer. Gathering her courage, she snapped photos of herself, using the mirror for her back.

Might not be today, and maybe not tomorrow. But someday, Adam Mansfield, there will be a reckoning.

Marla reapplied her makeup with a heavier hand this time. She slipped into a pale-green blouse that flattered her complexion and lifted the crisp collar up and under her hair. After covering her wrist with a wide silver bangle and brushing her bangs to the bruised side of her forehead, she stepped into the hall just as the front door opened.

Susan raced to meet her. Her daughter pursed her red-coated lips and batted her eyelashes before striking a complicated grand jeté.

"Susan, you're so weird," said her sister, who'd already wiped her face clean and let down her hair.

"No," said Marla, "just dramatic, like Dad and Grandma Claire. It's a gift. Excellent pose, Susan, but make-up is for rehearsals and recitals only."

"Aw, come on, Mom. That's not fair. How come you're wearing so much?"

Good. They'd noticed the makeup, not the bruise. But what if they did later ... in front of the guests? No. She couldn't bear the shame.

Sarah's eyes had been fixed on Marla since she came in, probably even spotted her flinch when she'd adjusted the bangle.

"Well, it's because I tripped over the shovel while I was gardening. Nothing for you to worry about. Where's your father?"

Susan giggled. "Oh ... he's just getting something out of the trunk for ..."

"Shush, Susan." Sarah shook her head. "Jeez, Mom, you should hire a gardener for the heavy stuff." Sarah, older than Susan by sixteen minutes, had always been the astute, sensitive one. Following her sister up the stairs, Sarah's phone lit up. "Looks like my school won the basketball game." She turned her head. "Mom, do you think I can play a real sport next year instead of dance?"

"Dance is a very strenuous, athletic discipline, Sarah. But if you'd prefer a change, I'll discuss it with your dad."

Her daughter smiled and took the rest of the steps two at a time.

Everyone deserved to follow their dreams. Marla had had to fight for piano lessons as a kid.

Her mother had balked. "I'm a rocker. I don't want to hear that boring, classical shit."

But her dad had sided with Marla and negotiated a deal. The large, walk-in pantry with the oval window would be converted into a piano room in exchange for a living room walk-out to the garden, plus a huge sliding-door pantry in the kitchen to hold the herbs for Claire's witchery.

After combing the local barns, Marla and her dad had come across a Canadian-made, *Mason and Risch* upright with original ivories and great inner workings. It fit the space perfectly. She'd practiced hard and made it to Grade Eight Conservatory.

Well, almost.

Marla flinched remembering the fiasco with the baseball bat. Her beloved piano was no more, and along with it went the music lessons.

So, yes, she'd lobby for Sarah, certain Adam would agree. No battles on the parenting front.

The door opened. "Hi, darling."

Adam's cheerful voice sent a shudder through her.

She turned to see him place a beautifully wrapped parcel on the hall console. "For you. It's the same colour and style as the one you have—the one you wore last night."

"You mean *had*, don't you?"

Marla grabbed the parcel and threw it on the floor. "Take it to Boston."

Adam smiled and whispered, "Come on. You know I didn't mean any harm. I love you."

She bristled and backed up. But not in time.

He trapped her against the wall, then fingered her bangs. "You always find a way of looking so beautiful. That's my girl."

Her impulse to smash him was replaced with a bark. "The Lams will be here in fifteen minutes. You've got just enough time to get rid of that box and open a bottle of wine. Make it French." She sounded braver than she felt.

"Whatever you say." His voice so sweet it would have made the devil, a believer. "I'll put this on your chair for later." Adam winked, picked up the package, and stopped in his tracks to savour the aroma wafting from the kitchen. "Mm. Smells like … Paris."

"Glad you remember the good old days."

Change is coming.

Chapter 2

The minute the doorbell rang, the girls thundered down the stairs. Pepper growled and stayed at a distance.

"What kind of guard dog are you?" said Adam, prodding Pepper forward with his slipper.

"He's old and a little cautious these days, Adam. Come on, boy."

Amy, Evelyn and Philip's daughter, entered with a joyful, "Hi everybody! Look what I brought."

Luring Pepper with a treat, the girls ran off squealing.

"Hi," said Philip. "My daughter sure loves that dog. She's starting to get big ideas of her own."

Evelyn gave Marla a warm hug but bumped against her forehead and made her wince.

"Sorry. Are you hurt?" said Evelyn before turning to stare at Adam. "What did you do to her?"

"Not guilty," he said, raising both arms in the air. "I haven't been home all day."

Marla grinned and wrapped her arms around Adam's neck. "My garden shovel was the evil one. Not Mr. Perfect."

Her guests laughed.

Why wouldn't they?

The floral display outside her door offered the perfect excuse. And as for Adam—a better family man there never was. He'd always demonstrated a fierce love for her and the kids. Kind, fair, charming, mannerly, funny. That's how people saw him. Mr. Perfect.

"Speaking of shovels, great job on the arrangements, Marla," said Philip. "Our house could use a little help."

"I promise," said Marla. She winked at Evelyn, knowing she'd already scheduled it on her calendar.

"Don't expect it this weekend, honey," said Evelyn. "Adam's going to Boston. Marla has to visit her parents. And I've got a full house."

"Right, I forgot," said Philip, handing Adam a bottle of *pinot noir* and sniffing as they walked into the kitchen. "Smells great in here. You're a lucky man, Adam."

"Not luck. It's that *Cordon Bleu* training. Thanks for the wine. Perfect pairing for tonight."

Philip put an arm around his wife and kissed her cheek. "Why don't we take a little trip to Paris for some of that ... training?"

"Are you complaining about my cooking, dear? Look at your belt," said Evelyn. "It's in the first notch."

Marla felt a pang of jealousy.

It had started out all love and romance for her and Adam. Sure, having kids had changed the dynamics, but wasn't that what Adam had wanted? She bit her lip. "You don't have to go to Cordon Bleu," she said. "Anyone who can read and measure, can cook. You should try it, Adam."

"Ah, but don't you remember the silver spoon—butlers, servants?" He laughed as he poured the iced vodka into martini glasses.

"Wish I'd known that when I met you." Marla shook a finger at him before pulling a tray out of the oven

Adam caught her eyes. "Well technically, you did. Don't you remember I lived above a diner in high school? All I had to do was slip downstairs and order anything I wanted. I also had a friend who often invited me over for Sunday night, roast-chicken dinners."

How cavalier. Calling Jimmy, a friend?

Marla grabbed the nearby cleaver and, with a loud chop, sliced a lemon in half. "Whoops," she said, continuing to cut jagged teeth into the halves before placing them on a platter.

Evelyn raised an eyebrow. Marla knew she'd have some explaining to do later. It had always been easy to talk to her friend about her mother's issues—sick, needy, and still a tyrant. But tell her about Adam? No.

Marla passed the canapés. "Try these."

Evelyn bit into one. "Mm, oysters. Delicious."

The men doubled up, devoured both, and smacked their lips.

Raising his glass, Adam toasted her. "Marla, you're the best."

She could feel her face redden as she picked up the basket of hot rolls. "Okay, dinner's ready. Adam, please bring in the cassoulet."

After setting the heavy pot on the table, he lifted the lid and announced. "This is my wife's signature dish. It made me fall in love with her."

Sarah frowned. "Come on, Dad. You fell in love with her way before that."

"Truth is, it was love at first sight for me. Mom's the one who took her time."

Marla needed to change the subject before she said something she'd regret. "Speaking of cooking, let's hear about the upcoming science project, girls."

"I'll tell you about it," laughed Evelyn. "It's about three girls, two boys, and baking soda. Doesn't that sound like trouble? Good thing I'll be there to supervise."

"I'm sorry to miss that one," teased Adam. "Evelyn gets to have all the fun. And speaking of fun," he said as he jumped up, "who'd like more wine?" He pretended to top up the girls' milk glasses.

Too bad he was such a good father. Marla wanted to hate Adam for everything.

Chapter 3

Early the next morning, Marla woke up thinking about how well the previous evening had gone. Adam had helped with cleanup, and to continue the peace, she'd followed him up to the bedroom. The new lavender nightie sat draped over her chair. *Well, that didn't happen!* Adam had also agreed that *her* sleeping in the guest bedroom would be a good idea (so she wouldn't disturb him, she'd said). Making sure to lock the door behind her, she'd buried herself under the covers and prayed for sleep or the salvation of amnesia.

Feeling refreshed and energized, she gathered her things, and tiptoed to the kitchen with Pepper at her side. Based on her dog's prior behaviour on long drives, she administered a mild sedative with his morning meal and scooted him to the backyard. Meanwhile she arranged her suitcase and a large picnic basket in the SUV before coaxing him into his cage. No incidents. And no sign of Adam.

What a relief.

First stop, the drive-thru. As she waited for her order, she unclipped and tousled her hair, letting it fall loosely over her shoulders. It gave her a sense of easing into wholeness. She slid a CD into the player. Mm—coffee and Carly Simon. Perfect road partners.

Carly's smooth voice sang the opening bars to *You're So Vain*.

Was there ever a more appropriate song for that miserable husband of hers?

Thank you for hooking me onto Carly all those years ago, Mom.

Marla laughed and sang along. If only her mother could hear her now, she'd be rolling her eyes in disgust because, of course, only Claire could sing.

As Marla hummed the next tune, she thought about transience, freedom, power. Qualities Carly sang about. Qualities Marla craved.

She'd gone through both tracks of the CD by the time she came to her exit and couldn't remember the last time she'd felt this relaxed. Maybe this weekend would be good medicine for her. A dose of tranquility.

The back roads that wound through the scenic hills of the escarpment had always been her favourite leg of the journey. As Marla slowed down to enjoy the landscape, her mother clouded her thoughts again. Such a terrible role model. But no one deserved to be sick.

"Type two diabetes," Marla's dad had told her a few years ago. "Dr. Beatty says it's a silent disease. Your mother may have had it for a while without knowing. But Marla, you don't need to worry, the doctor says it's not a death sentence. She just needs something to kick-start those beta cells along with a lifestyle change: diet, exercise, and no smoking or alcohol."

They'd both locked eyes and tried not to laugh. "Well, we know Mom takes her own remedies seriously, but do you think she'll follow Dr. Beatty's recommendations?"

The answer became clear. At age fifty-six, her mother's latest test results showed peripheral neuropathy, nerve damage, and poor circulation.

Had the disease progressed even more since then? Why else would her mother have summoned Marla to Stoneham this weekend? "Marla, I know you have a big city life, but would it hurt for you to help us out once in a while? I'm a sick lady—or don't you care?"

"Of course, I care." Marla's pinky finger had twitched.

"The doctor says I need to buy orthopedic shoes. Me, Marla, can you believe it? I'm not going to that foot clinic with anyone but you."

"I'll have to juggle my schedule. Let me see what I can do." The request couldn't have come at a worse time. She'd just landed her first big job and her boss expected her to come up with suggestions at the preliminary brainstorming session on Tuesday. If that wasn't enough, Adam had meetings in Boston and the girls' science assignment required adult supervision.

Thank God for Evelyn. What a good friend. Marla wished she had the nerve to share her secrets with her. But, no, it would only complicate Sarah and Susan's lives.

The road began to narrow as Marla approached the next hamlet that boasted some unique crafters, including a tin house with silly garden gnomes dotting an herb garden. The hamlet had always been a great place for afternoon drives for the locals, but interest had spread and had turned it into a tourist attraction. Good thing she'd left early. Two more kilometres of straight road and then ....

Marla took a deep breath as soon as she saw it. The quaint stone bridge that straddled Clarence Creek—the link to her past. It was a *Monet's Garden* moment, so beautiful in every season.

How could she pass it up?

She swung onto the gravel path at the foot of the bridge and stopped the car. Mindful of Pepper sleeping, she slipped out and walked to the middle of the bridge. The years had worn smooth grooves into the concrete coping, creating natural armrests. She leaned down on them and inhaled as she looked out at the tall grasses, budding shrubs, and overhanging willows that moved to the warm spring breezes and yes ... the swans were back.

Picture perfect!

To the right, the swinging rope from her childhood still hung there, and hidden between the ancient oaks, only Marla's eyes could see a corner of the matted grass where she and Jimmy had lain on that old tartan blanket of his. The days of just daydreaming together had given way to Jimmy's poetry readings during that last year of high school. Of course, Adam had instigated that change. Well, he wasn't wrong. She did love to hear the soft, velvety words tumbling from Jimmy's mouth. Blake and Byron had spoken to her then—what a romantic fool she'd been.

She stiffened, steeling her eyes away from the other side of the bridge. The side that faced the cemetery where a stone angel hovered over the grave of that poor soul who'd died in that horrific fire.

Marla's glance shifted past the bridge to the rooftops of mostly Victorian, two-storey homes that poked above a clump of maples. Stoneham, the town she'd grown up in.

Her dad had always been a decent man and believed in moderation. But her mother ... well, Marla could write a book about her. *The Bible According to Claire*. Moderation had never been in that book. Marla didn't want to seem cruel, but had hard living caught up with Claire? Was it payback? How sick would her mother look?

Marla heard a little bark and retraced her steps. Oh, the love-hate of this place. It was a struggle each time she returned to Stoneham, but as long as her parents lived here, she'd never escape her connection.

"Why don't you come to the city and leave the bad memories behind?" Marla had often said, with sincere hopes to have her parents near her.

Her dad's answer never changed. "No, Marla. Good or bad, memories belong to us no matter where we live. The Slater family has been here for decades. It's an Orange community, based on old world friendships, loyalties, and values. This is our home."

That same topic had oddly come up on a rare occasion when Jimmy had been invited for dinner. "I don't blame any of your generation for deciding to move away," her dad had said. "But young people should give it serious thought first. Stoneham needs professionals. Doctors, lawyers, teachers, engineers. Finish your education, then you can both decide."

Her mother had grunted, but her dad must have visualized them as a pair.

Yeah, right. If only.

The Scent of Lilacs

Pepper stirred again. "We're almost there, buddy. Don't forget, if Grandma snarls, you have to protect me, okay?" From the rearview, she saw him cock his head to one side as if to give that serious consideration.

Reaching the town line, Marla passed the wooden visitor sign. "Welcome to Stoneham, Population Five Thousand Three Hundred". The bulletin board read "Legion Oldies Dance, April 1st Get your tickets"; "Last week of Little League Baseball registration at arena." The list seemed endless. Her dad was right. Community spirit was alive and well.

She recalled the simple pleasures of her childhood. Horseback riding, carnivals, and county fairs. Teenage years had given way to swinging off the rope into Clarence Creek, go-carting, and drive-ins which included smoking and an occasional mickey of gin. But that's about as far as it went. Her mother's voice reverberated in her ear, "Don't try to pull anything on me, young lady. I know *all* the tricks."

No kidding.

The little risks *she'd* taken could never compare to her parents' exploits. They'd experienced the big, bad world and vowed to keep their daughter sheltered from it. Pretty much succeeded, too.

With the guilt of ruining her mother's life and the pinky promise to put her mother first, Marla had developed a brutal conscience. Respecting rules had kept her out of trouble all right, but weren't young people supposed to make mistakes and experience growing pains in order to make good choices in life?

You thought you'd protected me by passing me into Adam's good hands, but you blew it, Mom and Dad. Look at my life now!

Marla shrugged and turned the next corner. Glover Street—tidy rows of privet hedges and white-washed picket fences, testaments to the community's original need for order after the war. Her eyes darted from garden to garden. Today's delicate spring growth of forsythia and lilacs would give way to majestic English gardens by end of summer. Hollyhocks, foxgloves, morning glories. And there stood that big, old alder tree. Were the J and M in a heart still visible? Hard to pass these intimate places without feeling loss, even after all this time, and even though Marla had no business thinking about them.

"It wasn't meant to be, Pepper. My old boyfriend turned out to be a monster. Why did this happen?" She gritted her teeth. "Adam happened. Monsters are everywhere."

The unfolding foliage of the Slater's red maple came into view. It marked the front lawn of the only ranch bungalow on the street—another of Claire's thump-prints.

Her dad's arms were around her the minute she pulled into the driveway. "I missed you so much, kiddo."

"I missed you too, Dad. Mind letting Pepper out."

Her dad chatted as he lifted the cage and released the gate. "So, how was the drive?"

"Carly kept me company."

"Oh boy, woman power. Is that what I have to look forward to this weekend?"

"Mom and I will try to go easy on you."

"Sure, you will," he snickered.

Good humour, good company, good start.

"How are my beautiful granddaughters?"

"Really busy. They send buckets of hugs and kisses." She rolled her weekend bag up the path and stopped to smell the French lilac bush. She'd never seen it so out of control. Was her mother that sick? Ah, there she was, behind the screen door, arms akimbo. Marla braced herself.

"Taking your sweet time, aren't you?" said her mother, opening the door a crack. "Where's Pepper?"

Marla pointed.

"Come here, boy," said Claire. "You know who loves you."

The word 'love' slipped from her mother's lips so easily to a dog—but to her? Never.

Pepper poked his head out from behind a bush, padded up the steps, and licked her mother's face as she bent down to pet him.

Traitor!

The Scent of Lilacs

Marla snapped off a small branch of lilacs.

Her mother glared at her. "I asked your father to do the pruning, not you. Give me that."

Marla waved the branch under her mother's nose and stole a peck on her cheek. Age and illness had a way of fading people, and she'd expected to see that today. But Claire was an elusive woman, able to distort the mind's eye. A woman who refused to give up or grow old, regardless of how precarious her diagnosis might be.

Marla fingered a strand of her mother's hair. "The highlights look great, and the shoulder length really accentuates your cheekbones."

"Well, Ruth thought it was about time."

"Turn around. I want to see your outfit."

Her mother had cleverly hidden what had to be a thickening waistline under a turquoise shift. Lapping up the attention, Claire put her hand on her hip and turned one knee inward, the side split exposing her leg.

"Wow. Still showing them off?"

"Why not? You might be younger, but you sure haven't learned anything from me. Hope you have more than track pants in that suitcase."

Marla glanced down at herself. "Well, I have been driving for two hours. What did you want me to wear?" Sick or not, it was still bossy old Claire. "Don't worry, Mom. I'll wear the prom dress to town."

Could she hold out till Sunday?

"Mom, remind me. What time's the appointment at the foot clinic?"

"No appointment. I cancelled. Dr. Beatty will never get me to wear those shoes, Marla. He'll have me using a cane next."

"What? I thought this visit was urgent."

"Oh, so you need a reason to visit? Keeping me company, going shopping, having lunch at the new bistro aren't enough for you? What kind of child have I raised?"

Newsflash! You didn't. My father did.

"Sorry, I didn't know," whispered her dad, as he followed carrying the goody-basket Marla had brought.

"Never mind. I'm here now."

"I'm so glad you are, honey." He peeked under the checkered napkin and sniffed. "Mm. What did you bring this time?"

Marla lowered her voice. "Shh. Little things to go with some really great wine. Costello blue cheese, peppercorn *pâté*, olive tapenade, cornbread, Tuscan meatloaf …"

"There she goes again, Bill," said her mother. "I told you, she'd flaunt it. It's not meatloaf. It's 'Tuscan' meatloaf. She's a Mansfield, Bill."

Damn Claire's selective bat-ears.

Marla set her suitcase in the bedroom and returned with a book. "Evelyn sent this for you, Mom. It's called *Tea Ceremonies in China*. She said to tell you the book is sure to make your husband docile."

"I've got news for you. You may need that for Adam, but I don't need tea ceremonies to make *my* husband docile."

Her dad shook his head. "Oh great. Now your mother's reduced me to a mush-ball. Good thing the guys at the station aren't here. I'm the regional police chief, for Christ's sake. I'm supposed to give orders, not take them."

"Oh, I think they've already discovered the truth, Dad." Marla smiled, placed Pepper's bed in the corner, then left the room to freshen up.

The smell of coffee summoned her back. Her mother sat thumbing through Evelyn's book and looked up at her. "How are my girls?"

Her girls?

"They're excited about their upcoming ballet recital. They want to call you with the details themselves—it's on June the twelfth. Save the date. And Dad, it's a fancy night. You'll need a suit and tie." Marla pointed to his plaid shirt with the sleeves rolled up to expose his 'War Not' tattoo—a remnant of his early passive-protest days.

"Last time I looked, there was a men's store in town. Might have to dust off the racks, but I'll find something."

"Don't worry, Marla. We'll be there." Her mother waggled her shoulders. "My granddaughters have my DNA. I just have to teach them how to get noticed."

"Give Marla some credit, Claire. She's doing a great job with Sarah and Susan, *her way*. You've had your turn."

"Yeah, and look how that turned out. Maybe those girls will actually listen to me."

Marla balled her fists. "God, where's the wine?"

Her dad raised his little finger. "Take it easy, Marla. Your mom's just teasing."

"Don't let me start. And why do you always defend her?"

There goes the peaceful weekend she'd hoped for—already.

Her mother smiled, picked up her cup, and took a victory sip. "You really should switch to my herbal teas—with ice. You need to chill."

"How's Adam?" interrupted her dad. "Still keeping the Brinks trucks busy?"

Oh, if she could only blurt out her secrets right now, but no ... not the time or place. "Mom was right about Adam's business side. He's quite successful. In Boston this weekend for an exhibition by new artists. Thought he might come across some pieces to mix into his big Chicago auction in June. It's actually the same weekend as the recital, so he won't be attending the performance with us."

"Too bad. Won't the girls miss him?" said her mother.

"Of course, but they understand this auction is the event of the year for their dad. He'll get to see the video later. Besides, the twins have me to sort out their melodramas." Marla leaned back in the chair. "How'd you make it through all my stuff when I was growing up, Mom?"

Had she opened a can of worms?

"Oh, I ignored a lot and kept my eyes and ears open. And ... in those days, I could drink."

Now, that was closer to the truth.

"Well, too bad I won't get to see Adam at the recital," continued her mother. "I loved that man the minute I met him. He's so handsome and knows just how to treat a lady."

Knows how to treat a lady?

Marla choked on her coffee and grabbed a napkin.

"Are you okay?" said her dad, ruffling her hair as he'd done in childhood.

She flinched.

"What's wrong?"

"It's nothing. Just being my usual clumsy self."

How could her dad, a police chief, not recognize the clues? Should she say something? No, she wouldn't … she couldn't.

He lifted her bangs. "That's nasty. Seriously, what did you do?"

"Garden shovels make terrible dance partners."

Her mother shook her head. "Could only happen to you."

Marla tossed her mug into the dishwasher. "Okay, time to go. Stores must be open by now. I'll do a quick change and meet you at the door, Mom."

Moments later, Marla reappeared in a breezy cotton dress and a jean jacket.

"That's better," said her mother.

Approval—wow—amazing!

Flinging a turquoise pashmina over her shoulder, her mother strutted towards the door, several rows of silver bangles chiming her presence.

Holy smokes! For shoe shopping? What a diva!

Chapter 4

Marla kept her mouth shut as they drove into town, but she couldn't help making a comment when they got to Main Street. "I see Stoneham's finally letting in the big coffee franchises. Is Mabel's Bakery still open?"

"Of course. Not everybody's in a hurry, you know." They reached a storefront with an artistic display of modern footwear. "There, that's it. Pull over, Marla." Her mother scanned the shelves from the doorway and headed straight towards a pair of black, strappy wedges. "Look at these beauties."

"Mom," Marla snapped, "I thought you were supposed to buy sensible shoes? More like these ones." She picked up two pairs of flats and jangled them.

"Fine, I'll try them, just to get you and doc off my back. But I'm not leaving without those wedges." After trying on the flats and nodding, it didn't surprise Marla that the strappy ones would end up on her mother's feet. "Ooh, now that's more like it," said Claire, pulling aside the slit of her dress and pointing her toe again. "They match my outfit. Think I'll just keep them on."

"They look great, but shouldn't you break them in first?"

"Bistro's only a couple of blocks away. I'll be fine."

"Here, let me at least carry the bags."

Sure enough, each window they passed made her mother stop. "Smell that fudge." "Patty's knitting me an afghan like that one." "They make those cheeseboards right here in town."

The image of her dad waving his pinky finger flashed before her. Marla sighed, then wiped her forehead with the back of her hand. "Hey, Mom," she said, "it's too warm to walk. I'll get the car and we'll drive over. Besides, if the food's bad, we can make a quick getaway."

Her mother shook her head. "God forbid, you get a little sweaty. And you just can't accept that Stoneham might have a decent restaurant, can you? Nothing's ever good enough for you."

Marla almost dropped the bags. "Where *is* this place, Mother?"

"They built on the empty lot beside the hardware store. There's parking in the back."

Marla bolted to her car, collected her mother at the curb, and switched on the Carly CD hoping for strength transference—to help her erase her mother's brutal comments.

As she turned the corner and neared the bistro, something caught her eye. She swerved.

It couldn't be! Had to be mistake!

"Watch it," yelled Claire.

"Sorry, I got distracted." Marla straightened the wheel and pulled up in front of Peter's Pan and Grill.

Her mother was quick to open her door. "Go ahead and park. I'll let myself out."

A blessing. Stuck to the seat, Marla was confused and too embarrassed to mention what she saw for fear her mother would declare her delusional.

By the time Marla walked into the restaurant, her mother had the *maître d'* smitten. She knew her mother's power over men and this one was like putty in her hands.

"Meet my daughter, Marla."

The *maître d'* graciously clicked his heels and bowed. "Peter at your service. What a pleasure to have two of the most beautiful women in the world come into my establishment. Are they filming a movie in town?"

Oh boy. Here comes the old 'big city music career' routine.

"Thank you. I used to sing in Toronto years ago. Now I sing at Brody's on Saturday nights. Why don't you drop in some time? But make sure you eat here first. The only good thing at Brody's is the beer ... and the music, of course."

"I knew it," said Peter. "Please follow me." He escorted them to a table in the centre of the room.

The seat of power!

Her mother thanked him with a flutter of her eyelashes and a grin that grew her dimples to canyons, before scanning the room and waving to a couple of ladies at a corner table. For sure, this sighting of 'Claire the Celebrity' would soon hit the Stoneham grapevine.

Lunch would have been pleasant, should have been pleasant.

"My steak's delicious, Marla. How's your snapper?"

"You were right, Mom. The food here is excellent." And she meant it. "It's just that ..." she rubbed her temples.

"You need peppermint tea," her mother interrupted. "It'll help settle you."

Still on edge after the second cup, Marla glanced out the window, repeatedly crossing and uncrossing her legs.

Even her mother seemed to be percolating now, smoothing her dress with one hand and lightly tapping her spoon on the saucer with the other. "All right, Marla, I saw the truck too."

Her jaw dropped. "What?"

"You might as well know. Jimmy was released from jail. He showed up here a few weeks ago. Milt must have kept the truck for him. I had no idea we'd see it today."

Marla could hardly breathe.

"Milt's been alone since Pauline left. I heard he invited Jimmy to live with him. Loves that kid like a son and believes his nephew is innocent. Guess Jimmy works next door. If I'd known, I swear we'd never have come here. Wait till I speak to your father."

Marla's stomach heaved as she tried to filter through her mother's ramblings. Anger replaced the nausea. "You and Dad knew Jimmy was out of jail and didn't think to tell me? Jesus, Mom. He had a life sentence. Why is he out already?"

"Keep your voice down." Her mother peeked over her shoulder before she continued. "I was told they gave him early parole for good behaviour. Anyway, he's not your concern."

"I'm a grown woman. How dare you decide what I should or shouldn't know or care about?"

Her mother shifted in her chair and touched Marla's arm. "You're here for the weekend. Don't worry about Jimmy."

She nudged Claire's hand aside. "What do you mean? We had a history together. He was my soulmate, like you and Dad."

"Just a minute. Don't compare yourself to me. I'm a successful—"

"Don't make this about you again. Jimmy went to jail. The fire and everyone in this town took away his life. Now there's talk he's innocent?" Marla clenched her teeth. "You, Dad, Adam, the courts, everyone kept me from him. I would have known the truth if I could have just talked to him."

"Think you knew more than the courts? The evidence was there, Marla, right down to the zip ties and the lady's pearl necklace they found in his truck. Besides, aren't you glad Adam stuck by you?"

"I didn't want Adam. You said go for the rich boy. And I did. Not because he was rich, but because Jimmy was gone. Adam finally made me feel alive—as if I mattered and belonged. I trusted him." She gulped down some water and reached into her purse for her cell phone. "I have to talk to Dad."

Her mother caught her hand. "Let it go. Everyone's watching."

"Jimmy is next door and you want me to let it go? I still need answers."

"Don't upset your dad. We've had such a lovely time together. And anyway, what would you say to Jimmy right now? 'Sorry I didn't believe you?' 'Sorry I married someone else?' It's too late, Marla. Get a grip."

Dammit, she had a point. What would she say? She'd have to consider her words carefully before facing Jimmy.

It was an cighteen-degree day outside and although the restaurant was comfortably warm, Marla felt like ice. She grabbed her mother's pashmina and wrapped it tightly around her shoulders.

The Scent of Lilacs

Marla barreled into her parents' driveway and came to an abrupt halt.

Her dad dropped the hose. "Hey, take it easy."

"She knows, Bill. We saw Jimmy's truck at the hardware store." Her mother had already clambered out of the car. "You could have tipped me off."

"So, Dad, when were you planning to tell me about Jimmy? I'm so tired of being treated like a child. I let you two control me in the past. It won't happen again."

Her dad stood rubbing his forehead.

Marla gathered the bags and stomped into the house.

"Forget tea," said Marla, as she watched her mother fill the kettle. Instead, Marla uncorked the Argentinian malbec and grabbed a tumbler from the cupboard.

Her mother smirked. "Well, well. And you used to criticize me for that."

"You guys have driven me to it. But rest assured, Mother, I'll never be like you." Marla filled the glass to the brim and guzzled some down like water. "Okay, Dad. I'm listening."

He sat down and let out a deep sigh. "From what I've heard, Jimmy had a lot of support and turned out to be a model inmate. The fact that his family believed he was innocent and visited him constantly, made all the difference to his time in jail."

"I tried to visit too," said Marla, taking another gulp of her tonic. "There was a big X beside my name—he wouldn't see *me*."

"When he got out last year, Jimmy went to live up north with a family from the John Howard Society. Then a few weeks ago, he showed up at his uncle's. He's here to prove he's innocent. People in town think it takes a lot of courage to come back. They're willing to give him a chance."

"What are you saying, Dad? Has he been in jail for nothing? Is there proof?"

Her mother smacked the table. "I'm sick of keeping quiet, Bill. She says she's a big girl, so tell her. It's about time she knew everything."

"I've told her everything she needs to know, Claire. Just because Jimmy's out doesn't mean they've overturned his conviction. There's no new evidence."

Marla met his eyes. "Have you seen him?"

"He reports to a parole officer at my station every week. Word is that he's a calm, quiet, reserved man."

Her lip quivered. The calm, quiet, reserved parts of that image were clearly a given—but a man? She still thought of Jimmy in the past. Athletic body, so cute with his long, blonde, straggly hair and sparkling baby-blue eyes. A happy guy with a baseball cap. Always polite, kind, and unpretentious. She tried to fast forward his life. Of course, he was a man now. She tried to picture him.

What did he look like? Had he hardened? Would she recognize him? Would he even recognize her?

Her father broke into her thoughts. "Guess he's working to pay for a lawyer. Wants to reopen his case."

"Has ... has he ... asked about me?" she stammered.

"I have no way of knowing that."

"I don't get it. If Jimmy knew he was innocent, why couldn't he have just told me? I would have believed him and waited. Why did he cut me loose?"

"There, now you've got it," said her mother. "He didn't *want* you to waste your life waiting for him. Can't you understand that?"

"That was my decision to make. I hate him for not giving me a choice." Marla's heart ached. She dropped her head on the table and closed her eyes.

"Marla?"

She looked up. "What is it, Mom? Spit it out."

"It's something your father and I should have told you long ago. It won't make any difference now, but at least my conscience will be clear."

A conscience? Did her mother have one?

"No, Claire. Don't do this," her father cautioned.

"Haven't you both done enough damage to me? What now?"

"Look here, Marla." Her mother rubbed her forehead. "When Jimmy was arrested, your father was having a hard time with the Snow family. If we'd told you then, your relationship with Jimmy may have ended, and the consequences of the fire probably wouldn't have affected you. I wish we had."

"You're not making any sense."

"It's my fault Pauline left Milt. I was playing around with her husband. Your father was always working and I hated being alone. Milt offered me a ride on his motorcycle. I needed excitement. It just happened."

Marla closed her eyes. The scene in the living room so many years ago became vivid. Jimmy had made his usual nightly call. He'd mentioned her mother being at Milt's when he and Adam had shown up to show off Adam's new Mustang. Since Milt was a licenced mechanic as well as a farmer, Marla hadn't given it a second thought. After hanging up the telephone, she'd poked her head into the room where her parents had been relaxing. "Mom, what was wrong with your car today? Jimmy saw you at his uncle's."

She remembered how her father had immediately removed his reading glasses, sat up ramrod-straight, and clenched his teeth. "Now there's a good question, honey."

Her mother had stared back at him coolly and said, "Brakes," then turned to Marla with cut-eyes, "don't you have a piano to practice?"

For a long time after that night, the air in the house had been toxic.

How could she have been so naïve?

"Alone? Mom, you had me," Marla shouted. "I've never been enough for you, have I? Not good enough. Not pretty enough. Not exciting enough. I'm just your average, invisible person going nowhere. That's what you've always been afraid of, isn't it? That's why you didn't like Jimmy. Too ordinary. You thought your daughter would be a nobody. Or worse—better than you—and you couldn't have that, could you?"

"Come on, Marla. Try to understand."

"Oh, I understand you very well." She glanced at her father. "It's *him* I don't get. Why didn't he protect me from you?"

"You're out of line, Marla. You can disrespect me all you want, but not your father. You have no idea how much he fought for you. For me. For this family."

"And you rewarded him with adultery? How could he just forgive you?"

Wait! What had she just said? Wasn't she forgiving Adam? Ignoring his indiscretions? Protecting him? How could she admonish her parents? What about her own secrets? Secrets she couldn't talk about.

"Milt made me feel alive for a while," said her mother. "But your father and I are still together and we don't need you to judge us."

Her dad stared at Pepper sleeping in the corner, then sighed and said, "I knew your mother's appetite for excitement. Being adventurous was okay when we were young and free. But at home in Stoneham? It wasn't easy. I couldn't just throw away all the memories. I couldn't break up our family." He walked over and put his arms around her mother's neck. "Your mother is my life."

Marla had swallowed that bitter pill, too.

As he reached out to draw Marla into the hug, she squirmed and pushed him away.

"Okay," he blurted. "Milt and I had it out. But when you live in a small town, word gets around unless you bury it. That's what I did. I didn't want to make more trouble for the Snow family. When it came to Jimmy's crime, the courts took care of it, not me. I don't know why your mother chose to tell you this story, but it's for her sake more than yours, and it has no connection to the fire and murder."

Marla felt numb. "How do I know that spite or vengeance didn't interfere with the investigation? Jimmy's innocence depended on the truth."

"Come on, the investigators were from out of town. The evidence was stacked against him. There were no other suspects. Milt and I had our differences, but it had nothing to do with Jimmy's conviction. It's over, Marla. Get on with your life."

"Over? Then how do you explain why he's in Stoneham trying to clear his name? What am I supposed to do, pretend nothing happened?" Marla looked at her mother. "And you, how do you live with yourself?"

Her dad raised a finger. "Our mistakes are between *us*. We're human. We forgive. I'm sure you've made some mistakes yourself."

Marla shuddered.

"Marla, your father and I have done everything for you. We sacrificed our own ambitions when you came along. We gave you a good life. Enjoy it."

Marla jumped up and grabbed the leash from the nearby hook. "Come on, Pepper." She couldn't get away fast enough. Her thoughts shifted to her own family.

What if her parents knew Adam, really knew Adam? The one they approved of? What if they knew the truth about the real life of their daughter? Would they still have encouraged her to trade boring for rich?

When she re-entered the house, her parents were still deep in conversation at the kitchen table.

"Mom, Dad, this is all too much. I'm heading out in the morning. I'd brought my laptop to work on a project, but it's better if I do it at home."

"Marla," said her dad, "your mother and I never expected the weekend to turn out like this. We should have warned you about Jimmy being released and that you might run into him. But in our defence, we were only trying to protect you."

Her mother slapped the table. "Hold on, Bill. Why should we have warned her? What difference should Jimmy make after all these years?"

"Because I have a right to know about the people who've touched my life," shouted Marla.

Her mother pushed her chair back. "Maybe it is better you go home. Focus on your new job, and more importantly, your daughters. Not Jimmy."

To get through dinner, Marla consumed more liquid than food.

Would she sleep tonight?

Not a chance.

All she could think of was her mother's affair with Milt Snow, Jimmy back in Stoneham trying to clear his name, and this whole weekend debacle.

Although news of the infidelity had been an eye-opener, Marla knew Jimmy's conviction had nothing to do with her dad. It couldn't. The provincial police had handled the case, not the local police. Her mother had simply come clean to explain *why* they had wanted her to break up with Jimmy. Family ties with the Snows would have been far too uncomfortable for everyone.

As she tossed and turned, she forced herself to replay the events of the terrible fire of '89.

Was there anything else Marla could have added to help Jimmy's case? Had she told the detectives everything she knew at the time? Yes.

Someday ... someday she'd face Jimmy. Once and for all, she'd find out whether he really didn't love her, or whether her parents had been right—that he'd released her to live a normal life without him.

After a restless night, the clock finally struck six. Marla readied herself and carried her suitcase to the kitchen.

Her dad peered over the morning paper. "I've fed and walked Pepper and there's buttered raisin bread and fruit for you."

"Thanks, Dad. I'll take it to go."

"Already wrapped. Sorry, your mom didn't feel well enough to see you off. I told her to stay in bed."

"Good call. I really worry about her health. But with you at her side, she couldn't be in better hands. Please keep me in the loop."

"I will. Too bad we upset you this weekend. If I'd realized how Jimmy's return to Stoneham would have affected you, I'd have handled it differently."

"I know, Dad."

"Wisdom takes a lifetime."

As she crossed Clarence Creek, there was no stopping this time. No Carly tunes. No feeling of lightness. The falling rain reflected her mood. Her mother, father, Adam, Jimmy—so much pain.

Get it together. It's up to you to change! Be strong! Make Sarah and Susan strong.

Marla was soon chanting the words out loud, like a mantra.

The rain had stopped by the time she pulled into her garage and unloaded. Pepper waddled over to his familiar spot in the family room. She'd thought about calling Evelyn and shortening the girls' weekend stay-over. But no, she'd use the extra time to work on the landscape drawings. Besides, the girls wouldn't thank her.

The next morning, she greeted Evelyn with a grateful hug. The twins and Amy came running.

She could tell by the giggling that Susan was bursting to tell her something.

"All right, out with it."

"Mom, boys are so weird. They think they know more than we do about hard stuff like science."

"Yeah, Mrs. Mansfield," said Amy, her nose in the air. "Howie didn't measure properly. He put too much baking soda in the beaker."

"It was everywhere," continued Susan. "I tried to tell them about your baking rule, 'measure exactly or expect the unexpected'. Too bad they didn't listen."

Evelyn crossed her arms. "But we fixed them, didn't we? They had to clean up and reset the experiment."

"And *I* measured the next time," said Amy.

"Mom," said Sarah, "we learned a lot about the experiment, but I think we learned more about show-offs. They're bound to make mistakes."

Marla smiled as she drove them to school. Sarah already knew what had been taking Marla years to figure out.

The rest of the day was spent at her desk. This first assignment had to be timely and impressive. Her future depended on it. She used every last minute reviewing her work before doing the school run at the end of the day. All she could manage for dinner would be pre-cooked, store-bought chicken. The phone rang during cleanup.

Susan answered. "Hi, Dad, where are you?"

Marla slipped into the den, lifted the extension, and listened.

"Hi," said Adam. "How are my best girls?"

"Dad, we're your only girls. When are you coming home? We have so much to tell you."

"Sweetie, I'm stuck in Boston. I won't be home for a couple of days. Can you get your mom for me?"

"I'm here. Hang up, Susan." Marla waited to be sure she and Adam were alone before speaking. "I heard everything, Adam. Don't really appreciate you going off plan, though. I have things to do as well."

"Hey, you're a little curt, aren't you? How about giving your husband a proper greeting?"

"Enough, Adam. You knew I had a meeting scheduled for tomorrow." She sounded petulant, even to her own ears.

"Who cares? You damn well know you don't have to work. All I need is for you to be beautiful, take care of the girls, and be nice to me."

Marla closed her eyes. Under her breath she repeated, "I'm strong, I'll survive, I'll be free."

The mantra and the distance between them gave her courage. "Of course, Adam. What was I thinking? As long as you get what you want, nothing else matters."

"You've known that from the beginning, Red. Anyway, did you have a good weekend?"

The blue truck. She had to tell him.

"Adam, I have to talk to you about Jimmy."

Click ...

She held the receiver in the air.

One mention of Jimmy and the guy hangs up.

Chapter 5

Adam frowned at the glamorous blonde behind him. The pressure of her hand on his, had forced the call to end.

"That wasn't very nice of you, Gillian."

"Well, maybe this is," she said in her lusty Boston accent before grazing his neck with her tongue.

Mm—this woman had her ways.

She loosened his tie. "Remember Paris?"

How could he forget their first encounter?

"Shame on you, Gillian. So irreverent in front of van Gogh at the Musée d'Orsay. And me, an innocent young pup minding his own business."

"Nothing innocent about you that day, my love. What did you expect, standing in front of *Starry Night?* Such a romantic painting of lovers on the Rhone. And you, looking all sexy in that tight black turtleneck tucked into your schoolboy trousers. Couldn't wait to get you alone."

Adam pulled her hips closer. "And I couldn't wait to get my hands around you—your *neck*, to be exact." He remembered pausing to be sure he'd read her cues correctly. Hadn't wanted to end up facing the French *gendarme*. But the minute Gillian had asked about his cologne, he knew what was on her mind. It had nothing to do with art.

"Must admit, you surprised me—tying the scarf so tightly I couldn't breathe. Risky move."

He could feel her tingling as she said it.

"You surprised me too, madam. Gifting me Dorian Conte's painting. I've had nothing but good luck ever since."

"Don't ever forget it."

The thought of combining pleasure with exploiting Gillian's wealth through her husband's shipping firm, made Adam's heart race. He undid his shirt buttons and drew in a breath.

He knew she preferred French perfume, but tonight she'd worn the lilac just for him. It set him off. He snatched a handful of blonde hair and forced her down onto the plush carpet.

Gillian groaned. "Adam, you're such a bully. I adore you. Does your wife appreciate you like I do?"

"Remember the rule, Gillian. Stay out of my family life and I'll stay out of yours. All we want is fun and money. So, let's not ruin our perfect, symbiotic relationship."

If only Marla knew the truth. The smell of jasmine and orange blossom she'd questioned him about that day in Paris, *had* belonged to another woman. Not residue scent from the perfume factory he'd lied about. Well, he'd warned Marla he'd be out making business contacts while she attended *Le Cordon Bleu*. Good thing she had no idea what he'd meant. Wasn't quite sure of it himself, until the motherlode had landed in his lap.

Too bad Gillian had hung up on his wife tonight. No problem. He'd come up with a good excuse later. Didn't want to hear about Jimmy the Loser, anyway.

"Had enough?" he said, giving Gillian a sharp slap on her smooth backside before kissing her shoulder.

"I hate to leave, but I must. If I miss the opera with Gregory tonight, he'll be very disappointed. He might even punish me and not write that cheque tomorrow." She grinned. "The one to sponsor your auction?"

A sobering thought.

"You win." He lit a cigarette and lingered by the sofa, watching Gillian squeeze into her dress. The standards of perfection and flare of this older woman amazed him.

She reached for the door handle and tossed her cashmere sweater over her shoulder. Her hair followed in a single, sultry movement. "Tomorrow at one-thirty," she said, turning to lock eyes with him. "Contact our new prospect, darling. Use all your charm and the skills I taught you. This artist will be a big one." Gillian's voice trailed as she stepped into the hall.

Adam lifted his pants off the floor, rummaged through the pockets, and fingered a business card.

When he woke the next morning, he itched to call the number on the card, but waited until nine o'clock as a matter of proper business protocol.

"Is this Nalin Crawford?"

"Uh huh." The voice on the other end sounded groggy.

"This is Adam Mansfield. I was at the Young Hands—Warm Art Show last night. Your work really impressed me."

Her voice perked up. "Thank you."

"I'm putting together an auction in June in Chicago. I believe your work would be a good fit. But I'm flying out tomorrow, so my schedule's a little tight. Are you, by any chance, available to discuss some business this morning? I'd be happy to drop by your studio."

He heard a squeaking noise that sounded like a bed.

"I ... I could be ready for ten-thirty."

"Excellent. Looking forward to meeting you."

Since Nalin's studio was only a short cab ride from his hotel, Adam ordered breakfast and made a quick call to Marla.

No answer.

Where in hell could she be this early in the morning?

He checked his calendar. Evelyn's turn to drive the kids. Something about this Bob guy had begun to stink.

On the fourth ring, Marla picked up. "Uh huh?"

"Christ, is that any way to answer the phone?"

"Oh, so you hang up on me, but when I'm busy, I should drop... "

"Sorry. You're right," he interrupted. "I only hung up because I had an important call coming in. Anyway, great news, honey. I'll be home in time to pick up the girls from school tomorrow."

"My hero."

Adam ignored the chill in her voice.

"At least I'll make the meeting with my boss and won't have to beg Evelyn for another favour."

Bob, again.

"By the way, I'll be home late. Takeout, okay?"

"Fine. I really miss you, Red. Can't wait to get my arms around you and run my fingers through your beautiful hair." He paused, "By the way, what was that about Jimmy?"

"Never mind. It can wait."

"I thought so. Bye for now." He chuckled to himself. Nothing about Jimmy could ever be that important.

Adam's breakfast arrived. He ate hungrily and drowned it with a pot of coffee, then checked his watch again. Nine forty-five.

What would he wear to impress a twenty-year-old?

Gillian had always said, 'the tighter the better'. That meant t-shirt and jeans. Except he'd worn a black blazer and a bowtie to the art gala. Nalin might recognize him if he threw the blazer on with the jeans and … it would give him contemporary sophistication—make him irresistible.

Adam pictured his cool-looking father—shoulder-length, wavy, salt-and-pepper hair, slicked back to mimic the male students on campus. Always stylish and up-to-date, the professor had worn desert boots, flannel pants, and turtleneck sweaters. The tweed jackets with suede patches on the elbows had set him apart and had given him an uppity, equestrian look. Heads had turned everywhere they went together, including those of young, female students. His father had snagged his mother that way and … that rich old bag he'd finally married.

Yup, dressing for success had been one of Dad's more useful lessons.

Before he left his hotel room, Adam glanced in the mirror.

How could anyone say no to him?

The cabbie drove him through the artsy section of Boston and stopped in front of a live-work unit with unstructured curtains, a pot of geraniums, and a hand-painted sign that simply read "Nalin

The Scent of Lilacs

Crawford—Artist." He stepped up to the door, placed his right hand in his pant pocket, and lifted his left hand to touch the buzzer.

Whoops, the wedding band.

He slipped it off, pressed the button, and waited. The young woman opened the door on the first ring.

Holy crap!

He almost tripped over the threshold. Where had the demure, unassuming, mousy bit from the previous night gone? What a chameleon! Trendy, ripped jeans, and ... was she braless under that paint shirt? Black hair tied in braided pigtails and a smattering of freckles decorated her velvety, light-brown face. Made her look so whimsical, so exotic.

At the gallery, Adam and Gillian had spotted the outstanding qualities of Nalin's artwork the minute they'd walked in. Gillian had immediately cautioned him to ignore Nalin and her paintings so the other vultures wouldn't suspect their interest. They'd had a quick glass of champagne and left.

Through Gillian's masterclasses, Adam had learned exactly how to get what he wanted. She'd often corrected him. "What *we* want, darling. Never underestimate me. You know I can make or break you." Her threats bugged him. He'd dump the old broad someday. But for now, Gillian's contacts were paramount.

No doubt about Nalin's potential value to their business, though. His goal was to dazzle this young woman today. With his looks and skills, he'd gain her attention and ... her contract.

However, what he hadn't expected was for a goddess to appear from behind this door. It doubled his pleasure.

"Hello, Miss Crawford." Adam smiled as he handed her his business card.

"Hey, I remember seeing you at the show last night. You had on a bowtie and you were with a blonde lady, right?"

He smoothed his lapel. "Ah yes, the bowtie. Works every time. The blonde lady was Gillian, my business associate."

"Come on in, and please call me Nalin. There were so many people at the show, it was impossible to meet everyone. Besides, I think you two left early. Can I call you Adam?"

In his experience, chatterboxes were usually nervous. Had *he* caused it?

"Yes, of course. Please call me Adam. You're right, though. Gillian and I had to leave early for another event, but we talked about your work all night."

"Wow, that's so nice. It was my first big show." Nalin squinted and tilted her head sideways as if taking a mental snapshot of his face, then methodically moved her eyes down his body.

He cleared his throat.

She slid her hands into her jeans and shifted her feet. "Sorry for staring. Visualizing is such a bad habit of mine."

"No need to apologize. Your imagination is the reason I'm here."

"I was just about to make tea. Would you like some?"

"Yes. Thank you."

A meow came from a corner of the room. Adam turned to look. A large, grey tabby took a few steps forward and stopped to eye him before inching towards him.

Was this cat onto him?

Finally close enough, the cat circled, sniffed, and batted its tail against the bottom of his trousers. "Cats are always drawn to me." He chuckled, placing his hands behind his back and balling his fists.

"I'll let you two get acquainted while I get the tea organized."

Good thing Nalin had slipped out of sight for a moment.

Damn cat—brought back memories he thought he'd buried along with that bitch's calico after it showed up to leer at him while he'd been banished to his room to 'think about it'. What the fuck would a fourteen-year-old know about bric-à-brac? And, so what if he'd dropped a stupid painted jar and the arm had come off a naked dude?

Adam's face turned rigid as the memories flashed before him.

He'd wanted to vomit as his dough-breasted stepmother (Winnie, his father had called the 'stuffy') nearly fainted when she saw the broken pieces of her precious artifacts in that mausoleum of a mansion. His old man had gotten so mad, he'd sent Adam to his room and spent a half-hour lecturing him on respect.

Well, he'd fixed Winnie and her goddamned cat. Same supercilious attitude as her owner, prancing in and out of his room like some lucky lady. He'd waited till just the right moment, then used every ounce of his strength to slam the door shut. By the time his dad, stepmother, and the butler had reached his bedroom, Shalott was laying lifeless in a pool of blood on one side. Her elegant, fluffy tail on the other.

Nothing Adam hated more than cats. And now he had to play nice with Nalin's just to make a buck. "Well, aren't you a beauty?" he said, crouching down to scratch under its chin just as the young woman came back carrying a tray.

"I see you're fond of cats, Adam."

"I know exactly what they like. My stepmother had three of them. What's her name?" he said, watching the cat shake her tail, then amble away. "It is a she, isn't it?"

Nalin nodded and laughed as she placed the tray on a slice of highly polished tree trunk that served as a table. "Alta. She truly is haughty and arrogant, but she's good company."

Adam checked his watch. Although time was ticking, he had no intention of rushing this divine creature.

He scanned the room, a mixture of industrial and organic. "I can see why you chose this space," he said. "It's great." The breakfast island with three wooden stools separated the kitchen from the rest of the large, open area that boasted a sixteen-foot-high workroom and lounge. Unlit but well-used candles dotted the room. The curtains had been opened. Rainbows danced on walls as the sun scattered light through the crystal drops that dangled from the windows. The room felt ethereal.

But more to Adam's amazement and satisfaction, paintings were everywhere. "You're prolific. I'm glad I came to your studio."

An abstract triptych in vibrant fuchsia, green, and yellow acrylic caught his eyes. The thick single line pulled you in and weaved from one panel to the next, then looped back and forced you to repeat the cycle over and over. "Imagine sitting in a waiting room and staring at this. Time would pass without notice. Very clever. I've already got a buyer in mind for this."

On the wall next to the floor-to-ceiling fireplace hung six unframed oils that were three-by-five feet each. "These figures are simple yet so dynamic. You've captured powerful emotions. Anguish, despair, loneliness, passion, elation."

Three easels held works in progress, and holy smokes, leaning against another wall were two stacks of finished canvases. Adam rubbed his hands together and began flipping through them.

"Jeez, when do you sleep?"

Nalin smiled. "I'm a loner. Art makes me happy." She pointed to a circular staircase that led to a loft with an open metal railing to below. "There's a few more upstairs."

He stepped closer and looked up. A king-size, low-framed bed, loosely covered with a white duvet, was visible along with numerous paintings on a brick wall.

Paintings in a bedroom?

"A private collection?" Adam said. "Can I see those as well? I'd hate to lose out on anything."

"Let's have tea while it's hot," Nalin said. As she handed him a mug, her bare foot caught the edge of the sisal rug. She teetered slightly and seized his arm to catch her balance.

With one hand, he managed to swoop up the mug without spillage and stabilized her with the other.

"Jeez, I'm so clumsy."

"No worries." He set the mug on the table and pretended to ignore the incident. "Your work is compelling. You know, Gillian sets direction for innovative art throughout the world. Although this business is about the enjoyment and beauty of art, for serious collectors, it's about sniffing out investment potential. Gillian is extremely eager to promote you. You could be the next big discovery." As he spoke, how could he not notice Nalin's plump lips and perky breasts under the paint shirt? Something about this enchantress had him in her grips.

"I'm so excited!" she said. "What do you propose?"

Adam adjusted his blazer and moved into the pitch he'd rehearsed. "First, consider the triptych sold. For the auction, we'll start on an exclusive consignment basis. I'll pick out eight paintings and give you a retainer of twenty-five thousand dollars. I'm prepared to write a cheque today."

"That much?"

"Here's how it works. There's a preview prior to the show. I'll establish an opening bid to protect the integrity of your work. The bidding will go up based on interest. You'll get thirty percent of the final selling price. How do you feel about that?"

"Whoa, is my work that good?" She twirled, then covered her mouth. "You must think I'm so childish."

Adam touched her arm. "Anyone who paints the way you do is no child. The intensity of your feelings is strong. You throw it all on the canvas and bare your soul. You're fearless. You're real."

Nalin lowered herself on a bean bag next to the table and pointed him to the other side.

Having always been surrounded by the finest furniture, Adam had never been around anyone with a bean bag as a seat before, not even Marla. "Squishy, isn't it?" he said, adjusting himself till he found a comfortable position before picking up his mug. "So, tell me what inspires you."

"Hmm ... okay. I was a little nervous when you first came in, but now I think you're really cool."

"Well, thanks. You are too."

Everything Adam had gleaned about Nalin so far, pointed to her free spirit. He'd take a chance. "Do you smoke, Nalin?" He wasn't surprised that she accepted a few tokes.

Relaxed, but more conscious of time now, he stood up and helped Nalin to her feet. "Let's walk around. I'll choose some paintings and arrange for my movers to come and pick them up."

With Gillian's guest list in mind, Adam and Nalin placed the selection at the front door.

"I'd start the paperwork," he said, shifting his eyes to the loft, "but I'd really appreciate seeing what's upstairs before we finalize."

She nodded. "Follow me."

When he reached the top rung, he froze as his gaze swept around the room. The brick wall had seven paintings, three smaller ones on either side of a four-by-six. They all had sexual context and screamed for attention. But the painting in the centre lured him. Adam stood spellbound in front of the profile of a young woman, head tilted back, black eyelashes fanned out like distorted bars of a jail cell. From luscious, crimson lips triple in size, red droplets spilled onto the stark-white canvas. Scarlet tears cascaded from the corner of her eye and the hair, black at the roots, shot out in flames.

"Are you sure Salvador Dali didn't paint this? I have to sit before I faint."

Without waiting for permission, he dropped onto the edge of the bed and continued to study the painting. The flames seemed to jump out to lick his skin. Adam broke into a sweat, his heart pumping wildly as he removed his jacket. "Excuse the bluntness, but I have to know. A self-portrait?"

She blushed.

He patted the bed. "Tell me what you were thinking when you painted this."

Nalin sat, but kept a little distance. "I never thought I'd have to explain these paintings to anyone. Guess that's why I keep them up here. I call this one *Human Inferno*."

That's exactly how Adam felt—as if he'd been ignited.

"I believe in freedom and kindness, Adam. Once we're cut off from our birthing mothers and arrive at the age of reason, we walk through life alone."

Astounding. His own mother had thought the same way. Nalin had poked his 'Achilles heel'. To keep himself from slipping away, Adam clenched his jaw and took a cleansing breath.

Nalin knit her brows as she watched him. "Are you okay?"

"Yes, don't stop. I'm intrigued."

"It makes me crazy when someone tries to trap or cage me in. It goes against our primal instincts, our basic human nature."

Not only was Nalin expressing the heart of her work, but confirming his existential way of life after his mother's death. He needed to hear more.

"My old boyfriend became possessive. We broke up." She pointed to *Human Inferno*. "The blood in this painting represents my inner thirst for life experience. The tears, the letting go of deep sorrow and lost love. Artists, dream of moments of inspiration and one-mindedness. We call it 'white light'. I felt it the day I painted this." She glanced away, then back. "I'm glad you like it, Adam. But it's not for sale."

"I'm baffled. How can someone your age, find that kind of enlightenment? Sorry to say this, but your boyfriend was too closed-minded and weak for you. You need a strong partner, a man with experience, someone who shares your philosophy." Adam locked eyes with her. "We're actually a lot alike."

Nalin's closeness made him want nothing more than to fling this mysterious woman down and experience the red-hot passion in this painting. But he forced himself to stillness, trusting the rhythms of time, space, and free-will to unfold.

"Tell me more about your artistic journey."

She leaned back on the bed. "Not much more to tell, except, as I already mentioned, I spend a lot of time alone. I just let myself go and ... a brush is never far from my hands."

Adam stretched out on his side, staring into Nalin's liquid black eyes. "You are so beautiful, but I can't put my finger on your heritage."

No longer worried about decorum, he traced the strong line of her jaw, waiting for her to flinch or push his hand away. She didn't.

"You're so gentle," she said.

Marla had thought that about him at first too.

He touched a braid.

"I was born in Arizona," said Nalin. "Hair, eyes, creativity, and spirit come from my mother, part Native American and part Mexican. My dad, on the other hand—according to legend, because that's all I know of him—was a meandering Scot. I'm sure you see what he gave me."

"Beautiful freckles," said Adam.

"If you say so." She grinned. "And, of course, he left me his noble name. My mother must have heard Crowfoot instead of Crawford."

He admired the way Nalin seemed to have bounced back from life's lessons. Not knowing her father must have been hard for her.

At least his own father had somewhat stuck around. Although The Professor had never cared enough about Adam to pass on his name.

He clenched his jaw.

No matter. In the end, no more lessons from good old Dad.

"That's quite the story," Adam said. "What a fantastic biography for your brochures. I can see it now." He used his finger to write across the sky, as he shouted, "A Star is Born! Nalin Crawford, Dali's Right Hand! You're going places, young lady."

"Is this really happening?" Nalin ran her hand down his torso.

He froze. "Are you sure?"

"You're so honest and sensitive. I trust you. Can I tell you a little secret?" Her lips tickled his ears. "I was attracted to you the minute you stepped into my studio, maybe even last night. And if Alta likes you, so do I." She lifted her head to look into his eyes.

No need to overpower this woman. What followed was just a natural, cosmic collision of two free spirits stoked by *Human Inferno*.

"You are what you paint, young lady."

They lay side by side until a glimpse at her bedside clock sent Adam's heart racing.

"Hell," he said. "I really get your artwork and ... I completely get you." He jumped up. "But unfortunately, I have to go ... so I can make you famous."

"Sounds great." She laughed and pointed him to the shower.

There was something so pure and familiar about Nalin, just like his mother. He vowed to keep her work and image sacred.

His only problem now? Time and Gillian.

Shortly after two, Adam glanced at the registry at the front desk of the hotel. Gillian had arrived. He hit the elevator button, slung his jacket over his shoulder, and caught a glimpse of his spiky, wet hair and untucked t-shirt in the lobby mirror.

Ooh, baby! Wait till you see what I accomplished this morning.

He pictured Gillian sitting in his suite, drinking Dom Pérignon and reading the current issue of *Forbes*. He knew she liked to peruse the pages of the who's who in the fortune world. Some of the articles often featured people in her own social circle.

Adam shivered when he walked in.

Icy.

Curled up on the sofa with her legs tucked under her, Gillian hadn't even bothered to look up at him.

"Hello, sweetheart," he said, kissing the top of her head.

She flicked the magazine aside and stared out the window.

"Why are you so cranky?" he said, flopping down beside her. "You, told me not to come back without Nalin's contract. Here it is." Adam tossed the papers on her lap. "You should see the paintings I picked for the show. Nalin's work is amazing and … so is she." He chuckled and reached over to lift Gillian's chin. "What's wrong?"

"You're a naughty boy," she growled and slapped his hand away. "You've kept me waiting. Nobody keeps me waiting." The remains of the champagne landed on his face.

Game changer.

Adam lifted his t-shirt up to wipe himself, then viciously dug his nails into her arm. "Is that right? And nobody disrespects me." He pulled Gillian off the sofa and threw her face down onto the carpet, pinning her with the weight of his body. Clenching his fist, he gave a blow to the back of her head then her shoulder blade, enough to knock the wind out of her. She gasped and screamed, "No, Uncle Charlie, please! I'll be good."

Screams would bring hotel security.

He slammed his hand over her mouth while repeatedly jabbing his knee into the small of her back, then turned her over. Gillian's eyes, stunned and frightened, said it all.

"So, Uncle Charlie, huh? Is that why you like pain and power? I can be your Uncle Charlie." Adam slid off his belt and swung it so that the leather smacked against her thigh. She groaned, then sobbed. He'd never seen her break down like this before. Their wild, sadistic playtime had always made Gillian appear bulletproof. What had changed today?

Guess you're not the toughest broad on the planet. Scared of losing me to a younger woman? Pathetic.

Hard to believe the woman who yielded so much power in the art circles of the world had a simple weakness—fear of growing old. Just like his stepmother.

Although it revolted him, Adam had to maintain Gillian's loyalty and stroke her ego for the time being. He drew her towards him, tenderly wrapping her in his arms until her body softened.

Perhaps he'd gone too far today. It didn't really matter. Gillian had always been a broken woman. Not like his sweet, beautiful Marla.

"Gillian, you're the one who told me to use all my charm and the skills you taught me. So, I did. We both got what we wanted. Why did you break the rules? No possessiveness. No emotions. Remember? Why did you make me hurt you?"

Tears trickled down Gillian's cheeks.

Adam scrunched his face in the imagined pain of a victim. "You need to control your temper if you ever want to see me again."

"I'm so sorry, Adam." She feathered her hand down his chest and closed her eyes.

Adam picked up the magazine after Gillian left. The cheque he needed for the auction was inside.

Chapter 6

Marla couldn't wait for her family to see her transformation.

Using her elbow, she pushed down on the latch to open the front door and then slammed it shut with her foot. "Hello," she sang out.

"Hi, Mom. We're starving," shouted Sarah from the family room.

Marla slid off her shoes. "Can someone come and take these off my hands?"

Sarah let out a loud shriek the minute she rounded the corner.

Susan, steps behind her sister, yelled, "Mom, your hair! What did you do?"

The girls flanked her and fingered the short, black wisps that had replaced her long, auburn tresses.

"Wow, it's so cool. You even smell different!" said Sarah.

From the end of the hall, Pepper bared his teeth.

Her own dog didn't recognize her.

Adam poked his head out of the den and grinned. "Well, look at you. Girls, take the bags and run for it while I check out this stranger. She could be dangerous."

The twins squealed with laughter and ran to the kitchen with the bags.

"I needed a change," Marla said, stopping to fluff her pixie-cut. "Besides, men like variety. Don't they, Adam?" She gave him a crooked smile. "What do you think? Guess you won't call me Red anymore."

He leaned against the door with his hands in his pockets and kept one eye trained on her.

Not dramatic enough, Adam? Okay.

She stepped close to him and buried her head in his neck. "Go ahead and smell. I know lilac is your favorite," she mocked. "This is English rose. Am I still as fresh and intoxicating as the day we met?"

"Always, Marla," he said, pulling one hand out of his pocket to tilt her chin upwards before kissing her.

The girls could hear their conversation from the kitchen and giggled. Adam guided her into the den and closed the door.

Marla squirmed, but couldn't break his hold. "Show's over, take your hands off me now."

"Your haircut, your swagger. I love the performance. What's this about? Revenge for hanging up the phone on you? Jealousy? Or are you angry because I delayed your meeting with … Bob? I already apologized for that." Adam bent to whisper in her ear. "It's a risky game you're playing, sweetheart. I hope you're prepared. And yes … of course I remember the first day we met. You were so indignant when I smelled your neck." He tried to imitate her. "'Monsieur Mansfield, you are most certainly an alpha.' And the way you walked. Wow …" He rocked her from side to side. "Your ponytail swinging—so haughty, so righteous. Such a little lady. I had to have you. Jimmy didn't stand a chance after that."

Marla felt herself weaken as Adam squeezed tighter.

"That's just the way it is, Marla. That's the way it always will be. No use fighting. I always get what I want."

She pushed again. "Let go."

"In a minute. When I phoned you from Boston, you said you had something important you wanted to discuss. Something about Jimmy?"

"He's back," she blurted.

"That's it? That's your big news?"

Why was Adam snickering?

The Scent of Lilacs

"While I was in Stoneham this weekend, I saw his blue truck in town. My parents hadn't even bothered to tell me he'd been released."

"Marla, he got out over a year ago."

The floor beneath her seemed to tilt. She reached for the wall. "What? You knew? But how ... how could you know this? What's going on? Why didn't you tell me, Adam?"

He tousled her hair. "Since you surprised me today, I have a surprise for you too. But you'll need to sit down."

Marla searched his eyes. Their dazzling crystal blue had turned indigo, then pitch black. He sent a shiver down her spine.

"No. I'll stand."

"Suit yourself. I've kept in touch with Jimmy over the years," he said, his brow arched coyly. "Saw him every couple of months while he was in jail."

She scanned the room for the wastebasket. Adam followed her gaze. He picked up the basket, placed it in her hands, then opened the door a crack, "Girls, bring a glass of water. Mom doesn't feel well."

She heard the twins scrambling. "Mom, are you okay?"

Through deep breaths, she said, "Yeah, yeah, I'll be fine."

Susan handed Adam the water. "What's wrong with her, Dad?"

As they tried to peek in, he blocked their line of sight with his body. "Must be something she ate. I'll take care of her." He motioned for them to leave. "You two grab a snack and go up and do your homework. I'll call you down as soon as your mom's settled."

"But we want to help."

"Marla, tell them."

"Girls, listen to your dad."

"Okay, okay."

Marla heard them walk away then slipped to the floor—helpless, defeated.

"There, there," said Adam picking her up and helping her to the chair. "Take a drink, put your head down, and relax." Passing her the glass, he sat on the edge of the desk and patted her head as he swung his leg back and forth.

This isn't happening. This is someone else's horrible life.

But no, there it was. The devil's voice again. Right in the room with her.

"Yeah," he said. "Once the trial was over, I went to visit Jimmy in jail."

Marla stifled a moan, but as difficult as this was, she needed to hear every detail.

"I told him I was sorry things had turned out so badly and that I'd be there for him."

Tears flooded down her face as she stammered, "Did—did he ever ask about me?"

"Of course. The guy broke down lots of times. I set him straight, though. Told him to give you up so you could get on with your life."

Her lips quivered in disbelief.

"I didn't want him to have false hopes that an appeal would result in an acquittal." Adam lifted his palms in the air. "Jimmy had to face reality and accept he wasn't getting out of jail anytime soon. Anyway, he agreed it was only fair to you and that you deserved someone better."

"You think you're better? You're a monster." Marla jumped up and lunged at him, her fingers set to claw his face. "So, it wasn't just my parents who took Jimmy away from me. It was you." She wanted to scream, but with the girls upstairs, how could she?

Adam grabbed her wrists. "Come on, Marla. Think about it. Jimmy let you go and I was there to pick up the pieces."

"You're lying. He was in love with me."

"You may not believe it, but he asked me to take care of you. Said he figured we'd end up together anyway, that I had more to offer. Then he stopped asking about you. I kept him in the loop though, showed him wedding and baby pictures."

"You're making this up. No one could be so cruel." She shuddered as Adam continued spewing out his venom.

"Jimmy could've told me to get lost. Instead, he took my advice and started concentrating on his studies. I even brought him the books he needed to get through the courses. He has a degree in mechanical engineering, you know." Adam lifted her chin. "Marla, you might think I used him to get you, which I did, but he used me too. So, you see … everything turned out."

Adam pulled a tissue from the desk drawer. "Aw," he said, "your mascara is streaking like one of those tragic figures in dark comedy." He wiped her eyes and cheeks with it. "Darling, stop crying. You're a married woman. What will your children think?"

He pulled Marla to her feet. "I know how much family and commitment mean to you. My mother left me, but you won't." He laughed sardonically and twirled a strand of her hair. "Sweetie, let's not waste your little performance. Tonight, I'll make love to the new you. It'll be fun. Take a hot bath and I'll join you after the girls have gone to bed."

Marla covered her pinched face. Adam was right. Jimmy was in her past. She'd married Adam. *He* was the one she lived with.

"Hope you're prepared … risky game …" The words were hypnotic as she made her way up the staircase.

The next lucid moment she had was the scalding hot water she'd stepped into. She jumped out of the tub, her silent shriek catching in her throat. Had she done it deliberately to punish herself, or had she lost her mind? She stared down at her legs and raced to the shower stall. Lucky—this time.

She reset the bathwater, added Epsom salts, and plunged in. Could she go on like this?

Her children loved their father and she'd truly loved Adam when she'd married him. Shouldn't she keep her vows? And then there was Claire. The day she'd left her parents' home after high school, her mother had said, "You've judged me—let's see what you accomplish in your life." Would her mother's curse win out?

No bloody way.

Marla shivered, stepped out of the tub, wrapped a towel around herself, and took a hard look in the mirror. That same blank face stared back. Did the stranger really think cutting and colouring her hair would change her life? She turned away from the mirror, dabbed on Adam's favourite perfume, and slipped on the new lavender nightie.

The soft sounds of *Meditation from Thais* from her bedside radio lulled her to sleep. A gentle touch woke her just as the last few notes of the music faded away.

Was she dreaming? Was she back on Bretton Street ... those heady days of tennis, laughter, and love?

"I didn't hear you come in," said Marla, flipping onto her side to face Adam. They both lay quiet.

Life would be good again.

"Remember those nights on the sofa in my apartment, when we were students, Adam? We were so happy."

"You mean the nights I dazzled you with 'She walks in beauty, like the night'?"

She closed her eyes to conjure up the smell of his body and the feel of his breath as he'd declared his love for her in poetry.

"Yes. What was the last line?"

Adam stroked her cheek. "A mind at peace with all below, a heart whose love is innocent."

His whispers brought back warm, fuzzy feelings—feelings to numb her revulsion.

Adam's breathing quickened. He kissed her. Hard, tense, smothering. The kisses Marla remembered had been luscious and delicate, like soft ice-cream. They'd been kisses that had awakened her passion. She'd learned to love Lord Byron. She'd learned to love Adam.

Now, here she was, loathing him, forcing herself to submit.

Oh, what's that? Sonatina in F? Yes!

Marla could see the notes in front of her plainly. Her body and mind separated. She slipped back, back to Stoneham.

Her parents had been ecstatic when she and Adam had announced their engagement. She twisted the ring with her thumb as she lay in bed, accepting Adam's hungry advances.

Oh, yes, yes, what about the ring?

She remembered the day they were all together to formalize their wedding plans. Her dad had held Adam's hand—crushing it, to be more specific. What had he said that made Adam suck in his cheeks? At the time she'd viewed it as the creation of a powerful family bond, a new version of the pinky promise, to protect *her*.

Hah, what a joke.

She'd married for love and could almost feel the way Adam had held her on their wedding night.

"Marla, where are you?" said Adam, as he traced the curves of her hips.

"Just catching my breath." She kissed his neck, then let her mind drift away with Chopin's *Nocturne Op. 9* until the room and her mind finally stilled.

She dared to open her eyes.

Yes, she'd married someone she'd once thought was her hero.

Heaven, help her now.

Chapter 7

Marla wheeled into the studio parking lot and jumped out of the car. "Hurry up, girls. You can't be late for rehearsal. It's too close to the recital date." She looked up at the threatening sky and handed them each a backpack.

"Not our fault," said Sarah.

"What's up with you, Mom?" added Susan. "Dad told us to let him know if you ever start acting weird. I think always being late is a bit weird. Don't you, Sarah?"

Marla froze.

Sarah shot her sister a dirty look. "No. Mom's just trying to finish her project."

A drop of rain fell on Marla's forehead. "Quick, girls. Enjoy your practice. I'll be in the car. Keep your tights on afterwards, you can change at home."

As the girls rushed off, she blew two ritual kisses into the air.

So, Adam, now you're turning Sarah and Susan against me? Our daughters are your little spies?

Marla couldn't deny she'd neglected them lately, but only because her job teetered on the timely completion of this assignment. Had Adam noticed her changes and become suspicious?

Even that morning, he'd flashed a wolfish grin. "You're getting carried away with your work, sweetie. Be careful."

"You know I can't live without you," she'd said. "We're a team, Adam."

The girls had final exams coming up as well as daily ballet rehearsals. She really needed Adam on side.

Marla watched her daughters disappear and jumped into the car seat in time to escape the deluge. Five after four, and it would still take a few more minutes to load her laptop and do a quick review. When Bob had approached her about the tender, he'd said, "It's a challenge, but from what I've seen so far, I think you're up to the job, Marla." Had she incorporated all the criteria—playground, fountains, washrooms, walkways and ramps, lampposts, disposal, benches, special events area? Yes, everything was here.

"Sorry I'm late," Marla said when Bob picked up.

"Family first. You warned me when you started."

"Thanks for being so understanding. So, what do you think?"

"Looks really good. I like the modern waterfall. Very ... Zen. Pebbled or plain concrete for the pad?"

"Covered on the options page, along with costs and photos."

"What about the benches? Moveable or screwed into the concrete?"

"Check the fine print, Bob," she said. She heard him rustle some papers.

He cleared his throat. "Just testing. I see hard costs are within budget. What can you do with the soft costs?"

"Working on that right now. The drafts will be on your desk tomorrow."

"Tease me with something to visualize."

"The park should be urbanized so that the impact of yearly maintenance on the taxpayer is minimal. No wormy willows or messy walnuts. Historical and indigenous have to give way to function. You know it'll be beautiful."

"No doubt. Everything about you is beautiful." He threw in a little chuckle.

Awkward comment, but she often heard Bob compliment people.

"By the way," Marla said, "if you're in the downtown area, check out Gallery One. There's a painting of Central Park. The setting is serene and romantic. It's my inspiration for this project."

"Hang on, I'll write down the details. Gallery One? Isn't that your husband's gallery?"

"Yup. But the painting may be auctioned off soon."

While she waited for him to write things down, Marla checked her watch again. The girls would be out in an hour. Would she have time to finish the work?

"Dazzle them, Marla. And if you keep the city coffers healthy, you'll come out a star."

"I'll try. Shouldn't I get to work now?"

Her bold rapport surprised even her. But if this was the voice of freedom, she liked it.

"Yes, ma'am," Bob said. "You're starting to worry me and you aren't even a partner."

His words left Marla breathless. Someone actually recognized her talents. Forget about just gardening awards like her mother had received in Stoneham. She could actually become a partner.

Ooh, Claire wouldn't like that.

Marla completed the drawings and, as a matter of habit, backed up her work and tossed the memory stick into the glove compartment.

The studio door opened. She heard the girls squealing as they ran towards her in the rain.

Her bright, healthy, beautiful daughters, identical in most ways. Both had Adam's dark curly hair and her creamy complexion. Their grey eyes, however, had always posed a genetic mystery.

Marla stared at the twins in the back seat from the rearview mirror and smiled at their slight, but noticeable differences. Physically, Sarah was a little thicker and had a small cowlick at her hairline, while slender Susan had inherited Grandpa Bill's cute freckle on her earlobe. Despite their differences, unique personalities, and normal sister scuffles, she marveled at how well Sarah and Susan got along with each other.

Growing up, Marla had often wished she'd had a sibling to share her life with. But her mother had made it painfully clear that would never happen. "One mistake is enough for me."

The rain continued as they drove off.

"Is Dad home for dinner tonight?" said Susan.

Marla blinked. For some reason, the dampness made her arm ache a little. The new bruise had faded, but it was still a little tender. She'd been exhausted and had refused Adam's advances when he arrived home from a night flight the previous week.

"Too tired, eh? I told you. You could work as long it didn't interfere with us. So now what do you expect from me? You must want trouble."

Marla's heart had fluttered as she'd kept her distance. "You're always so angry, Adam. I can't go on pretending this is normal. Maybe you should get counselling." The suggestion was meant to be helpful, solve their problems. Instead, it had earned her a way-too-firm squeeze of the arm.

"I explained. I warned you. And you tell me I need help. Get out of my bed."

Gladly.

His behaviour towards Sarah and Susan had never been less than perfect, but towards her … it was all about power and control.

Could she prove his abusiveness without calling the cops or visiting an emergency room? Even then, he'd somehow change the narrative—explain it away as an accident or clumsiness. With the life she led, no one would feel sorry for her, either. Certainly not her mother who'd blame her for not being good enough to hold onto a dreamy man like Adam. Her dad eventually might, but he'd have a hard time believing Adam would have had the nerve to defy the authority of a police-chief father-in-law, especially after their 'little talk'.

Someday, someday … Adam would make a fatal mistake. Then she'd wipe the floor with him … along with the lilac perfume, Lord Byron, and all his goddamned bullshit.

"Mom."

Susan's voice.
"Mom, we asked you if Dad would be home tonight."
"Yes, he sure will. And I hope he's satisfied with a grilled cheese sandwich. What about you, girls? Grilled cheese, okay?"
"Sure, Mom. The quicker the better," said Sarah, "we have an assignment."

While the girls listened to music on the radio for most of the ride home, Marla's mantra, *I will be free,* echoed as she blinked away the snapshots of her life.

Adam's adjacent locker at Stoneham High; Jimmy's old blue truck; Jimmy's good-bye letter; Adam's '88 Mustang; her parents hippy-days photo on the hall console; her hiding place in her bedroom closet to block out her mother's chilling backstories; her father's badge and what it stood for; but, mostly, the giant hole in her heart.

Marla felt a hand on her shoulder.
"Earth to Mom?" said Susan.
Would they consider daydreaming weird and report it to Adam as well?
"Oh, sorry, girls. I'm not trying to ignore you. It's just that I've got a lot on mind right now. Can't wait to get this presentation over with."
"I really hope you win the contract," said Sarah. "You deserve it."
"Commitment and hard work are what it takes in life when you want something badly enough."

Susan closed her eyes and wrapped her arms around herself. "Think I'll just marry a rich man," she said wistfully.

They had a laugh over the light comment, but Marla knew 'rich' was not the answer to anyone's prayers.

As the girls discussed their homework with each other, she gritted her teeth.

So, I'm acting weird, am I?

Adam was standing in the hall with his suit jacket on and his tie in his hands when they entered. Marla could barely look at him.

"Surprise, ladies," he announced. "Since you've all been working so hard, I'm taking you to Pizza e Piatti tonight. Not a fancy place, but no jeans and no tights."

"Jeez, I wish you'd have checked with me first. The girls have homework and this is such an important night for me."

"Stop complaining, the reservation is made. Change and let's go."

Within forty minutes, the four of them sat in a cozy booth, staring at heaping plates of cannelloni, veal parmigiana, and roasted veggies. The charming old-world ambiance and divine aromas changed her mood. "Good call, Adam. This is better than what I had planned."

"I knew it would be," he said, as he sat facing her. He'd dismissed the waiter and poured the wine himself. "Okay, what's the homework, girls?"

"Glad you asked, Dad," said Susan. "We need your help. We have to do a chart that traces our physical traits to our families. We pretty well know about Mom's, but we're not sure about yours. You never talk about them."

Adam shifted in his seat.

"Did anyone in your family have grey eyes?" said Sarah.

What a coincidence. Marla had just been thinking about that.

The deadpan look that usually foreshadowed Adam's disappearing act at the mention of his family took on a placid expression.

Odd.

"My father, your grandfather, had smoky eyes just like yours, girls."

Well, hallelujah, finally.

"Do you have a photo of him we could see?" said Susan.

"Sorry, no photos."

"Not even in that bankers' box in your closet?" Marla took a sip of wine to make the question appear casual. She believed in respect and privacy and had never touched that box, but it had never stopped her from wondering.

"That box is full of legal documents. Hands off—all of you. Is that clear?"

Susan cringed and moved closer to Marla, but Sarah had chosen to sit beside her dad. "Please don't be mad, Dad. We're just curious."

Adam patted her back. "I know. But I mean it. Now let me tell you about my family."

Was Marla hearing things?

"You already know my mother died when I was eight," he said. "I'll dig up the photo of her when we get home. Anyway, I was three when she taught me to read and by the time I reached kindergarten, I could read the newspaper. By eight, I'd already gone through Dickens and Shakespeare."

None of that came as a surprise. His intellectual abilities had never been in question. After all, he was reading the high school *Curriculum Prospectus* by his locker when she'd first met him. Something no one she'd ever known had done, or at least cared to do in public.

Between sips of chianti, Adam continued. "You girls played with Barbie dolls when you were little. I played with Dinky cars. Too bad I didn't have twin boys." He winked at Sarah and Susan. "I would have spoiled them like my father spoiled me. Every time I finished a book, he bought me a new car. I had a huge collection. My favourite was a black Mustang, like the one I had in high school." He glanced across the table. "Remember it, honey?"

Susan sounded impressed. "You had a black Mustang, Dad?"

Marla and Adam both nodded.

"Anyway," said Adam. "My mom would run the car through my hair, telling me that my brain was the highway to success. And believe me, girls, she was correct. It is. She used to tickle me and we laughed a lot." He turned to tickle Sarah.

So, the Mustang did have a connection to his family. Adam had had a good reason to keep and use it as their wedding-day getaway car.

The new-found knowledge, Adam's lightness of mood tonight, the beaming faces of the girls, and the happiness of the moment made Marla believe anything was possible.

Had she been making up all that bad stuff?

"Your grandmother's name was Isabel," he continued, "and she was an amazing artist and poet. Received a scholarship to university. That's where she met my dad. A couple of years later, I came along. Now you know why I love literature and art so much, and why I opened my own gallery. I followed in my parents' footsteps. Just like Susan loves ballet and Sarah—remind me what you love?"

Sarah nudged him. "Come on, Dad. Cut it out."

"Never mind, you'll find it." He patted Sarah on the back again.

To lend support, Marla reached over to touch Sarah's hand and noticed Adam rolling his eyes and twisting his neck.

Uh-oh. Bad sign.

"I ... I wish my mother had lived longer." He wiped his mouth.

"What happened after your mother died?" said Susan.

"Marla, it's getting late. Order the gelato and a couple of espressos. I'll be right back."

She watched Adam shuffle off.

Destination Neverland?

Adam leaned against the sink.

He could see himself clearly on that morning so long ago. A little stick boy with shoulder-length curly hair in his favourite Cookie Monster pajamas—two sizes too small. He loved that his mother had been different than the other moms at school and the park. She'd made a dramatic statement everywhere she went. Vintage clothing and hair well below her waist. To add to that, she carried everything in a basket, including him as a baby, she'd told him. The man who'd turned out to be his dad, had been intrigued by her uniqueness, even though he'd later called her a 'non-conformist'.

Whether she fit in or not hadn't mattered to Adam. He loved his mother unconditionally. But why hadn't she loved her little boy back?

He spat into the sink and rubbed his temples.

Isabel would wake him up every morning singing her usual medley of Raffi songs. But that day ... nothing. No kiss on the forehead. No ruffling his hair. No tickling his feet. He thought she might still be asleep, as the apartment only he and his mother shared, was so quiet. Adam had jumped out of bed, tiptoed to her room, and crept up to her—close enough to see her wide-open, beautiful blue eyes, staring up at the ceiling.

"Momma!" *he'd yelled as he touched her cold arm.* "Momma, I have to go to school. The bus is coming. Momma. You have to go to work." *Her image and the words had burned into his memory.*

In her left hand, she'd held a small red book with a note in it. Adam took the book from her and pressed it against his chest. Something had dripped from her wrist.

He'd screamed. Then ... nothing.

The neighbours said they'd found him paralyzed with terror and slumped on the floor beside her bed, her blood trickling on him as he'd held her hand.

When he'd finally come to, he was on a hard gurney in a sterile room, looking up at strangers in white coats.

Sarah and Susan both reached out to touch their dad when he returned.

"Susan, you asked what happened next," said Adam in a calm voice. "I'll tell you. Doctors. Doctors and," he gulped, "my father were there for me."

Who was this man, now willing to share his secrets?

"Your grandpa was sad when your grandma died, but he taught me that, in life, you have to move on. With those soft, grey eyes, my dad was a man of mystery about the campus and caught the attention of a very rich lady who shared his love for art and literature. After they married, I went to live with them," he said. "Big mansion, tennis court, swimming pool, servants, and three cats. We had the best of everything."

"Wow, Dad. You were pretty lucky. At least you had your dad around," said Sarah.

"Lucky? Yeah, sure—that was me. Unfortunately, my dad was a very busy man. He had to go to all lot of fancy parties with his lady. Didn't have time for family photos. That's really all I can tell you about him, except that he would have wanted you to study hard and do really well in school. He'd made sure I had."

"Is that why you're so smart?" said Susan.

"I was born smart and ... like I told you ... books. I went to the best schools that money could buy and travelled abroad on school breaks and even special holidays. As soon as we'd gobbled the turkey and Christmas pudding, our chauffeur would shuffle me off to the airport and poof ... I was gone. My father taught me many things. Made me what I am today. But ... dads don't last forever. Your grandpa got sick and died."

Sarah and Susan's smiles turned downward.

"Then I moved to Stoneham to finish high school," said Adam. "That's where I met your mother and fell in love. I knew she was the one for me." He glanced over at her, "And here *you* are, girls." He stood up. "I think you can get your homework done now. Let's go."

The question of grey eyes from his daughters had impelled Adam to open up tonight.

But they've just scratched the surface, haven't they, Adam?

Chapter 8

After staying up late to finish the soft costs of the big project, Marla woke up exhausted but eager to present her work. Thankfully she'd switched her pickup day with Evelyn and Adam had agreed to collect the girls from dance.

Pepper lay sprawled across the entrance of the den when she walked in. She placed the containers of food and her computer on the counter.

"Smells like lasagna and garlic bread," said Susan. "Can we eat at the breakfast bar?"

"Suits me. I'm going to get changed."

She could hear whispers from the den as she passed it. "I have to go Gillian. My wife's home. See you soon."

Adam winked at Marla and mouthed, *work*.

Hmm—jasmine perfume lady. At least he's loyal.

It wasn't until she'd polished off a slice of lasagna that Marla gave thought to her laptop. She blinked. "Where's my computer?"

"Dad put it in the den for you," said Susan, still nibbling on a piece of bread.

Her spine prickled. She charged down the hall and clicked on the project page.

Empty.

"No!" she shouted.

The girls and Adam came running.

"Something wrong, honey?" said Adam.

His look of concern confused her for a moment. But she knew him too well.

"What did you do, Adam?"

He looked at the twins. "I think your mother's working too hard. Please make her some tea and ... put ice in it. Grandma Claire would say she needs to chill." As soon as they stepped out of the room, he closed the door and turned the computer towards him.

He knew the password?

After pressing a few keys, Adam stepped away and stared at her with a cagey grin. "See, it's still there."

"That was a dirty trick." Her eyes welled up.

"Oh, come on, it was a joke. You've been too serious lately. It's important to have fun and keep life interesting. Feeds my soul."

What soul?!

Marla pictured the memory stick in her glove compartment and sighed.

Waiting for the city's decision to award the contract, Marla walked on pins and needles for the rest of the week. She couldn't wait for the phone to ring today. Adam offered to close the gallery early and fill in for her pick-up duties.

Thoughtful.

At six o'clock, she closed Guy de Maupassant's *The Necklace*, one of her old French schoolbooks. The pathos at the end of that piece had made her reflective and must have shown on her face as her family burst into the house.

"Oh no," said Adam. "Guess things didn't go so well today."

Susan and Sarah ran to hug her. "Don't worry, Mom. You'll get the next one."

Unlike the one-sided relationship with her own mother, Marla and the twins outwardly showed their love and support for each other. Her heart swelled with pride.

Adam may have done a lot of bad things, but together, she and Adam had created something wonderful. Sarah and Susan were worth any pain she had to endure.

"Ahem," Marla coughed. With their arms still around her, she walked them towards the dining room and opened the French doors.

"Ah," yelled the girls. "You got it!"

"Yes, we did. And there's king crab and baked Alaska to celebrate." She had a lump in her throat. "Thank you, everyone. I couldn't have done it without your patience and understanding."

"Aw, and I was looking forward to takeout," said Adam.

The girls laughed and pulled him into the hug.

Was this how marriage was supposed to be?
She'd hold onto these feelings for as long as possible.

In fact, she'd willed herself to stay positive, knowing Adam's departure to Chicago was around the corner.

Marla looked into the dressing room mirror that day. Her short, spiky hair had grown to a longer, shaggy version of itself. Nothing she could do about the length, but dyed back to its natural auburn, she'd begun to recognize herself again.

Regardless of Adam's recent good nature, *yippee* crossed her mind. "Limo's here," she hollered. Marla followed him to the foyer. "You've put a lot of work into this auction. I hope you and Gillian get what you deserve." She'd never spoken the woman's name before.

He tilted his head and smiled.

"Come on, Adam, I may be submissive, but I have eyes and ears. Who's the other one you talk to?" She tapped her temple. "Oh, yes, Nalin."

"Very good," he laughed. "Art's a multi-billion-dollar business, sweetie. My associates and I fully intend to collect our share of it. Don't take it personally. It's win-win for everyone. Enjoy your week with the girls. I've already wished them well." He locked eyes with her and stretched out his arm.

Marla stepped back.

"What, not today?"

Adam settled into the limo.

Marla, Marla.

She acted so much bolder whenever he had to leave.

The lengthy ride to the airport gave him the opportunity to make some calls and check his notes. Adam had been pleased with the final catalogue that detailed the artwork, along with biographies and certificates of authenticity. Was the auctioneer in transit? *Yes.* And the hotel manager had just confirmed caterers, technicians, movers, handlers, security, and administrative staff had all arrived.

Good. Everyone and everything in order.

Now to review his juicy international guest list. Courtesy of Gillian.

Marla had learned to assume nothing. Her only defence against the battery of surprise attacks on her. They reared up from every corner of her life. *Surprise,* Jimmy was back in Stoneham. *Surprise,* her mother had been Milt Snow's lover. *Surprise,* Adam had been visiting Jimmy for twelve years. *Surprise,* Adam had lied and cheated. *Surprise,* her own husband had attempted to sabotage her computer and potentially her career.

The minute Adam left the house, a weight lifted off Marla's shoulders. She called her parents. "Hi, Dad. What time are you and Mom coming tomorrow?"

"Around eleven."

"Sounds good. Don't forget your suit, tie, and swim trunks."

"What would I do without the women in my life?"

She pictured him shaking his head as he said it.

The next day, she woke early. Recital day jitters led her to the kitchen. Baking, just like her mother's tea-making, made her mindful. Besides, her dad would appreciate fresh scones and croissants. As the aromas filled the room, she noticed Pepper drooling. "Didn't mean to torture you, buddy. How about you wait outside?" She put him on a long leash and tethered him in the front yard.

Wasn't long before she heard barking. Eleven already? What would Claire be like today? Civilized?

She could only hope.

"Oh God, look at your hair. What a mess."

"Thanks, Mom."

Her mother barged past her. "Where are those girls?" She put one foot on the stairs, then paused and lowered it.

Had Claire finally accepted her limitations?

"Look, you don't have to climb Mount Everest, Mom."

"Aren't you the sensitive one."

"I was just about to say you won't need the guest room or go upstairs at all. You can use the pull-out sofa in the family room and the pool shower by the back door."

Her mother slipped her moccasins on. "What is that blasted music those girls are listening to? I thought you'd gotten that classical crap out of your system along with that damn …"

"Language, Mom. Stop it."

"She's right," said her father, shaking his finger in the air.

"She's all yours, Bill."

Images of the day Marla had taken the baseball bat from the umbrella stand and smashed her beloved piano made her cringe.

She'd been fragile, her nerves raw, when Jimmy had been arrested. Wouldn't anyone crack if they'd been forbidden to see their boyfriend and told to practise for a stupid piano exam, instead? It wasn't as if her mother had wanted to hear her play. Their musical tastes differed.

She tried to push those thoughts aside. "Yes, Mother, thanks to you, I did give up the piano. I've also been grateful that Sarah and Susan never asked for lessons. But breaking my piano wasn't a form of exorcism. It will never cleanse me of Bach and Beethoven."

"And I gave up my gig at Brody's for this? If it wasn't for Susan and Sarah, you'd never put me through *Swan Lake*." Her mother stood up, raised her right arm, brought her fist to rest against her mouth, and belted out the loudest, most soulful version of *Midnight Train to Georgia* Marla had ever heard. Her mother truly could have been, should have been, an international star.

Oh God, it wasn't as if she'd asked to be born.

The twins flew down the staircase shrieking, "Grandma, Grandpa!"

"You finally heard me," said her mother.

"I think the whole street heard you, Mom."

"Girls, get the makeup. I'll show you how to get noticed. It's all about eye contact and … talent, of course. Your mother didn't have it, but something tells me you took after me and your dad."

Sarah and Susan both whipped their heads around to see what Marla's reaction would be.

She forced a smile. "I put three stools in the powder room, ladies. Have fun."

"Right, this is the Mansfield house. I'd forgotten you need a ballroom to go potty."

The girls giggled and headed for the stairs.

Her dad avoided her eyes. "Think I'll read the paper in the family room."

"Wait, Dad. Adam cranked up the heat in the pool. Why don't you go for a swim instead?"

He nodded.

"I'll make some coffee and join you."

By the time she'd changed into a bathing suit, prepared the tray, and sat down, her dad had already gone for a dip and was drying himself off.

"Good call. That was refreshing." He stretched out on the lounge next to her, bit into a pastry, and licked his fingers. "Mm, so good. I'll have to thank Adam again for sending you to cooking school. Should have sent your mother with you. Don't tell her I said that." He took another bite. "Now talk to me, kiddo. I know your new career is taking off. What stage are you at?"

"The engineers have finished the soils testing. As soon as the site is scrubbed, they'll start with undergrounds, sewers, water, and hydro. My job is to make sure the plans are being followed and take the project from A to Z."

"Your mother and I are really proud of you."

"Thanks." Marla raised an eyebrow. "Did Mom actually say that?" When Bill shifted in his chair, she knew the answer. "Never mind. Doesn't matter."

He squeezed her hand. "How's Adam doing, sweetie? Tell me about the auction. A shame both events had to be on the same weekend. You could have gone with him."

Her dad had no idea how much she'd like to be a fly on the wall in that hotel. "His biggest show yet. He and Gillian …"

"Who's Gillian?"

"His associate." Marla's tongue tasted sour. "She's a wealthy socialite from Boston. Husband has a shipping company and she handles his investments. Adam met her in Paris the first year we were married." She stiffened. "Anyway," she continued, "for this exhibition, they managed to get their hands on a Warhol and a Jackson Pollock."

"Soup cans and drip paintings."

She winked. "You'd like the museum-quality pieces from his stepmother's private collection. And a prolific French artist named Dorian Conte is being featured too."

"Never heard of him."

"He was Gillian's new contact twelve years ago when she and Adam met. Adam acquired a painting from Dorian called *Heat of the Night*. It's still hanging in Gallery One as Adam's good luck charm. You should see Dorian's work. The man has the uncanny ability to flawlessly reproduce the masters, a *savant*."

Her dad frowned. "I've heard of people like that. Not accusing anybody, but art forgery is on the increase. Hope the guy is signing his own name and not passing reproductions off as originals."

"I wondered about that at first, too. But no, Dorian's work is widely collected throughout the world. Even hanging in government buildings. Must be legit. And there's a young, contemporary painter named Nalin Crawford who's about to blow the art world away. If you have any money to invest, she'd be the one."

"Honey. It's music, not art, that makes me happy. My guitar, a beer, your mother at my side."

The Scent of Lilacs

Marla felt a tug on her heart and looked up at him.

"And, of course, seeing my daughter and my granddaughters." He yawned. "Sorry, I didn't mean to be rude. I worked last night and it was a long drive here this morning."

She wanted to say, "Take a nap," but this was her chance for a heart-to-heart before she lost her nerve. "I think you'll find this interesting. Adam has a couple of limited editions, signed sketches from your favourite musician's art portfolio."

He gave her a knowing look. "Wow, they're sure to bring in the big bucks. From what I remember, they were pretty erotic pictures." He rubbed his chin. "Hmm, guess your husband's doing alright. And guess my little girl married the right man."

The right man?

Marla flung off her robe and dove into the water.

Chapter 9

By four o'clock, Marla had already showered and applied her makeup. She popped her head into the girls' rooms, "It's time. Meet you at the front door."

Hampered by ballet bags, costumes, and their meticulously coiffed chignons, the girls walked down the stairs gingerly and received gentle hugs from the grandparents as they filed out the door.

"Knock them dead," shouted Claire.

Marla jangled the keys. "I'll be back by five and you two should relax. It'll be a long night."

Her parents' car was not in the driveway when she returned.

Oh, great.

As she turned off the engine, they pulled up behind her. "You do know we have to leave in an hour, don't you?"

"Pfft—no sweat," said her dad. "We drove over to check out our old stomping grounds."

"Yeah, when life was free and exciting." Her mother shook her head and glanced at her. "Lighten up, kid. All you ever do is worry."

Maybe Marla was being uptight, but timing and perfection were the Mansfield traits she'd learned to live by. "Sorry, performance night. We can't be late."

Marla slipped into her cocktail dress and faced the mirror. As she snapped on her pearl and diamond earrings, she heard a faint knock on her bedroom door. Her dad stood there with his white shirt not yet tucked into his suit pants.

"What do you need, Dad?"

"Wow," he said. "You look sensational."

"Thanks." She watched his expression change to a half-smile.

"You're going to kill me," he blurted. "I remembered the trunks, the suit, the tie—just like you said. But I forgot the cufflinks. Any chance I could borrow a pair from Adam?"

She cleared her throat. "Of course. Not sure what we'll find, though."

Yes, she did.

Her dad followed her into the closet and walked around the perimeter with his mouth gaping. "Holy smokes. I've never seen anything like this. Does he actually live here? No man can be this neat."

"Adam can."

She opened the drawer where she'd last seen the intricately carved rosewood box with the black-velvet liner she'd given him on their wedding day. Still there. She lifted the top. No cufflinks, but what was this?

Adam's wedding ring.

Marla flushed. "Guess he forgot it."

"Probably did. We men forget lots of things." Her dad peered into the box and laughed. "Hey, look. The handcuffs from your wedding day."

"Never know when you might need those." Marla laughed. "Well, as you can see, there's more than one tie clip in this box, but no cufflinks." About to close the lid, she spotted a small brass key with a tassel.

"I think I know what this belongs to. Adam had the cabinetmaker install a locked drawer within a drawer. It has a false cabinet front that unhinges with the press of a corner and drops down to reveal an inner metal box." She maneuvered the workings as she talked. The key fit.

Her dad scratched his head. "It's a vault."

"Let's see if we get lucky." Marla fiddled with the sequencing.

Adam had never bothered to change the combination. Guess he trusted her.

She pulled the box open. The cufflinks were there, all right, at least six pairs of them. But Marla couldn't make sense of the rest of the jewellery.

"This all yours?" said her dad, after a moment's thought. "Quite a stash. Is it real?"

She trembled. "It's not mine and ... Adam's never mentioned jewellery in his business."

"I'm sure there's a good explanation. Someone clearing out their estate, maybe."

"Could be." Marla pointed to the onyx cufflinks. "I think these may work for you, but hold on before you touch them." She rushed to get the Polaroid camera. "I'll just take a quick photo."

Her father knit his brows. "Why do you need to do that? Would Adam be upset if he knew I'd borrowed them?"

"Not upset," she lied, "I just want to put them back exactly as we found them." She tried not to look at him. "Adam likes his privacy. Understandable, right?"

"If you say so. It's not normal to me."

Marla took the photo then passed him the cufflinks.

"Your hands are shaking, Marla. Is this still about the wedding ring? He just forgot."

"Hey, you two," her mother shouted from the foot of the stairs. "Hurry up. It's a quarter to." She paused. "Marla, a fancy car just pulled into the driveway."

Her dad stiffened. "Are you expecting someone, Marla?"

"It's the limo," she said, trying to put a smile on her face. "Adam wanted us to go to the theatre in style. He's also arranged for a swanky late-night dinner after the show."

She could feel the butterflies coming back. The Boston muses, the wedding ring, and now ... unexplained jewellery? Would she make it through the night?

Bill squeezed her hand. "Come on, sweetie. To hell with the drawer. It's probably nothing. If you're still concerned, we can check it out later. Let's enjoy the performance and celebrate the good things in life." He shook his head. "I'm such an ass. I could kick myself for forgetting my cufflinks."

"No, Dad—opening the drawers, opened our eyes."

Marla and her parents stepped out of the limo and made it to their seats just as the orchestra began to tune up. She looked around the packed theatre to where the Lams and her boss were seated and gave them each a nod before the curtains rose and swept her away.

At intermission, she pointed to a quiet spot near the staircase. "I'll be over there, Dad. The restrooms are to the left." She could see Amy, Evelyn, and Philip waving to her from the snack bar. Bob approached from another wing.

"Marla," said Bob, carrying two bouquets of flowers. "Best performance of *Swan Lake* I've ever seen."

"Sure, sure. I'll bet it's the only *Swan Lake* you've ever seen."

"Busted." He laughed. "You've worked so hard juggling for this recital and still managed to complete the assignment on time. I had to come and see what this was all about."

"Thanks for your support."

"I'm a single guy and don't know what it's like to raise children, but you're certainly doing a great job with yours. Not really surprised, though. You do everything well."

Back from the restrooms, her dad steered her mother towards the staircase before heading to the drink counter.

"Thank you, Bob," said Marla. "Meet my mother, Claire Slater. She can take *all* the credit for me and the girls. She'll tell you it's all about DNA. Mother, this is my boss, Bob Wyllie."

Claire gave Bob a flirtatious smile. "Wonderful to meet you." She placed her hand on his arm. "And congratulations on being awarded the city contract. My daughter's been telling me all about it."

My daughter?

"I'll bet you had something to do with Marla's talents in that department. She's told me how much you've influenced her passion for landscaping. I should be thanking *you*."

Oh, brother.

"Mom, what did you think of the dancing?" said Marla.

"Marvelous." Her mother turned to face Bob. "Weren't my grandchildren superb? That *pas-de-deux* with the prince was breathtaking." Her mother put her hand on her heart and swayed. "And ... what do you call those turns on point, the ones where they swing their legs out, Marla?"

"*Fouettés*, Mother. But I'm sure Bob doesn't need a ballet lesson."

"Marla, if only you'd listened to me like the twins do."

She noticed the corners of Bob's lips twitching.

For sure, he'd gotten a clear picture of Claire. No need to enlighten him further.

After the performance and decadent dinner, complete with champagne and Shirley Temples, Marla looked at her watch as they turned into the driveway.

Midnight.

Her dad carried in the bags while she helped her mother to a stool. "I think the girls will need a wagon to bring in all those flowers and ... one for Adam's roses."

She gathered some large vases from the server and added water. "Just plunk them in, girls. We can pretty them up tomorrow."

"Madame said the video of the performance will be ready next week so we can show Dad. And guess what?" Susan's voice sounded so wistful. "There was someone watching from the National Ballet."

Her mother raised her brow. "Well, let's hope someone in this family makes it big."

Sarah gave her sister a hug. "I hope it's you, Susan. I'm done with dancing."

Marla kissed the tops of the girls' heads. "We're so proud of both of you. Now, do me a favour and sleep till noon."

"Goodnight and sweet dreams," said Claire before pulling a nightie out of her suitcase. "You coming, Bill?"

"Mom, I need Dad to fix something in my bedroom first."

"Well, just hurry up," said her mother, as she walked towards the sofa that had already been pulled out and set up for her.

"Dad," Marla whispered, "Adam left a bottle of XO at the bar. I'll get the tool box."

Marla checked on the girls. Already fast asleep. She closed her bedroom door.

Her dad took a sip of his drink, then placed it on the bureau and began fidgeting with his wedding band.

"What's wrong?"

"I know this may seem odd to you, but do you have a couple of nylon stockings or thin hankies?"

"Dad, you told me not to worry, and now you're saying we shouldn't leave fingerprints? You're scaring me."

She came back with two pairs of trouser socks and handed him one.

"Perfect," he said. "You ready?"

She nodded and went through the mechanics of reopening the vault.

No, she hadn't imagined it.

There was the jewellery, neatly arranged in sets. She'd brought her cellphone up this time. "Let me take some shots. It has to be put back perfectly"

Her dad nodded. "You'd make a great cop."

The first thing Marla lifted was a pearl bracelet and earrings.

Odd, no matching necklace.

Next to them was another necklace and bracelet in white gold and turquoise. She picked up the bracelet and turned it over. "I think I can explain this one. It has IM on it. Adam's mother's name was Isabel

Mansfield. I've never seen a picture of her, but he said she had black hair and blue eyes like him. I can just imagine her wearing these."

Her dad then picked up a ring with a large emerald, translucent and intense. The bracelet beside it was studded with smaller but similar high-quality gems.

"These have markings. A heart with DK in the middle. Who's DK?"

They both scratched their heads.

"Wow, look at those. They're dazzling," said Marla. She looked closer. "Diamond, topaz, opal, ruby, sapphire. They're like the royal crown jewels of England."

"What a collection. Let's not touch the necklaces. They're not usually engraved." Instead, Bill picked up a diamond ring. "This says GK."

She took the ring out of his hand. "So, DK and GK must be a married couple."

GK?

She felt light-headed. "Dad, I have to sit down." She made it to the bed. "Oh my god! It ... it's hers."

Her dad rubbed her back. "Whose?"

"Gladys Kingsley. The lady who died in the fire back in '89." The words sat on her tongue like ashes.

"What? That can't be right." His face matched the confusion in his voice.

"Boo." A soft voice sounded from the doorway.

They both rushed out of the closet.

"Claire?" said her dad. "How did you get up those stairs? You should have called me."

"Did you want me to wake the kids? I couldn't sleep. See, Marla, I can even climb Mount Everest when I want to. What are you guys doing?"

Her dad put his hands on her mother's shoulders. "Now look, don't overreact. We're checking out some things in Adam's closet that maybe ... shouldn't be there."

Claire hobbled behind them and eyed the gaping drawer. "Jesus!"

"I came up to borrow a pair of cufflinks from Adam," explained her dad, "and this is what we found. We don't know what the implications are, but there's one bit of information that has us really baffled." He brought a stool in from the bathroom. "Sit down, Claire."

Marla held up the ring. "Mom, this ring belongs to the lady who died in the fire at Stoneham Manor and it's … it's in Adam's drawer. I never come into his closet. He asked me not to. So, I … I had no idea any of this was here."

Her mother immediately opened her mouth then clamped it shut.

Was her mother about to chastise her for allowing Adam to hide secrets? Say that this would never have happened to her?

"What … what were you going to say, Mom? How could I be so stupid? How could I not have known?" Marla's voice got louder with each breath.

Her dad raised his hands. "Shush … the girls."

Marla glared at her mother with fire in her belly. "I suppose you wouldn't let anyone tell *you* what you can and can't do in your own home. I'll … I'll show you why." She unzipped her dress and turned her back to her parents. "That's why. That's the wonderful man you both wanted me to marry. See? I wasn't clumsy after all. Now you know. What do you think of Adam now? Is he still better than Jimmy?"

Her dad bit his lip and gathered her in his arms. His tears soaked her hair.

Marla looked up. Claire was glassy-eyed and trembling. A trickle escaped the corner of an eye, wound its way down her cheek, and fell from her chin. Another followed.

She eased out of her dad's arms. "Dad's right. We can't let the girls hear us. We have to protect them. This has been going on for a long time. I've kept it to myself till now."

The sadness in her dad's face grew to anger. He punched a fist into his palm, his jaw so tight the veins in his neck popped. "I swear I'll get that bastard. Why didn't you tell me, Marla?"

"Humiliation, fear, family. Pick one. I just couldn't. I learned to live with it." She gathered her strength and continued, "Look, I don't need your pity. I need your help." She held up the ring. "This ... we have to get to the bottom of this before Adam gets back from Chicago."

Marla scanned the closet. "There's something else I have to do."

There it was, in the corner, behind the tie-rack. The trunk. The kind that reminded her of early Atlantic immigrant crossings. The forbidden bankers' box would be inside. She crouched down and lifted the arm of the tie-rack, careful not to disturb the small fortune in designer ties Adam collected. She seemed to remember a small magnetic tin. Years ago, the girls had discovered the key when they were playing hide and seek. They'd gotten as far as opening the trunk before Adam caught them. The girls saw a side of him that meant business. The next day, he'd taken them to the zoo and they'd had a grand old time together. But ... after the scorching she'd gotten from Adam about it later, that trunk had repelled her like molten lava. Until now.

Marla ran her hand across each metal bar of the rack. "Aha, found it. Dad, this trunk is really heavy. Give me a hand."

Together, they nudged it over just far enough to open. Luckily, the trunk had left an indent in the pile of the carpet. They'd have no trouble putting it back where it belonged.

"Thanks. I've got it now, Dad," she said, stepping in front of him. Her hands felt clammy as she unbuckled the crisscrossed belts, unlocked it, and lifted the lid.

Her dad peered over her shoulder.

Adam hadn't lied. Just like he'd said, neatly organized folders with tabs. Marla fingered each without opening them. The last few folders intrigued her. She pulled them out and placed them on the carpet. Something grey beneath the now-empty space caught her eye.

"Dad, I'll hold these files back while you get whatever's under there."

He shimmied out an old, hard briefcase. "Somebody's been around the world. Look at the travel stickers." He tried budging the clasps. "It's locked."

She walked back to the vault. Just as she thought. A small flat key, easy to miss amongst the glitter. "Okay, here we go."

Leather notebooks and a small red journal!

She gasped. "Jimmy had talked about seeing the journal at GK's place and the notebooks look like the very ones Jimmy had borrowed."

"Whose journal would it be?"

"Adam's ... Adam's mother's ..." Marla stammered. She read the first page.

"'To My Beloved', with the initials 'IM' in the corner."

Such an intimate title.

Although Marla felt a qualm of shame to be intruding on IM, this book might hold some answers. She flipped through the handwritten calligraphy and stopped.

His kiss,
A butterfly on my lips and the tiny blissful place within me.
It holds me captive.

The words tasted like a spoonful of crème brûlée.

"You look strange, Marla," said her dad.

She could feel her face redden, but not with anger. "This woman was so in love. Listen to this."

He approaches
Titanic, powerful, wicked
His hubris
Delicious
I hold my breath
Then step forward to embrace him

Her mother gave her a *beyond me* look. "What the hell is that jibber-jabber?"

"A beautiful love poem. It means Isabel Mansfield recognized her lover's distasteful qualities and accepted him with total abandon."

Funny how words like *titanic, powerful, and wicked* also applied to Adam's personality. It was as if Adam and the man his mother loved were cut from the same cloth. Marla turned to the last entry in the book.

The leaves, the petals, the tears
Fall.
They cover me
As you walk away

She gasped. "Isabel knew exactly what she was about to do. It was the last thing she wrote before she killed herself."

Her parents looked at each other with blank faces. "What does this book have to do with anything?" said her dad. "And if this had been in Gladys's possession, what is it doing here?"

"Mom, Dad. I can't expect either of you to understand." Marla pointed. "This is the briefcase."

Bill shook his head. "We're going in circles."

"Don't you remember the details about Jimmy and Gladys Kingsley?"

"Of course. I know Jimmy killed Gladys Kingsley, set fire to Stoneham Manor, and went to jail for it. But what does *that* have to do with Adam?"

Chapter 10

"Enough of Adam's lies," said Marla. "The answer to everything is in this box. I'm ready to find out what."

Her mother opened her mouth and shut it again. After a moment's pause, Claire stood and threw her hands up. "I've had enough. It's been a long day and Pepper needs to be let out."

"I'll go with you," said her dad.

With a tear-stained face, her mother lifted Marla's chin. "I don't know what Adam's trying to get away with, but by God, I'll find a way to make him pay. You can count on it."

There had never been anything her mother had vowed that hadn't come to pass.

The words sounded so heartfelt Marla longed for the safety of her mother's arms. But tonight, the secrets in this closet left no room for melt-downs. She changed into a track suit and fingered the first file. *St. James Clinic.* By the time her father returned, she was buried in paper. "Dad, do you realize my husband, your son-in-law, the father of my children, might be a criminal?"

"Don't jump to conclusions, Marla. *Habeas corpus.* The law says you need proof. There's definitely a concern here, but let's find out what before you accuse your husband of something so god-awful."

"Really, Dad? You've already seen the bruises. The man is capable of more than you can imagine. Those investigators missed some key evidence in '89. I'm sure of it."

"I don't see how. But the question is, what are all these things doing in your house?"

Marla lifted the pearl bracelet again. "Dad, did the pearls and clasp of the necklace they found in Jimmy's truck, look like these?"

"Pearls are pearls, aren't they?"

"No. Don't you find it odd the necklace to this set is missing?"

"If you say so. But if it hadn't been claimed, the necklace they found back then, will likely have been auctioned off. The photos should still be in the archives, though. Look, you've gone through a lot for one day. Adam's not back till next week. I'll flush out this necklace business tomorrow."

Marla shivered. "I'm so worried about the girls. I hope they don't catch us in here."

"Don't dig any further. If we want the case to be airtight, you'll have to follow protocol. We'll resume in the morning."

Her dad poured them each another shot of brandy and left the room.

She swallowed hers in one gulp. The liquid burned through her body and tempered her mind as she got into bed.

Marla heard her dad's gentle knock, then the clunk of the coffee cups on the bureau.

"In here." Her head throbbed as she lay curled on the carpet in Adam's closet. Through heavy eyelids, she saw Bill freeze at the sight of her, then collapse to his knees. "No, no, no. I told you to wait for me."

"I couldn't. There's so much I need to show and tell you." She grabbed his arm for support and stood up.

"After you've had some coffee."

They both sat on the edge of her bed. A few sips calmed her enough to organize her thoughts. "Dad," she said, "Mansfield wasn't Adam's father's name."

"What do you mean?" He almost choked as he swallowed his coffee.

"Isabel Mansfield was a single mom. Her Death Certificate is in the folder." She squeezed her eyes shut for a moment.

To think, all these years, she'd been living in the dark—not knowing who Adam and his family really were.

These reports finally provided missing details she'd always wondered about.

"This will shock you, just like it did me, Dad. St. James wasn't an ordinary hospital or clinic. It was a mental health facility for children."

"What are you saying?"

"From ages eight to ten, Adam spent over two years under the care of a Dr. Fyodor Volinoff."

Bill sighed. "When you and Adam became serious about each other, I checked him out. Background was a bit hazy, but there were no red flags. I mean, who would try to fool a cop?" His chest heaved. "Anyway, his driver's license showed he was two years older than the other kids in your grade level. I figured it had something to do with different school systems or time off for travel. Now I see where he lost those years."

"He had me fooled, too. Didn't know his real age for the longest time. Then, well ..." she crossed her arms, "his age didn't matter to me after that. Now I see how important it really was. Did you learn anything about the Mansfield name back then?"

"A few details about his mother's birth and death. The obituary said nothing about how she died. I could've dug deeper, and now I wish I had, but when I found Adam Mansfield listed under all the private schools, he'd said he'd attended, I figured he was truthful. I didn't find any criminal record, not even a parking ticket. I believed what he'd told us ... that he was an only child with deceased parents. I left it at that."

"Yup, Adam is very convincing."

"Okay, so who was his father?"

Marla sucked in a breath and trembled, afraid of what she was about to reveal. "DK."

"DK? K for Kingsley?"

She nodded.

"Adam had a connection to Gladys Kingsley?" His hands flew to his head.

"Turned out Donald Kingsley was his mother's professor at the university and Adam's biological father. Older teacher fraternizing with his student. A big no-no. No wonder he didn't marry Isabel. He may have been worried about losing his job."

"I'll be damned."

"After his mother's death and subsequent therapy, Dr. Volinoff released Adam to the care of his father, who was by then married to Gladys." She handed him a paper. "Look at this document. It shows Adam's father had taken custody, but no name change. Adam remained a Mansfield."

She handed her father another folder labelled *Academics*.

He skimmed it. "Every school says he was brilliant. Yet he bounced around and never stayed put."

"Bad behaviour and influencing others. The reports show parents demanded his expulsion. Gladys threatened to withdraw financial support. If that didn't work, she'd simply find Adam another placement ... guess money talks in that circle. And so it went, until his father died and Adam moved to Stoneham. Could you imagine what he must have gone through as a little guy, losing his mother that way and having a father who didn't take responsibility for his son until he had to? When I think about it, Adam always described his stepmother as *Winnie the Witch*. He must have hated her. Those reasons alone would have caused anyone to break down. Sad what we do to each other."

"Marla, there's no excuse for what he's done to *you*."

"I know. He's a monster and scares me, but now I know why."

"Get this 'sorry' business out of your head. He's guilty of assault and we're going to find out what else. So many questions need to be answered—like, what was he doing in Stoneham in the first place?"

"Especially if he hated Gladys for luring his father away. First from his mother, then from him. Guess Adam's mother couldn't hold a candle to a rich socialite and philanthropist, even if the lady was a good ten years his dad's senior. I remember the article in the Stoneham newspaper had her at age seventy-five. Sounds like DK played with the young one, but the old one had more to offer. No wonder Adam always said, 'I sure learned a lot from my dad.' He didn't mean good things at all. So much for a proper upbringing."

"What a gold-digger."

"That explains his mother's emotional state. She felt abandoned and broken-hearted. All these years, Adam blamed himself for his mother's death. Thought he wasn't loveable enough. He had so much pain."

A terrible thought went through Marla's mind.

Adam's violence seemed to always spring from moments he'd felt inadequate or betrayed. Like when he couldn't find lilacs on her birthday and substituted a rose. Her look of disappointment must have made him lose it. Or not wanting her to work for fear she'd distance herself from him. Had *she* replaced his mother?

Marla looked at the box. Still so many files to read through.

She had to stay strong. There were bound to be more shocking details.

She flipped open another folder. There it was, the photo of Isabel Mansfield wearing the turquoise jewellery. "Look at this, Dad."

"Wow. Adam has an amazing resemblance to her."

"You know, Sarah and Susan were looking for family-tree information recently for a school project. He said he had a photo of his mother. V*oilà*." Had he already shown it to the girls?

Marla slipped it into her back pocket.

Her dad shook his head. "So, Adam's a Kingsley. This sheds a whole different light on that fire. Something really stinks."

"I know, Dad. I'm frightened."

"You and the kids are getting out of this house."

"Adam won't be back till next week. So, for now we're safe. Besides, the girls have final exams. I can't take them out of school until Thursday. Then the following Monday, they're leaving for three weeks of sports camp. That'll help."

"Okay, bring them to Stoneham after school ends on Thursday. They can keep your mother company."

"Good idea. I'll drive them to camp from there. How will we keep Adam at bay?"

Her dad put his hands on her shoulders. "As long as you stay with us, he won't dare show himself in Stoneham. But first, you're going to report the assaults and charge him. Here's where physical proof comes in. Photos."

"Dad, I've already done that."

"Are they dated?"

"Yes." Marla dropped her head. "Remember the last time I came to visit you?"

"You had a bruise on your forehead and said it was a shovel."

"I was embarrassed and didn't want you to worry."

"I believed you, Marla. How long has this been going on?"

She stiffened. "Since I accused him of having affairs ... year one."

He smacked his forehead. "You shouldn't have stayed with him, Marla."

"I know that now. But the twins came along." She covered her face. "It happens. The next day, it blows over, and you couldn't find a more wonderful husband and father. I've always felt so confused about what to do. Over time, I learned to avoid his triggers. When I don't, he feels threatened and reacts."

"And ... his father-in-law a police chief." He closed his eyes and shook his head. "Does anyone else know about this, or even suspect it?"

"Well, I've never been to the doctor, if that's what you mean. Adam's very careful." Marla paused. "You know, I think Evelyn might suspect something."

"What do you mean, might?"

"She's commented on the bruises under my arms in the change room at the tennis club. I've managed to deflect the truth, but she looks at me with shifty eyes. Then she makes a point of fussing about how lucky I am. That Adam's a perfect gentleman—too good to be true. I think she's waiting for me to confess. I got close a couple of times then chickened out."

"It's time to tell her, Marla."

"You're right. I will." She walked over to her dresser and scuttled through a drawer. "Dad, I've kept a diary, but I'd never want to share it unless I have to. Besides the photos I took, I also have a couple of ... mementos."

The telephone rang.

"Mom," shouted Susan from the end of the hall. "It's Dad."

Her father tossed her a look of authority, "I'll put it on speaker and talk first, Marla."

He stepped out and stared down the hall at Susan. "I brought your mom some coffee, but she's in the bathroom right now. I'll talk to your dad until she comes out. Hang up as soon as I pick up. Okay, sweetie?"

Susan nodded and disappeared.

He re-entered the bedroom, closed the door, and after picking up, he waited for Susan's phone to click off. "Adam, my man. How's the auction going? Are you a gazillionaire, yet?"

"Well, in fact, things are going extremely well, Bill."

"That's great. But speaking of great, your daughters were fantastic last night. You'd have been very proud of them. Hold on, Adam. Marla's coming. You're on speaker."

"I'm here, Adam," she choked.

"Everything okay, Marla?"

"Yeah, yeah, I'm ..."

Her dad jumped in again while she summoned her courage. "Like I was saying, Sarah and Susan were great. We had such a spectacular night. Claire and I want to thank you for your thoughtfulness. The limo, the fabulous restaurant—you spoiled us. I'll never get Claire to come home now."

Adam laughed. "My pleasure. Nothing but the best for my family," he said. "Please say hello to Claire for me. Marla, can I talk to you for a minute?"

"Bye from me, Adam," said her dad. "You take it easy, now. We'll be seeing you real soon."

"We're alone now," murmured Marla.

"What's wrong? You don't sound right."

"Just tired. Guess the last few weeks have finally caught up with me."

"I'll fix that. We made a killing this week. Start packing. Soon as the girls are at camp ... it's you, me, and Paris. We're going to hop on the TGV train to Provence—*des truffes noires, Chateauneuf du Pape, beaucoup d'amour ... ça va?*"

"Sounds dreamy. You should have seen the girls last night. Very impressive. And holy smokes, Adam, the flowers you sent? Sarah and Susan were over the moon."

"I know. They already thanked me. I seem to remember *you* flipping over flowers once upon a time."

"Must be how you cast your spells. Listen, Adam, I've decided to take the girls to Stoneham when they finish school on Thursday. I'll drive them to camp from there."

"How come? I was looking forward to seeing my children."

"My mother wants to spend more time with them. All of a sudden, she's kid-friendly."

"Claire? Not bloody likely, but go ahead." Adam cleared his throat. "So, tell me. You're not by any chance planning to meet up with Jimmy, are you?"

"Where did that come from? I have nothing more to say to him. Look, if you don't want me to go ..."

"I said go. See you next week, Red and ... start packing."

God, he sounded so sincere.

Chapter 11

Marla's dad wiped the last of the breakfast dishes. "Okay, let's hit the road, Claire. See you in Stoneham everyone and ... good luck on those exams, girls."

Her mother raised a fist to her mouth and sang a spirited, *"Oh, yeah!"*
Claire would go out the way she came in. A celebrity.
The girls laughed, said their good-byes, and raced up the stairs.
"Dad, I'll be waiting for your call," said Marla.
He pointed his finger at her. "Do your homework and stay calm."
"Won't be easy. I'll have to wait till the girls are in school."
She walked to the passenger side of the car. Her mother had already buckled up.
"Great having you here, Mom."
Her mother's usual response had never sounded so feeble.
"I ... I know."
Had she imagined the subsequent sigh and sniffle?

Marla called her dad the minute she was alone the next morning.
"Just about to call you. We got lucky, Marla. The chief inspector found the case box and you were right. The clasp in your photo of the bracelet matched the clasp on the necklace in Jimmy's truck. The team is suspicious enough to bring Adam in for questioning.

Since they can only trace the jewellery through insurance papers, they'll need time."

"What next?"

"Detectives will be dispatched to your house."

"Dad, I can't do this," Marla moaned.

"Yes, you can. For many reasons, least of all Jimmy. Canada has no statute of limitations on crimes like robbery or murder. Jimmy may have been wrongly convicted. You must do this." He paused. "I'm sorry for accepting Jimmy's guilt so quickly and preventing you from seeing him. At the time, we couldn't let you get involved in such a terrible situation. I have to admit, both your mom and I were blinded by Adam. It's sad, but true. After what I've seen now, we owe it to Jimmy to tear this case apart."

Her father would never know how much that meant to her.

"These new developments are very delicate, though. Especially in light of the publicity for locking up someone who may have been innocent." He sighed. "There'll be hell to pay and heads will roll."

"You mean yours?"

"No, but I still feel terrible." He paused. "Marla ... let's talk about the assault charges now. You'll have to go to the station. The officers there will ask you tough questions, make you very uncomfortable. But it's their job. With Adam out of town, they'll wait till he returns to press charges."

"Do you think the Crown will consider it serious enough? I've heard it's a grey area for women. Not to mention that men have always twisted things in their favour—the secret old boys' network."

"Not anymore. There's zero tolerance for spousal abuse, especially with kids involved. Just be honest, don't let them trip you up, and provide them with the evidence."

She'd only created the Memento Box to one day throw in Adam's face. She'd never dreamed it would be used against him in court.

"I sure hope I can do this." Marla's eyes darted to every corner of the room. "I get such an uneasy feeling. Could Adam be watching me?"

"No worries, Marla. I didn't tell you, but I checked for devices when you slipped out. Closet is clear of surveillance. That man really trusts you."

"I've never given him reason to doubt me. All right, Dad. I'll do it. Hope he doesn't show up unexpectedly."

"He's too busy making money, Marla. Keep your phone on. I'd have a car there so fast he wouldn't have time to blow his nose."

Her father's words settled her.

"This should never have happened to you. I'll never forgive myself."

She could hear the remorse in his voice. "How could anyone predict a situation like this? Adam is no ordinary artist. He's a con-artist. Dad, there's only a small window before the girls come home. I'd better get back to work. Call you later."

Marla sat down at her desk and sifted through the medical gobbledygook. A line from Dr. Fyodor Volinoff's psychiatric reports popped out at her.

Killed the pet cat.

She blinked and read it again.

Client: Adam Mansfield, Male, Age Fourteen.

Presenting Problem: Stepmother, Mrs. Kingsley, reports client deliberately broke two artifacts in her home. Client was sent to his room by father, Donald Kingsley. According to Mrs. Kingsley, client became angry, and in retaliation for being chastised for deliberately breaking priceless artifacts, he killed the pet cat. Mrs. Kingsley believes client timed the cat's exit from his bedroom and violently slammed the door on it, severing its tail, letting the cat bleed to death. Mr. and Mrs. Kingsley observed client showed no remorse. Parents fear further violence.

Diagnostic Impressions: These symptoms are consistent with a diagnosis of Conduct Disorder. This is quite concerning as he exhibits antisocial tendencies that could develop into Antisocial, Personality Disorder in adulthood if not addressed. This is likely the result of severe attachment ruptures due to his mother's suicide, father's emotional neglect, and conflict with stepmother.

Recommendation: admittance to St. James Clinic for observation and therapy.

Medication: mood stabilizer – Risperidone.

Holy smokes. Major relapse at fourteen.

Twelve years with a man capable of this?

No longer able to hold back her terror, Marla exploded. Her cries like a banshee. Poor Pepper trembled and yowled alongside her. Oh god, the police could arrive any minute. She splashed water on her face, applied makeup to mask the puffiness, and forced herself to continue the search while she waited.

Adam's academic reports were next. Marla stared at his photos—so clean-cut and preppy. He was described in superlative terms, until the tone changed. Smoking and distributing cannabis, bullying, falsifying signatures, cheating, spreading rumors, and vandalism. Gladys had stepped in and blamed it on the incompetence of the teachers and administrators instead of getting to the root of the problem.

Couldn't they see he was a child crying out for his father's attention? She now knew why Adam called her Winnie the Witch. If they'd only handled him with some kindness and given him a sense of belonging, he could have been a different person. A better person.

Marla switched to the wealth management file. Financial statements, investments, deeds, surveys—all interesting. But the real-estate section caught her attention. It included photos of the beautiful condo she and Adam had first lived in. It gave her a moment of peaceful reflection. Another showed a sprawling Tudor mansion. The one Adam was raised in? The estate sold for ten million dollars, with the proceeds eventually transferring to Donald's account. Did that mean the inheritance had filtered down to Adam?

If that wasn't enough, the artwork portfolio that had transferred to Donald Kingsley was even more shocking. Adam had only hung some of Dorian Conte's reproductions in their home, but she'd seen a few masterpieces in Gallery One and the Picasso in the hall of Adam's condo. According to the documents, Adam's father also had a private collection in prestigious galleries around the world. Some of them had been donated, but many were just on loan, and therefore liquid enough to get his hands on. The paper trail showed the artwork had originally belonged to Gladys's previous husbands. Donald's professor salary certainly could never have afforded such luxury. Gladys paid a hefty price for the love of a younger man. What a score for Donald.

Adam had always been a flashy guy with deep pockets, but *whew*, the kind of wealth described in this file was beyond her imagination.

Would Marla find surprises in Donald Kingsley's will as well? As she scrolled down, she noticed the date.

What the hell?

Strange to be of sound mind and body, then die of a heart attack so soon afterwards. Was Adam the named beneficiary to this fortune?

You bet—along with a name Marla didn't recognize.

The scrunch of wheels in her driveway gave her a start. *Police.* She checked her face in the mirror again, took a deep breath, and answered the door.

Time to bite the bullet. Probably easy compared to the bombs she knew would go off in the next few days.

"Thanks for meeting me here, Evelyn." Marla gave her friend a lingering hug and guided her to a corner booth.

Evelyn tapped her fingers on the table as the waitress took their orders.

"Okay. What's going on?"

"It's Adam."

"Is he sick?"

"No, health is good. But ... my life with him isn't." Marla opened her handbag, took out a large manila envelope, and pulled out the photos.

Evelyn's jaw dropped. The sadness on her face deepened as she studied them.

"I'm sorry I lied to you. I thought it would stop. Now things are out of control. I need your help."

"Marla, it's me that should apologize. I'm a damn fool and a coward. I had a bad feeling when I saw those bruises in the change room. I should have pushed for the truth. How could he do that? I knew he was too good to be true." Evelyn grabbed her hands and squeezed. "The girls—please tell me he's not hurting them."

"No, never, I promise. But *I* can't go on."

"And you shouldn't. I'm ashamed of myself, but I'm here to help now. What can I do?"

"I've already filed a report with the police and Crown Prosecutor. The justice of the peace set some conditions so that Adam can't come anywhere near me, the girls, or the house until things are sorted out. I feel safe for now."

Evelyn kept her eyes riveted.

"The attorney suggested I line up a witness. You're the only one I could think of. I know you didn't see it happen, but at least you could tell them what you noticed."

"Oh, Marla, I've been suspicious, but you always had a good excuse ready. Any time we were together, you two were so lovey-dovey, who was I to question you? Even the last time we came for dinner, you said the evil shovel, not Mr. Perfect, was at fault. Jesus, Marla. Do the girls know?"

"Please, Ev. You have to keep this a secret for a while, even from Philip."

"Listen to me, Marla. You've got to tell the girls."

"How can I possibly let them think so badly of their father?"

"It'll come out. You know how news travels. How would you like them to find out from a stranger? Or worse—have Adam feed them some lies?"

Their lunch arrived. Marla placed the envelope back in her purse.

The Scent of Lilacs

Her friend was right. There could be a slip-up and ... she'd constantly be looking over her shoulder. But with Adam still away and the girls off to camp soon, she'd have time to figure it out.

Evelyn buttered a roll, then pushed it away.

Marla patted Evelyn's hand. "I understand how it looks, but now that I've started the process, I feel a strength I didn't know existed." She bit into a shrimp. "Please eat. It'll work out."

By end of week, a warrant and summons to appear in court were in place. She knew that with no medical reports, bruises alone weren't enough to keep Adam in jail longer than overnight or until his lawyer took action. The wheels were in motion—no turning back.

Chapter 12

Marla's head spun. She'd filtered through Adam's documents, filed police reports, worked on drawings, cooked meals, dealt with the stress of exam week, and packed for camp—all by Thursday.

Amazing what you can accomplish with a gun to your head.

"Okay, girls, we're here," she said, turning into her parents' driveway.

As soon as she cut the engine, Susan jumped out, released Pepper, and yelled, "There you go, Pepper. Freedom!" Flinging her hands onto the grass, Susan executed a perfect cartwheel.

"Ditto," shouted Sarah, "no more school and no more dancing." Running to join her sister, Sarah performed an impressive back flip.

"Wow," said Marla. "I've never seen you do that before, Sarah. Maybe gymnastics is your thing, honey?"

"I'd love that, Mom."

"Okay. New game-plan. Grab your bags, girls. Let's find out what Grandma has in store for you this weekend."

Behind the screen, the front door had been left open. With all the barking and noise, it was a wonder her parents hadn't rushed outside.

When they walked in, it only took one whiff to understand why.

"Grandma Slater's Shepherd's Pie! Smells great," said Sarah, scooping up a finger-full of mashed potato.

Susan reached for the ends of her grandad's apron ties.

"I knew you two would be trouble," he said. His fake scowl was followed by laughter.

Marla savoured the happy moments that continued throughout dinner.

There hadn't been many lately.

"Okay girls, dessert later. We have more important things to do now," said Claire. She gave them each a wink and scraped her chair back. "Bill, you and Marla are on cleanup."

"What else is new, boss? Is it alright if Marla and I finish our wine on the porch first?"

Marla sat down on the swing and swirled her glass. "I left the documents in the car until the girls go to bed. What's happening on your end?"

Her dad sat across from her on the bench. "The only thing the force allegedly has on that … jerk … is possession of stolen property." He took a sip of his wine. "Was there any mention of jewellery in the will, Marla?"

"None. Gladys was very shrewd." She stopped rocking and leaned forward. "According to the files, she transferred a sizeable portion of wealth to Donald in a prenuptial agreement. Adam inherited some of that immediately after his father's death. That's when he moved to Stoneham and bought the Mustang. The rest of the inheritance transferred to him in March. He bought the downtown condo next. Can't tell you how shocked I was the night Adam first took me to see it."

"No kidding. I remember our visits there after you got married. The Picasso, the expensive furniture, the spectacular views of the skyline—something out of *Architectural Digest*. Had no idea he was so wealthy."

"I know. He had money to buy cars, the trip to Paris, a new house, opened Gallery One, and didn't even want me to work. And there's much more where that came from, including millions in artwork."

"Whew. Adam's father must have been some catch for Gladys."

Marla sighed. "Imagine how careful Adam had to be all this time not to slip up and reveal his parents' real names. Nicknames were the only ones he'd ever mentioned."

"Hell of a chess player. What else did you learn?"

"Adam always described his father as dramatic, charming, distinguished-looking—an intellectual with lots of accomplishments. Twice a widow and likely a billionaire, Gladys could afford to snag a younger trophy husband like Donald. Kids weren't in her plans, though. She swept Adam aside. Boarding school, travel, and made him a ward of the butler. Sad, isn't it? Hence, 'angry boy, angry man'."

Her dad pulled a pad from his shirt pocket and made a few notes.

"Wait till you hear this. Gladys must have assumed Donald had a guilty conscience for being a lousy father. To please him more, she added a proviso to her will that stated if Donald predeceased her, Adam would become the beneficiary of the balance of her estate. But Gladys changed her mind after Donald died. I found the codicil in the file. Paperwork shows Adam contested the will, but didn't win." They locked eyes. "Good enough motive, Dad?"

He raised his brows as he emptied his glass. "It sure sounds plausible."

"Now what?"

"We bring him in. Through the insurance, police have already confirmed the jewellery belonged to Gladys. Now they need to figure out how Adam got it. Cops are on his trail and waiting for his return. After you drop the girls at camp on Monday, I want you to come right back here."

"Of course, I will."

On Saturday evening, Marla elbowed her way to the bar at Brody's.

"Marla, me darlin.' You've been away too long, lass," said Connor Brody, a short, barrel-chested man with rosy cheeks and a kind smile. "What will it be, Murphy's or Kilkenny?"

Pubs—the seat of the soul in every small town.

Her mother waved her over and rolled her eyes. "Marla, you look so … um … polished. Jeans are okay, but did you have to wear a navy blazer? And jeez, lose the scarf, will you?"

"You know, I fit in just fine at home, but ..." She eyed her mother from top to toe—leather vest over her t-shirt, long peasant skirt, and cowboy boots. "I'd forgotten Brody's had a dress code, Mother."

Her dad coughed and slapped the back of his guitar. "Time to give this baby a ride."

The noise in the room hushed. Her mother centred herself then burst into a Joplin squeal.

The crowd exploded. Yup, Claire sure knew how to start a party. As the final chords of *Piece of My Heart* trailed, Marla joined the frenzy with a two-finger whistle.

Brody's, her parents, this wild music—great medicine for her fragile heart.

She sat back and let the golden liquid slide down her throat to work its magic, while the musical duo moved on to *Me and Bobby McGee* and *Cry Baby*. It had been a long time since she'd felt this mellow. After the second beer, she sauntered towards the washroom and glanced up at the entrance.

No! Impossible!

She groped her way back to the stage.

Catching her dad's eyes, she gave a sideways tilt of her head to signal the entrance.

He dropped his guitar and flew to the bar with Marla in tow. "Connor, police business. Run the tapes," he said, as he pulled out his phone and made a call.

Adam's presence held Marla captive. Her feet nailed to the floor. A shadow shifted behind Adam.

Marla gasped as the spotlight hit the face. The face she'd tried for years to forget. Older now—more mature. His sandy hair shorter, but the clipped beard that covered his otherwise smooth jawline couldn't hide the face she knew so well. Her legs turned to jelly. She held onto the bar for support.

Pocketing his phone, her dad grabbed onto her. "Marla, I've got you."

Her mother stepped to her other side.

Adam waved and snaked his way around the tables.

For sure he'd been home. How had she left his closet? Had she put everything back in place? Had he opened his drawers? Could he tell the trunk had been moved?

Marla's stomach knotted.

"Listen carefully," said her dad. "OPP is on the way. I'll do the talking."

"What about J—?"

He cut her off. "Never mind him. Follow my lead and don't interfere. Once Adam's in custody, I'll head to the station to follow up. You take your mother straight home and stay there. Clear?"

They both nodded.

"Now smile."

As she watched Adam strut towards her, some of the women in the room craned their necks to stare at her husband—the body and face of Adonis. Adam lapped it up like a peacock.

"What are you doing here?" she sputtered.

"I missed you, Red." He gave her a hungry squeeze.

Her dad interrupted their intimate moment. "Adam, good to see you. Have you come straight from the airport?"

"Pretty well. Limo dropped me off at home. Didn't even go in. I just threw my suitcase into the car, stopped at your house to see my girls and … here I am."

Marla had inherited her mother's height. Her chin rested squarely on Adam's shoulder. It gave her a clear view of the phantom hovering at the entrance. Even from a distance, she could see the remorse and pain in Jimmy's eyes still held kindness. In that split second, twelve years of doubt, uncertainty, and resentment dissolved.

If only Jimmy knew he'd pushed her into the arms of the wrong man. She yearned to run to him.

But wrapped in her husband's arms, how could she?

"Did Jimmy know I'd be here?" said Marla.

"Of course not," snickered Adam. "At the door, I just fed him a line about how you must have found a last-minute sitter for the girls. Guy still believes everything I say."

Her blood boiled.

Wait—Adam had brought Jimmy here for a reason—to get a reaction. Okay then.

"Jimmy," Marla called out and waved.

Adam's grip tightened around her.

Her old boyfriend looked straight at her.

She smiled and gave him a thumbs-up.

He gave her a military salute then slipped out of sight.

"I thought it only appropriate that I should be the one to arrange a little reunion," said Adam.

She recalled the telephone conversation after the recital.

This was no coincidence.

As Adam bent to kiss her, she clamped her lips shut.

He lifted her chin. "Don't be mad. Now that we're here, let's have a good time."

Her dad stepped in. "No. That's it for tonight. Not every day my son-in-law comes to visit. We have a lot to catch up on. Let's go." He put his arm around Adam's shoulder and nudged him forward.

Adam gave Marla a questioning glance and shrugged.

She shrugged back.

Adam felt stumped. Bill's buddy-buddy attitude tonight seemed off. And why was he pressing down so hard on his shoulder?

"Were the girls excited to see you?" said Bill.

"They sure were. Funny enough, though, they didn't mind me leaving to join you here. I think Fiona was giving them boyfriend tips."

He spotted Jimmy under the halo of a lamppost. Waiting for a lift no doubt. He'd picked him up at Milt's knowing Jimmy would have to find his own way back. Guy wouldn't be too comfortable staying at Brody's after the surprise he'd arranged for him. Adam had said, "Come for a beer—just the two of us."

Jeez, why was Bill digging his fingers into his shoulder?

"Bit aggressive, no?"

"Oh—sorry." His father-in-law loosened his grip, but hung on.

"Where in hell are we going, Bill? My car's not over here."

Adam had barely finished the sentence when a black and white cruiser roared into the lot and screeched to a halt right beside them. Good thing no one inside Brody's could hear over the music, but outside, all eyes turned towards the scene with him in the middle.

The driver door of the cop car opened almost before the wheels stopped spinning, while his partner came around the trunk.

"This our man, Bill?"

His father-in-law took on a cold, hostile stare. "Yup, he's all yours."

The officer yanked Adam's arm behind his back, pushed him against the cruiser, and handcuffed him.

"Is this a joke?" yelled Adam.

"What's his name again, Bill?"

Alerted by the sounds of the scuffle and curious to see who was being detained, Jimmy raced towards the scene. He arrived just as Bill answered.

"Adam Mansfield—Kingsley case."

Adam willed himself not to flinch or move a muscle, but his brain was on fire.

Kingsley? How could Bill know that?

Jimmy's jaw dropped and his eyes blazed. "What the fuck is he talking about, Adam? What have you got to do with Kingsley?"

Adam had always wondered how the guy would react if he knew.

Bill grabbed Jimmy's shoulders and held him back. "You're on parole. Shut up and stay out of this."

Pain shot up Adam's back as someone whipped him around.

"Adam Mansfield?"

"Yeah."

"You're under arrest for possession of stolen property. You have the right ..."

What in hell had they stumbled on to cause this?

The officer repeated the question. "Do you understand?"

"I heard you," he snarled. "I don't know what game you're playing, but you're making a big mistake." He broke into a laugh.

Drew Durban would end this shit-storm in a minute.

"Think this is funny?" said the officer. "We'll see about that." He shoved him into the cruiser and slammed the door shut.

Adam scanned the inside of the cruiser, remembering the first and only time he'd been in one. Twelve years ago, on his wedding day. Nothing had changed. No handle on the inside, mesh grill between the front and back, and again with the bloody handcuffs. He hadn't minded the feel of cold metal the first time, a gag for the amusement of the wedding guests. Bill had been gentle back then. Adam had even kept the engraved cuffs in the drawer in his closet, as a souvenir.

That was it!

Bill had asked if he'd come straight from the airport. His father-in-law had just spent the weekend at the Mansfield house. Must have needed something. No wonder Marla seemed nervous. It wasn't the shock of the reunion with Jimmy. Jesus Christ! She knew exactly what was going down. Based on twelve years of marriage, this should never have happened. He'd tested and monitored Marla's obedience carefully. Even his love taps had never deterred her.

Bill set up this sting and led him right into the hands of the cops. Marla hadn't even tried to save him from this embarrassing arrest.

She'd crossed the line.

Adam sat motionless in the cruiser, his mind racing. Hell, he was a master chess player and could anticipate several moves ahead.

But this arrest? Hadn't seen it coming.

All those years, the jewellery had been safe at the bank. He'd only placed it in his drawer because his damn pawn broker had wanted photos for a client. A crooked smile broke on his face. No harm, the Bill of Sale would be proof enough.

The two goons hauled him out of the cruiser and dragged him inside the station.

No point struggling. Why give them the satisfaction of holding power over him?

"Boys," said the sergeant, waiting for them at the entrance with his hands behind his back. "Take the man's keys and send someone to pick up his car at Brody's. We have a warrant to search it. Then process and lock him up tight."

Before Adam could protest, they rifled through his pockets and emptied the contents onto the counter. An officer crouched down to remove the laces from his shoes. "Wouldn't want you to hang yourself."

He'd expected that. Dr. Volinoff had done the same thing at the clinic.

A surge of anger swept through him.

After fingerprints and photos, they led him to a cell, removed his handcuffs, and gave him a little shove. "In you go." Like a dog.

"Where's Bill?" Adam shouted as the door slammed behind him.

"Chief Slater has nothing to do with this."

"Then who's behind this nonsense?"

"Warrant came from the city."

"I want my lawyer," he shouted.

The officer looked down at his notepad to make sure he'd been properly vetted on that request. "No problem."

Adam dialed Drew Durban's number. Voicemail.

Of course, estate and tax lawyers weren't available 24/7 like those other guys. Likely wouldn't hear back till Monday.

"What's wrong? Can't reach him? Would you like us to call a duty lawyer?"

"No."

Waste of time. They wouldn't get him out any faster.

"Make yourself comfortable, then. We'll write up the report."

Adam bared his teeth the minute he was alone. Stark and dimly lit, the cell smelled of a putrid mixture of urine and disinfectant. Reminded him of that room he'd been locked up in so long ago. It sickened him. He sat down on the edge of the cot and closed his eyes. But as the odours persisted, so did his memories.

Fourteen years old. What did they expect? Testosterone and adrenaline off the chart. Hatred and revenge for two asshole guardians who'd put him there. All because of a dumb old cat. He swore to never let it happen again. But here he was. This time because of his wife, her father, and these brutal henchmen.

Dr. Volinoff had offered Adam medication back then. He'd gladly accept that kind of deliverance right now.

Marla trembled as she and her mother stood outside Brody's watching Adam's take-down. She'd expected force to be exerted on Adam, but why was her dad restraining Jimmy?

She had to find out.

Following her dad's instructions, she waited for Jimmy, her dad, and the cruiser to leave, then drove her mother home. Her heart pounded as she pulled into her parents' driveway. "Mom, send Fiona out and please watch the girls."

For once—no protest.

After dropping off the sitter, Marla sped to the Stoneham satellite station. She knew there'd only be the usual handful of local force that took care of minor infractions, but as Regional Chief, her dad still held jurisdiction.

"What the hell are you doing here?" he shouted when he spotted her.

"I have to know what's going on. Where's Adam?"

"OPP station next door."

She hesitated. "And Jimmy?"

"Milt took him home. He'd better not be anywhere near here. I told him to call his lawyer—there've been developments."

"How did he take it?"

"Like a wild-man." He swiped a hand across his mouth. "I don't blame him. Imagine finding new clues after twelve years in jail."

Marla sighed and dropped onto a chair.

The clerk held up the phone. "Call for you, Chief."

"I'll take it in the empty office. Someone, please get this girl a coffee."

A few sips seemed to help, but her dad's sombre face when he returned, sent her spiralling again. "What's happened?"

"Adam couldn't reach his lawyer." Her dad met her eyes. "Two teams will be arriving. One regarding the alleged theft. Another with the judge's warrant for the assault charges."

She shuddered.

"I'd give anything to see Adam squirm when they lean into him." Her dad's smirk changed to a frown. "Except, we both know what a sly fox Adam is. I hope the charges stick."

Marla sighed. "Jeez, Dad. Why did Adam have to show up here? How will I explain this to Sarah and Susan?"

"We'll figure it out. Let's go. I'll be right behind you. Hope your mother has something strong in that medicine cabinet of hers."

Not even Pepper came to greet them when they arrived. A pot of pungent tea sat steeping. Her dad must have called ahead.

"Hope this tea does the trick," said Marla. She remembered the time her mother had knocked her out with some infusion when Jimmy had been arrested. Unfortunately, this tea had no such effect. She tossed and turned. How would she tell the girls their dad was a thief and maybe a lot more? She'd never been a good liar. Every strategy she came up with had flaws. She finally gave up and opened the blinds.

Red sun ... bad omen.

Maybe things would be easier with a good breakfast. She tiptoed into the kitchen and rooted through the fridge.

By the time her mother joined her, Marla had already finished a whole pot of coffee and was placing a tray of bacon in the oven to stay warm.

"Just what you need to wind you up, Marla—caffeine." Her mother shook her head. "Sometimes I wonder ... Come on Pepper, let's get Grandpa and get out of here."

Sarah, still in pajamas, sauntered into the kitchen and sat with her feet on the chair. Susan trailed behind her. "Mm. Something smells good. I'm starving."

The Scent of Lilacs

"Hey, I heard you two had fun with Fiona last night. Care to share?" said Marla as she scrambled some eggs.

"Stuff you already know, Mom."

Sarah giggled, poured a glass of juice, and walked to the front door. "Hey, Dad's car's gone," said Sarah. She sounded surprised and disappointed. "Where did he go so early?"

Just then, Marla's parents returned from the back entrance.

"Eggs ready yet?" said her dad.

"Dishing them out right now."

"You didn't answer Sarah's question, Mom. Where's Dad?" said Susan.

No getting out of it now.

"There's a shipment coming in today. He had to go back to clear customs."

"On a Sunday?"

Marla nodded.

"Well, at least we got to see him. I'll call his cell."

"Best not to. He's got a lot on his mind. He'll call when he's free."

Her dad gave Marla a *not likely* glance.

She cleared her throat. "So, girls. Tomorrow's the big day. Are you ready for camp?"

Her dad's phone buzzed.

"I'll take it in the other room."

He was barely gone a minute.

Her belly filled with butterflies as soon as she saw his pinched face.

"Everything okay, Grandpa?" said Sarah.

"The truth is your mom and I have to run an errand. We'll bring home some treats from Mabel's Bakery. Chocolate *éclairs*?"

The girls gave him a thumbs-up.

Marla grabbed her purse and followed him out the door.

At the empty lot, half-way down he street, her dad pulled over.

Marla held her breath. "Okay, what's up?"

"Adam's lawyer must have checked his voice messages and called the station. Apparently, there's a document at the bank that exonerates Adam. His lawyer plans to access and deliver it on Monday. If detectives find the papers in order, they'll have to let Adam go." Bill shook his head. "Guy's always a step ahead."

"H-how could this be?"

"Simple. The Bill of Sale shows Gladys gifted the jewellery and briefcase to Adam."

"No. This can't happen." Marla clutched her hair. "The charge was supposed to keep him behind bars long enough to investigate Adam's involvement in the fire and Gladys's murder. Now what?"

"We're going to have to focus on the abuse. The second team will lay the assault charge, but they can only detain him until they're sure there's no threat to you or the girls. He'll be subpoenaed to appear in court to make a plea. Come Monday, he'll likely be let out on both charges."

Her heart raced. "Then what?"

"Once he's released, Adam is not allowed to make contact with you or the girls until he appears before a judge and new orders are decided on. Marla, that means you can't approach him either."

She balled her fists. "Too bad. I want to tear his eyes out. To think I was prepared to tell the girls their father was a thief. Imagine how Sarah and Susan would've reacted. Thank goodness I waited." She looked up. "So, Dad—three weeks is all the investigators have to find out the truth. Otherwise, the only complaint will be about me and I doubt that will land him in jail."

Her dad touched her hand. "Marla, there's something else you need to know."

She sat on the edge of the seat. "You're scaring me, Dad."

"This is a dangerous time in domestic cases. It's usually after charges are laid that the abuser is most likely to go off the rails—attack the wife, kidnap kids, or much, much worse."

"No. He wouldn't harm the girls. And ... Adam hasn't done more than use his hand on me. Never anything life-threatening. And when it happens, it's like ... like he's a caged animal, not a person. Certainly not the man I married."

"I know, but maybe that's because you've always accepted him back. Turning him in could make him snap. You could be in real danger." He pointed his finger at her. "Stay clear, you hear me? Don't provoke him and take every precaution. As a matter of fact, your best defense is to live with us for a while."

Her chin quivered. Her dad was right. What would Adam do if he thought she'd abandoned him ... like his mother had?

Bill looked at his watch.

The *éclairs*!

Chapter 13

Adam glanced at the clock Monday morning as he sat in the interrogation room, surrounded by detectives. His stomach grumbled. All they'd given him was a weak coffee and a dry muffin. The door opened.

"Get me out of here, Drew."

"You've got it, my friend." His lawyer tossed an envelope onto the table. "This charge is bogus. Read and release this man."

The lead detective examined the Bill of Sale. A glum expression crossed his face. "Adam Mansfield. You're free to go."

Adam scraped his chair back. "Thank Christ."

The staff sergeant had been watching from the doorway with a twisted grin. He raised his hand. "Not so fast, Mr. Mansfield. Detective Hawkins and her partners are also here to visit you."

Adam gave Drew a hard look.

A stocky police woman stomped towards him and stared as if she wanted to scrape the dirt off her boot. "State your name."

"Adam Mansfield."

Where in hell was this going?

"Adam Mansfield, you're under arrest for the assault of …"

He could forgive and forget the jewellery charge brought on by Marla as a misunderstanding, but this was total betrayal.

"Adam Mansfield, do you understand the charges?" barked Detective Hawkins.

"Do you think I'm stupid?"

Drew adjusted his glasses. "Adam, what are they talking about?"

"Ah, it's nothing."

Getting ready to grandstand, Detective Hawkins cleared her throat. "Adam Mansfield ..." She read the recognizance and summons out loud.

Her attitude prickled him. He flopped onto a chair, crossed his ankles, and laced his fingers behind his head. "It's all bull."

"Mr. Durban. We'll wait outside the door while you confer with your client."

The detectives filed out.

The more Drew read and looked at photos, the more his chest heaved.

Pfft. You'd think the guy had never touched anyone in his life.

Drew finally took off his glasses and stared at Adam with cold disgust. "I didn't come prepared to deal with this type of case. Why didn't you tell me this over the phone?"

"You think I knew about it?" he shouted. "Who expects their wife to go squealing to the police over what ... love taps?" He could feel his nerves ready to snap. Who did Drew think he was, to question his behaviour? Maybe he should remind Drew about who funded his lifestyle. Now that Adam really needed him, his lawyer was backing away—as if he was too good to dirty his soft country-club hands.

"Okay, let's get you out of here, then figure what's next, Adam." Drew opened the door. "Alright, Detective, my client will abide by the conditions. He will not approach his wife or children and will appear in court as the summons dictates."

Detective Hawkins folded her arms across her chest and nodded. "Then we'll see you in court."

Adam tucked in his shirt and followed Drew to the front desk. Bile rose in his throat as he demanded his belongings. The slower the clerk moved, the angrier he got. Another ten frustrating minutes passed to get what they'd taken from him. He snatched his car keys, pocketed his wallet, and marched outside in time to hear Drew say good-bye to someone on his phone.

Adam sneered as he met Drew's eyes. "I appreciate you coming. As usual, I intend to pay you well. But it seems to me you don't have the stomach for this sort of business. If this is beyond your scope, I can easily have my files transferred to someone else—someone hungrier. You see, I need a lawyer who's in my camp—one hundred percent."

"When I came today," said Drew "I figured the document from the bank was a simple 'get out of jail' card for a crime you didn't commit. I was glad to help." Drew shifted his feet. "We've been together a long time. I've watched you grow from boy to man and tried to help you handle the tough blows in your life. But this charge? I don't know … it's not my thing."

"Your choice."

After a moment's silence, Drew shrugged. "Look, I'm not going to abandon you. I just spoke with my colleague, Randy Wade. You can trust me to keep your finances in order while Randy takes care of this matter. Deal?"

He waited for Drew to sweat a little before agreeing.

"One more thing, Adam. I'd like to make a recommendation. Dr. Volinoff helped you in the past … I think you could use his guidance right now."

Sanctimonious jackass.

"Dr. Volinoff and I are none of your business," barked Adam before sliding behind the wheel of his car. He gunned the engine and sped away. From his rearview, he watched Drew brushing the dust off his suit, his eyes wide and mouth ajar.

Adam rolled down the window and spat. This miserable weekend had been all Marla's fault. He needed to teach her a lesson. She'd probably be on her way to camp with the girls this morning. But after that?

Adam punched a number into his phone. "Hey," he said.

A raspy voice answered, "Where the hell are you?"

"Christ. Spent the last couple of nights in the Stoneham slammer."

"What? You're here in town?"

"Meet me at Clarence Creek in half an hour, and bring me something to eat."

The Scent of Lilacs

Adam pulled over to the familiar, secluded spot behind the willow where he used to keep his eyes on his prize in the distance—Marla sitting on a blanket with that jerk Jimmy. He closed his eyes and could almost smell her. Hard to believe what she'd just done to him.

But why? They were life partners. Why else had fate put her locker beside his? He'd moulded the redhead to fit his plans. Made her depend on him so badly, she'd never leave him—not like his goddamned mother had. No, this drama had to be just another of Marla's gags, like her haircut episode. They'd laugh about it someday.

He glanced at his watch then opened the glove compartment.

Bloody cops.

Everything was out of place. With kids around, he'd been careful to hide his stash. He fumbled under the dash.

Still there, just as he expected. Nothing thorough about these officers of the law, especially in the middle of the night.

Adam walked to a picnic table at the edge of the creek, sat down and lit a joint.

That's better.

Wasn't long before the vintage Cadillac rumbled to a stop beside his Benz.

Ah, my benevolent caregiver.

At least Oliver was no traitor. Such a dignified man. But make no mistake—a wild, bred-in-the-bone, impulsive streak ran through him—like now, snatching the joint from Adam's mouth and taking the last draw.

"You look terrible, son. Have I taught you nothing about image?"

"Kind of hard, where I've been," laughed Adam. "What did you bring me?"

"Pastrami on rye and a soft drink."

Adam opened the brown paper bag. "Thanks. Remember the old days? No one could beat those wacky combinations you used to make me. I mean who feeds a child, salami with aubergines and hot pickled peppers?" He laughed and took a big bite of his sandwich.

"I was simply exposing you to a cultural experience. Part of your education. So, what brought you to the Stoneham Slammer Hotel? It better not affect me."

"Well, yes and no. Marla and Bill found the jewellery in my closet."

The old man's eyes popped. "Please, don't tell me it's gone."

"My bloody wife connected the pearl bracelet to the fire and necklace found in Jimmy's truck. I was arrested for possession."

"No!"

"Not to worry, my friend, we're both safe. Drew drove up with Gladys's original Bill of Sale. The jewellery's locked up at the station in the city. I'll claim it when I get back." Adam took another savage bite.

"I told you to get rid of ..."

"Never mind the 'I told you so'," interrupted Adam. "Plans are in motion. As soon as I have your cut, I'll call you."

"Good," grunted Oliver. "Now, what about the wife? Can you get her under control?"

"It's a little complicated. My dear, *loving* wife ... also charged me with assault. Groundless, of course."

"I should say so."

"Drew's colleague will get me off, then I'll figure out how to smooth things over with that shrew." Adam wolfed down the rest of his sandwich.

"Something tells me there's more bothering you."

"You're right. Now that the police connect me to the Kingsley case, they're going to start snooping. Even Jimmy knows. I did everything I could to cover our tracks, but we'd better both be careful."

"Christ Almighty. After all this time? I have no intention of spending my last few years locked up."

A car drove over the bridge, turned onto the gravel, and stopped.

Adam frowned. "Cops?"

"Laughing, joking, and taking photos? Nah, probably newlyweds. Must be mad."

"I totally agree," Adam kicked a rock into the creek. "Starts off great, then ... ah, never mind. Cops couldn't find any evidence before, and they won't now—as long as you and I keep our distance. Look, I have to go. Thanks for the sandwich. I'll be in touch."

Every time Adam saw Oliver, he realized it could be the last. Although fit and still boasting about his manhood, the geezer *was* in his eighties. He couldn't last forever ...

Adam smacked the steering wheel. Something or someone had caused his wife to mistrust him. He stewed about it all the way home and finally rolled up to the curb in front of his condo. Needing to blow off steam, he entered the lobby, removed his shirt and ran up the four flights of stairs in his tee. Breathless and sweating, he jiggled the key in the lock.

Music? Yes, of course—he'd forgotten. His gallery staff had accompanied him to Chicago and kind-hearted Nalin had stepped up to man Gallery One.

There she was at the breakfast bar, drinking a cup of tea and sketching. His heart skipped at the way she looked. Flip-flops, sweater hanging loosely over her shoulders, soft jersey skirt clinging to her hips, tawny skin gleaming, and her black hair shining from a recent shower. Normally, Adam would be all over her. But not after what he'd been through this weekend—and not with his t-shirt sticking to his chest.

Nalin jumped up. "Hey, this is nice. I wasn't expecting you yet."

He set the envelope containing the police reports on the hall console and caught a glimpse of his reflection in the mirror. He looked as vile as he felt. Even though he raised his hands in protest, Nalin circled her arms around his neck.

Adam kissed her coolly.

"What's wrong?"

"Just tired."

"Adam, I want to thank you," she said.

"What for?"

"For making me a pile of money last week. You were right. You said my art would sell, but I didn't realize I'd hit the jackpot."

"I know art, young lady." And she really was young, barely twenty-one. In the short time he'd known her, she'd blossomed both in business and pleasure.

Adam visualized *Human Inferno* hanging on the brick wall of her loft. The woman was hot and ... talented. But more importantly, her free spirit reminded him of his own mother.

Strong, powerful women had crept like shadows in and out of his life. But Marla had been different—someone real, sincere, and above all, a constant.

Why had she gone and spoiled things? Would she desert him, too?

"Join me for a drink?" he said, pouring a double shot of vodka over a couple of ice cubes.

"No. Too early."

He took a couple of sips.

Hm—needed that.

"Thanks for helping me out at the gallery, sweetheart."

"Least I could do. Oh, guess what?" Nalin squealed. "I sold the Central Park painting I called you about."

"Good girl. Who bought it?"

"A really nice guy. Said your wife suggested it to him."

Adam swallowed and almost choked on the ice cube. "Bob Wyllie?"

"Yeah, that was him. Who is he?"

"Marla's boss."

"Said not to tell her. It was going to be a surprise."

What the hell? Had Marla asked her boss to spy on him?

Adam looked into Nalin's eyes, but all he could see was Marla, the bitch who'd betrayed him.

I answer to no one, damnit.

He grabbed Nalin by the hair and gave her a savage kiss, then pushed her down onto the carpet.

"Adam," she yelled. "What are you doing? Stop."

"No. Take it or leave it. I'm sick of you women."

"Women?"

While holding her firmly down with his body, he unbuckled his belt.

Nalin screamed and fought back like a vicious beast. Somehow her arm slipped from under him. She pushed against his chest and dug her nails into his arms, clawing and drawing skin and blood.

Good thing he'd had the condo sound-proofed so he could crank up the volume of his beloved symphonies. Noise drawing attention would not be an issue. But Nalin's screeching? Couldn't take it. He smacked her across the mouth. "Easier on you if you shut up and stay still."

Nalin whimpered and stared at him with terror in her eyes.

Adam froze.

This was Nalin. Anyone but her. He'd promised himself.

He loosened his grip and flopped over on his back. "I'm so sorry. Never meant for this to happen."

Nalin sprang to her feet and ran to gather her things.

"Please don't go," he called.

"Adam. You've hurt me. I'm all about peace and love …" Her swollen and bloody lip quivered. "I don't know what triggered this, but I'm not sticking around. By the way, I believe in karma. We get what we deserve in life."

Adam rose from the floor. "It's my wife!" he yelled, running his fingers through his hair and pacing across the room. "Charged me with assault."

Nalin's jaw dropped.

Damn. Should have kept his trap shut.

A tear trickled down her face as she threw his apartment keys onto the table and bolted out.

Although he made no attempt to stop her, he couldn't help but watch from behind the curtain. Someone in a black suit approached her at the curb. They both peered up in Adam's direction. When he looked out again, Nalin was stepping into a taxi. She disappeared without even a glance back.

Adam yanked off his t-shirt and headed for the shower. The water streamed down on him, hot and soothing. He lingered for a while, washing Nalin from his mind and his life.

Good riddance.

Adam wiped himself dry and peered into his closet. Hard to believe he'd soon have to fill it with everything he owned. *Bloody wife. If the court date hadn't been set, he'd have pushed it forward himself.*

Throwing on a fresh shirt and jeans, he rubbed his hands together, grabbed the police envelope, and picked up his car keys.

On to more important matters—money, money, money.

It wasn't long before Adam walked into the designated police detachment, identified himself, and presented his documents. The sideways glances the cops gave him made him want to shout something nasty. But no, he still needed to stay in their good graces in order to collect the jewellery and arrange to enter the matrimonial home.

Smooth sailing. With the precious pouch safely under his arm, his hostilities had been placated. Next—a trip to his buyer, an electronic money-transfer of the cool *mil* to his account, a partial withdrawal, and a quick stop to drop some loot into his gallery vault.

And that, ladies and gentlemen, would complete Gladys's contribution.

His Fine Arts Degree that had included Theatre Arts, had paid off again. Adam grinned, thinking about how his sob story had convinced the cops to contact Marla. Her quick permission had stung him a little. But—one problem at a time.

The van and the police vehicle he'd organized had already arrived by the time he got to the family home. He asked the movers to wait till he'd cleared out his personal items before coming up to pack the rest. Cops must have taken pity and gave him some privacy.

Adam entered his closet. Although his vault had been emptied, the brilliant Bill of Sale had been his ticket to retrieve his valuables and complete the transaction. Sweet. He looked around. Nothing else appeared out of place. He opened his gym bag and filled it with his small accessories.

Now to gather his prized possessions.

Adam removed the key from the tie rack and remembering how, over the years, the trunk had gotten heavier with the addition of each new file, he inhaled, squatted for leverage, and lifted the handles. He gasped as he tumbled and landed backwards on the carpet.

The files, valise, his mother's beloved journal—all gone!

Chapter 14

After dropping Sarah and Susan off at camp, Marla settled into her car for the drive back to Stoneham. Her dad's words echoed. "Don't put yourself in danger. Come straight here."

She drummed her fingers on the steering wheel.

It was the sensible thing to do. But would a couple of extra hours make much difference?

The police had called her to request a one-time home visit from Adam.

The sooner the better. Yet, she'd have to see it to believe it.

Marla jammed the key into the ignition and raced to the city. Every second counted.

Turning onto her street, she rolled to a stop behind a car parked along the curb. No one would notice her here. She, however, had a clear view of the activity ahead. Three vehicles pulled out of her driveway and moved northbound. Adam's Benz, followed by a small moving van, and what had to be an unmarked police car.

Okay, she'd seen what she came for—he'd moved out.

Except, where was he going on such short notice?

Adam always said 'knowledge is power'. So … she followed the procession, zigzagging lanes on the highway to stay out of sight.

He seemed to be headed towards his old condo. Couldn't be.

Yet, sure enough, that's where they ended up. The bugger hadn't sold it at all.

He'd kept a love nest.

The Scent of Lilacs

Marla smacked the seat.

What else had he hidden from her?

Keeping her distance, she watched Adam enter the lobby. The movers began unloading racks and containers of his precious finery.

Too bad your real treasures are gone, Adam. You have no valise or bankers' box, do you?

She could only imagine his fury at having found the trunk empty.

A clicking noise from across the street caught her attention. She turned to see a man in a grey Chevy snapping photos of the moving truck.

A private eye in a black suit?

Her father had trained her to be observant, but she barely had time to note the license plate number when the detective slipped his sunglasses on, made a U-turn, and parked right behind her. As she peered at him through her rearview, he waved. She nodded back, but had no intention of leaving the safety of her vehicle to identify him.

A white vintage car slid into the space the Chevy had just vacated. The impressive emblem and markings on the front grill gave away the make. A Cadillac Eldorado Biarritz in mint condition. She'd learned a lot about cars from Jimmy. He would have been proud of her ability to recognize this one. The Caddy door flew open. Out hopped a gentleman wearing a baby-blue dress shirt and knife-pleated polyester-slacks. His country-club appearance looked out of place in this urban setting, but she highly doubted that blending in or conforming to city norms was on this old man's radar. He threw his sear-sucker blazer over his shoulder, placed a white fedora on his head, and slipped inside Adam's building.

Before long, she heard clicking again and turned. Chevy man had his camera aimed at Adam's fourth floor window. Holy smokes—that same gentleman in the white hat was pacing back and forth with a drink glass in his hand. In the twelve years of marriage, Adam had never brought any grandfatherly person into their home.

Who was it?

Antonia Giglio

"Hey, Ollie. Nice hat," said Adam as he held the door open. He snatched the fedora and placed it on his own head, then preened in front of the mirror.

"Don't get any big ideas. Looks better on me, kid," said Oliver. He slid the closet door open and hung up his jacket. "Where's the scotch?"

Adam tossed the hat back to Oliver. "You know where it is. Get it yourself. I've got the delivery to take care of."

"Still your butler, am I?"

The movers wheeled in a rack. "Where do we put these, sir?"

Adam pointed to the bedroom and followed them. By the time he returned, Oliver had sorted through the liquor cabinet and stood cradling a bottle like a fragile newborn.

"Jeez. Didn't waste any time finding your favourite, did you?"

"Never mind that pedestrian brand." Oliver shook his finger at him. "You've been holding out on me, man. This baby aged slowly. Tweny-five years!" He licked his lips and rocked it from side to side. "If I remember correctly, this edition was awarded an honour in '95. How the hell did you get your hands on one? I'd expected it to be in the guarded possession of nobility. How much, Adam? Three ... four hundred dollars?"

"Think bigger, Ollie."

"Christ."

"A little contra deal, in lieu of a crappy piece of art. One of Dorian's discards. A score, eh?"

"You bet. Aren't I worthy of a little taste?"

Adam rescued the bottle from Oliver's clutches, set it on the counter, and stood back to admire it. After a moment's thought, he rubbed his hands together. "Okay, let's pop this baby." He removed the wrapping, shimmied out the cork, and passed the bottle to Oliver. "You deserve the first nosing, my friend."

With his eyes shut, the old man inhaled, then placed the back of his hand on his forehead and pretended to faint. "Ah ... peat, citrus, smoke, caramel. The path to heaven."

"Cut the drama and get the glasses, Ollie." Adam grabbed the bottle, held it under his own nose, and nodded. "By the way, to be sure ... heaven's not in your future."

"No worries. When the time comes, I'll confess and wipe the slate clean. Many before me have turned to sainthood that way."

Adam's exact thought.

But we just can't have confessions, can we?

"Special occasion," said Adam. "Use the Baccarat."

Oliver poured them each a generous dram and handed one to Adam.

"What shall we drink to—long life and the money to enjoy it?"

"Well, that may be easy for you to say, young man."

"Nice one, Ollie. Then I defer to you to come up with something brainy."

"Why don't we just drink to good times, friends old and new, and the masterful Celt who perfected this stuff?"

"*Slange Var.*"

The old man held his glass in the air and slowly swirled it around and around. "Look at these fine legs, crawling and cascading like delicate little tendrils." Oliver then took a mouthful and chewed it methodically before swallowing.

Thanks to his mother, Adam had grown to love words and images. They were the biggest gifts she'd given him. That's why her journal had meant so much ... the thoughts and inspirations she'd lived by. He'd memorized every entry, some written before he was even born. He stiffened as rage surged through him. Someone would pay for taking away his most prized possession.

"Ahem," said Oliver, with a dignified pose and demeanour.

Oh boy, he was in for a profound dissertation.

"Smoke, barley, licorice, treacle with a hint of floral and a taste of the sea. Finishes long ... and rich. I sure hope they have buckets of this wherever I rest my head." Oliver clicked his tongue and winked. "And ... maybe Gladys will be standing there, waiting to serve me."

"I don't believe they have happy hour in hell."

If nothing else, he'd remember Oliver had lifted his spirits today.

After the last trolley wheeled out, Adam closed the door and watched the old man empty his glass before setting it down and greedily eyeing the remainder of the bottle.

Don't worry, buddy. You'll get to enjoy every last drop.

With lips curled and eyes glossy, his eccentric friend strutted to the mirror, adjusted the hat at different angles, and made Bogart faces with each turn.

Pompous ass, look at him—even the tilt has to be just right.

"You might be a man of mystery to your lady friends, Ollie, but you ain't foolin' me."

"Have you forgotten what I taught you, son? In order to make a lasting impression, you must play the part."

"Oh, I remember what you taught me very well. Master classes from you *and* my father." Adam tightened his jaw.

Yeah—good old Professor Donald Kingsley, dressed to kill and prancing around the campus with his bloody pipe and those black glasses he didn't even need. Mr. Academia. Thought he was God's gift to anything in a skirt—including sweet, young Isabel. His stomach churned. *Yup, Professor Kingsley knocked up his mother then moved on to old moneybags.*

He slugged back his scotch and poured another.

I fixed you, though, didn't I, Dad? We had such a nice chat the night I coaxed you into signing your worldly assets over to me and Ollie. Too bad your heart gave out right afterwards, and, well—you just couldn't reach your nitro in time, could you?

Finally satisfied with the position of his hat, Oliver topped up his glass and paced back and forth in front of the window.

"Sit down, Ollie. You're making me nervous."

Oliver threw his hat back onto the ottoman.

"What the hell is wrong with you?" said Adam.

"I can't stop thinking about Gladys. Do you realize this is her last payoff? Making me a little teary-eyed."

"Boohoo. After all these years?"

"What can I say? I'm a sensitive guy."

"Yeah, me too."

"I miss that gal. What a beauty and ... dynamite in bed."

"You in bed with Gladys? Now I know you're delusional."

"I take offence, young man. How could *you* be aware of what went on in the Kingsley house? They shipped you off to boarding schools and had you globetrotting every chance they could. You weren't a very welcome member of the family, as I remember."

"Careful." Adam shook his finger. "You're pissing me off."

"Let me remind you that I was with Gladys long before your father arrived on the scene. I moved with her from husband to husband. I provided loyalty, stability, and excellent service. She rewarded me well." Oliver gave him a shameless look and took another mouthful of scotch.

"What about her loyalty? Didn't that matter?"

"You mean all those younger men who drooled over her money? Didn't bother me one bit. Besides, they made her feel youthful. I was always a whisper away."

"Well, too late for regrets. She's dead."

Gladys, Gladys, Gladys.

Adam was sick of hearing about her. What if this guy spilled something to the wrong person? They'd both end up screwed.

Oliver bent his head. "I've tried to replace Gladys, but no one comes close."

"Here. This will make you forget." Adam poured him another drink.

Oliver's mood changed, but for the worse. "You know, your father was stingy and pretentious ... a real cad. Look how he took advantage of your mother. Stupid, naïve broad."

Adam stiffened. "Hold it. I despised my father, but no one gets to talk about my mother like that and get away with it. Not even you."

"I beg your pardon. I simply meant to acknowledge your difficult childhood."

"I couldn't have made it without you," mocked Adam, in hopes of shutting the guy up.

Oliver continued regardless. "I generally had no fondness for children. But you ... you were different. Something of a delinquent son to me, if I may say so?"

"Who, me?"

Oliver laughed. "Clever lad. You knew exactly how to manipulate Donald and Gladys. They really weren't cut out for parenting. I don't know who suffered more, you or them. It was all quite entertaining."

Still smarting from the previous comment about his mother, this crack about him being a delinquent enflamed Adam even more. Yet the babbling old fogy didn't seem to notice he'd gone too far.

"Indeed, I felt pity for you," said Oliver, tilting his head sideways to look at him. "I did everything I could to make up for your wretched predicament."

Adam bit the inside of his cheek to keep his cool.

"We had fun, though, didn't we? After all, who taught you to play chess, tennis, and well, anything a dad was supposed to teach you?"

"I owed you for that. Hence our prosperous relationship. Did I not provide you with a lofty inheritance? I'd say we were even. Now stop living in the past."

Adam rubbed his chin. Tonight, Ollie's nostalgia may have been a result of the liquor, but it was far too disturbing to ignore. The cops were hovering, and the way this old man's lips were flapping, Oliver could prove to be a dangerous liability. He'd definitely outlived his usefulness. What to do? He pondered his options as Oliver rambled on.

"Gladys couldn't stand to be alone after your old man died. That siren enticed me to go with her to Stoneham Manor. She was right about it being a posh residence for seniors. And, at her expense, she set me up in a great room with a fabulous view of the valley. I really thought she'd changed though. That she'd picked me to spend our last years together before we rode off into the twilight." Oliver gritted his teeth. "But that woman still wouldn't let me sit with her in the dining room. Always on the hunt for the young ones. Christ, even Walter, the maintenance man. Mid-thirties, already bald and tattooed like a gangster—jeez. What did she see in him? Then Jimmy Snow came on the scene. Blondie thought he was special."

Adam frowned, remembering how Jimmy had done odd jobs for Gladys. In return, she'd loaned Jimmy *his* father's notes to study from. It had been hard for Adam to keep his mouth shut and not let on his connection.

Oliver sipped his scotch. "Oh, I knew she wasn't in bed with either one of them."

"Of course not. Why would she ruin her reputation?"

"True," said Oliver, "but she loved to rub it in the noses of her female rivals and it made the other men squirrley. She made me furious. Your plan came at just the right time, Adam. I decided if I couldn't have Gladys, I'd settle for her money and blow it on having fun." Oliver clicked his tongue and winked again.

Just like adjusting his hat, the clicking had been another of the old man's signature gestures.

Would he miss those antics someday?

"You're right, Oliver. We both did what we had to do. I hated that bitch for many reasons. The unforgiveable one—she had my mother's journal." Adam rubbed the back of his neck. "I knew she'd never let *you* near it, Ollie. So, I got it back my way."

Oliver glared at him.

"Don't give me that look. I did her a favour, didn't I? Sent her back to my old man." Adam took a deep breath. "Did I ever tell you …" he cast his eyes downward, "when my mother died … there was a note. It said she left the journal and her love to me. *Me*, Oliver. That book belonged to *me*. So, I got it back. And now …" His chest heaved as he smashed his fist against the wall. The plaster crumbled to the floor. "Now the cops have it. Marla let them take it right out of my closet." He noticed Oliver's hand tremble. "What, scared?"

"No, no," said Oliver with what looked like contrived bravado. "You have a perfect right to be angry. Son, I'm certain you'll find a way to retrieve it. You've done it before. You can do it again."

"Goddamned right, I will."

"You know, Gladys treated me badly, too."

Mother of Christ, Gladys again?

"Thought we'd work it out in the end, but it was impossible. She considered me beneath her status." Oliver waved his fist in the air and growled, "She deserved what she got."

"That's the spirit. Gladys is history. Now let's forget her by concluding our business." Adam strode into the bedroom to get his briefcase and returned whistling *If I Were a Rich Man*.

Oliver laughed. "Waited too long for this."

"Stop moaning. You're financially set for life. I made sure of that. This is just a little bonus." Adam opened his briefcase, took out a stack of bills, and handed them over to his butler's outstretched hands.

The old man fanned the money and frowned. "This can't be all of it."

Crap, the guy could still add and subtract.

He smacked his forehead. "Sorry, Ollie, with all the confusion today, I must have miscounted. What do I owe you? I'll run over to the gallery for it."

"Well, this is a third, so do the math." Oliver frowned. "That's not like you, Adam. You're starting to worry me."

"Stop nagging. Tell you what. Go to my room and take a nap. I'll call when I'm leaving the gallery. We can meet at our old rendezvous point. If you step on it afterwards, you might even catch a date."

Oliver looked at his watch, then headed towards the washroom. "Well, snap to it, lad. The booze and all this talk about Gladys, is making me hot under the collar and … below the belt."

Adam smiled. *Could have done without that image.*

"While you're freshening up, I'll pull your car into my parking spot downstairs, Ollie. It'll save you the trouble of going through the lobby."

"Good idea."

"Mind if I borrow the fedora?" *And the jacket?*

Oliver gave him a two-finger salute. "If you like it so much, I'll leave it for you in my will."

Oh, the irony.

Chapter 15

Crouched behind the steering wheel of her car, Marla kept her eyes on the fourth-floor window even after the movers had driven off. From her rearview, she caught glimpses of the detective doing the same.

As the minutes ticked by without activity, the burden of staying hidden was making her jittery. The phone rang.

"Hey, just thinking of you, Dad."

"What a coincidence."

Marla ignored his tone. "Sorry to worry you. When I called the office this morning, Bob said he needed to see me today."

"Is your job more important than your life or your children?"

"Of course not."

Yet, look what she'd have missed if she hadn't followed her instincts? With her own eyes, Marla had seen Adam clear out his belongings and found he still owned the uptown condo. And what about the old man in the fedora in Adam's apartment and the spy in the Chevy?

No. She had no regrets, but couldn't let on. "Dad, set a place for me at dinner. I'll explain later."

Her phone lit up again. "Hi, Bob. Is the meeting arranged?"

"Surveyors are at the park right now."

"Be there in thirty minutes."

Still wondering who the detective was, Marla saluted him, looked around to make sure it was safe, and pulled away.

Bob was waiting for her by his car when she arrived at the site. "Marla, I don't mean to be rude, but you don't look well. What's wrong?"

"Oh, the girls have gone to camp for three weeks," she said. "Separation anxiety. They're rarely out of my sight."

"Seems to me a little free time might do you good."

If he only knew how right he was.

She glanced at her watch.

"Okay, okay. I get the hint. Let's get started. The tripod is aimed at a stake where the proposed stage will be built. See if it lines up."

After greeting the team, Marla bent over and peered through the level. "Not quite right. I recommend adding one more row of stone and capping the fountain with a two-inch ledge to bring the wall to the height of the stage. It'll create a clean plane over the chairs."

Bob took a minute to check for himself. "I agree. Done." He relayed final instructions to the contractors and ushered her away. "What's next, Marla?"

"Plantings. We should start early enough in the season to get things well-rooted." She hated telling lies, even partial ones, but what choice did she have? "Unfortunately, I have to go back to Stoneham today. My mother's not well. You know, Bob, she uses her local nursery and tree farm for her projects. Apparently, it's one of the biggest suppliers in southern Ontario and ... she seems to have some pull for quick service with the owner of Bud's Tree Farm. What do you think?"

"As long as the stock is good quality, mirrors the budget, and they give a strong guarantee, I have no problem."

"Great. I'll email you the reports and quote later in the week."

"By the way," he said, pulling an office telephone pad from his shirt pocket, "I brought your messages. Had a feeling you might not make it to the office."

"Thanks. I really appreciate that." Marla tossed them into her shoulder bag and walked beside him to her car.

The Scent of Lilacs

"Now, get out of here, or you'll end up on the highway in rush hour."

What a good man. Bob really cared about her well-being.

Marla had no intention of telling him she had to stop at her house to gather some clothes first. As she pulled into the driveway, she remembered her phone messages and quickly glanced through them. Nothing urgent jumped out until the last one ... at one-thirty that day.

Nalin Crawford. Must speak. Call ...

Marla broke into a cold sweat. Her heart pounded. How was she supposed to face a woman who was sleeping with her husband?

Her fingers trembled as she pressed the numbers.

"Hello," said a soft voice.

She'd handle this harlot with curtness.

"Marla Mansfield, returning your call."

"Mrs. Mansfield, you don't know me ..."

"Yes, I do."

She heard a cough.

"I don't expect you to be nice to me, but please hear me out. I'm calling to offer my support."

"For what?"

"I know you've charged Adam with assault."

She knew?

"This is really embarrassing ... I didn't mean to hurt you, Mrs. Mansfield. Adam never wore a wedding ring when I first met him, so I assumed he was single. When I found out about you, I was led to believe that you and Adam had one of those liberal marriages. Anyway, by then, he'd already captured my heart. I don't expect you to understand me or my ways. I look for moments of light in both my artwork and my personal relationships. To me, Adam *was* light."

Marla's head spun. *Why in hell was this woman telling her this crap?*

Nalin sighed and continued. "Today, I saw a side of him that frightened me. Adam told me you reported him to the police. He became furious and took it out on me. Tried to hurt me. I have a fat lip, cuts, and bruises. I managed to get out of his condo before anything worse happened. Went straight to the police and filed a complaint."

Her dad had been right to warn her. This woman proved it. Even though this Nalin lady filled Marla with anger and humiliation, she also felt a bit of sympathy. Nalin was another person caught in Adam's web. First as a muse and now as a victim.

"Mrs. Mansfield, are you still there?"

"Yes," she choked.

"Adam had always been kind and gentle with me. Guess I didn't know him as well as I thought. No one should get away with abuse—including Adam. I'm prepared to testify against him in court if you want."

Marla's lawyer and her dad had said she needed proof against Adam. Well, here it was. Nalin's testimony would certainly leave no doubt about Adam's guilt and misogyny.

"Miss Crawford," she said, "your call took a lot of courage. I appreciate you coming forward. I'll accept your help and have my lawyer contact you."

"Mrs. Mansfield ... I'm so sorry."

Marla turned on the radio but struggled to keep her mind on the highway. She gave the steering wheel an impulsive tug. The car veered to the right and hit the shoulder. Startled, she eased it back onto the pavement.

Another move like that could be fatal. Did she want to leave her kids in Adam's hands? Marla clicked the radio off and kept her eyes glued to the road.

When she finally reached her exit, she slowed down. My God, her life story read more like fiction with each passing day. How could her marriage go from crazy love to restraining orders? Adam had always said guys looked for trust and loyalty in a woman. She had plenty of that to a fault and he used her weakness to control her.

Well—no more. Confidence, bravery, logic. That's what she had to embrace.

And she needed to pass that message on to her girls. Their lives were about to turn upside down. Marla would have to tell them about their father. About the violence, adultery, robbery, arson, and possibly ... murder. Sarah and Susan had arrived at camp as two pampered and innocent young girls. In three weeks, they'd come home to separated parents and a jailbird father.

She shook her head, trying to wish these thoughts away. Pretend it was someone else's family. The pounding in her chest and her tear-stained face told Marla otherwise.

No. This was her life.

Would her children believe or trust her? She slapped the seat. Why had she let it get this far? Was it the humiliation of not wanting her parents to see her as a failure?

She was still dwelling on her miserable excuses when Milt Snow's farm crept into view. She slowed down to a crawl, removed her sunglasses, and rolled down the window to glance over. The apple orchard, green and inviting in the late afternoon shadow, sent her spiraling down memory lane.

Was Jimmy actually just feet away?

Her parents expected her for dinner.

Shouldn't she keep going?

Yes, except ... 'dinner' wouldn't get her the answers she needed.

Marla tightened her grip and turned into the entrance. With her foot on the accelerator, she sped down Milt's driveway and came to a halt in front of the farmhouse.

No sign of Milt, but ... the blue truck was there.

She jumped out of the car and marched forward. By the time she reached the steps, there he was.

Jimmy—the man.

Her mouth opened, but nothing came out.

Without hesitation or permission, he rushed towards her, swept her into his arms, and kissed her—long and deep. She dropped her arms, letting them dangle by her side. This is what she'd been missing all these years. His warmth, tenderness, comfort. Being wrapped in his arms like the cozy sweater she remembered. Tears trickled down her cheeks, her heart swelling ...

Wake up. You're dreaming. If only he'd really done that.

Instead, he stood there, his eyes searching Marla's.

"How could you, Jimmy?" she said, pushing her fists into his chest. "How could you just abandon me like that? I went to the police station. I went to the jailhouse. I sent you letters. You shut me out, Jimmy. Why?"

His eyes dampened. "I didn't know what was happening to me. I was living a nightmare. I couldn't ruin your life as well, Marla."

"You didn't ruin my life. Adam did," she yelled. "He ruined both our lives. Had me completely fooled and he may have framed you."

Her legs wobbled. She sat down on the porch step and buried her face in her hands.

Jimmy sat down beside her and twirled a strand of her hair with his finger. Marla swatted his hand away.

"I ... I've suffered so much, Marla," he said, his voice catching. "Locked up, separated from you, knowing you were with another man. Imagine how I felt every time Adam came to see me in prison. He showed me your wedding photos. You under the Eiffel Tower. Pictures of your kids. You living the life I wanted for us." He balled his fist. "I wanted to be the one to surprise you with a trip to Paris someday, for an anniversary or a birthday. Make your wishes come true." He paused a moment to compose himself, then continued. "So, I set some goals, buried my head in books, and studied with a vengeance. It was the only way I could get through it."

"You gave me up. Handed me to Adam, told him he was the better man for me."

"It's true, but I didn't stop loving you. When they released me, I never expected to get you back. I only wanted to prove to you that I didn't commit those crimes. Marla, you knew me. I couldn't have hurt anyone. I cared about those people at Stoneham Manor."

The summer heat beat down on her. She fanned herself. "Jimmy, I don't know how, but Adam's in the middle of all of this. Everything changed when he came to town. Let's walk through the orchard. It's shadier. I have a lot to tell you."

With every detail that emerged, Jimmy's tension increased. He batted at flies and kicked the heads off the dandelions. "I can't believe the detectives missed all that."

"It's because Adam's name didn't match up to connect him. He had it all worked out so no one could trace him to the people in that building."

"My lawyers fought hard. There was no evidence against anyone *but* me at the time. I'm the one who went to jail for nothing. Lost years of my life. So many unanswered questions. I mean, how did he get there if he had no car? Did he have help? Did he know someone inside the residence? The planning and execution had to be ridiculous."

"Jimmy, we both know he's brilliant. But the whole force is on alert. I saw a detective following him. It's just a matter of time. We have to be patient. That bastard *will* make a mistake."

Jimmy gave her a curious look. "Marla, your language has changed. Never heard you swear like that before."

"Yeah, well, life happened." She'd explain the rest of her fury another time.

As they reached the porch again, Jimmy tilted his head towards the door. "Come inside. I want to show you something."

What if Milt showed up?

Regardless of the risk, Marla followed Jimmy to the dining room. The oak trestle-table had been pushed against the wall and stacked with piles of folders. Before she had a chance to examine anything, the sound of tires crunched down the laneway. She rushed to the front window and peeked out.

Chevy man! Walking up the steps with his camera slung over his shoulder and a large envelope in his hand!

She sprinted out and yelled, "Why'd you follow me?"

He shook his head. "I didn't. After you left, the clunker pulled into your husband's underground parking lot. Figured he was planning to stay for a while, so I left. And now ... here *you* are."

"My husband? How do you know Adam's my husband? Who are you and what are you doing here?"

She felt Jimmy's hand on her shoulder. "Wait ..."

The mystery man interrupted him. "Take it easy, Marla."

"You know my name? What's going on?"

The stranger had a puzzled look on his face. "I thought you recognized me when you waved to me earlier."

Jimmy had been standing there with a grin.

"Marla," said Jimmy, "this is my brother, Jeff. He's with my lawyer's firm, helping out with the investigation."

Marla covered her mouth. "I thought you were a city detective, tracking Adam. If I'd paid attention to your face and not your suit and sunglasses, I might have seen the resemblance."

"Jimmy, do you want me to come back later or show you what I have now?" said Jeff.

"We're all on the same page. Come in."

She remembered the last time she and Jeff had spoken, the day he'd hung up on her. The police had just taken Jimmy to jail. Jeff had assumed it was her dad's doing. No wonder he hadn't wanted to talk to a Slater.

"I think we could use some coffee," said Jimmy. "Get organized, Jeff. I'll be right back."

Time to call her dad. No point telling him where she was though. He'd probably send a squad car.

As she hung up, Jimmy returned with a neatly arranged tray that included proper cups and saucers, napkins, and biscuits.

All those years in jail and he still managed to hold onto his mother's gentleness and social graces. What strength, dignity, and goodness!

After pouring coffee into Marla's cup, he caught her eye. "Do you believe I'm innocent?"

"You bet."

He filled the other two cups and looked at her again. "That helps, Marla. Jeff and my lawyer have been searching for missing evidence for a long time. Nothing came up until that night at Brody's. Knowing Adam's connection to Gladys Kingsley changed everything."

The Scent of Lilacs

Jeff pinned a photo to the bulletin board. "Look at this, Marla."

"Okay. That's the man we saw at the condo today with Adam."

He pinned up a second one. "And this is one I snapped of him at Clarence Creek the Monday after the Brody incident. My colleague and I followed Adam there after he had been released. We pretended to be newly-weds taking photos. The Caddy showed up shortly afterwards."

She raised her eyebrows. "He's from Stoneham?"

"Marla," said Jimmy. "Remember the story I told you about the old guy at the seniors' residence who had a five-step plan to seduce women?"

"Oliver? I never did get to meet that nasty man. I can't believe it." She sank into a chair. "So, tell me. What does Oliver have to do with Adam? And ... what was this guy doing at Adam's condo today?"

"The man's full name is William Michael Francis O..."

"Stop," she shouted. "O for Oliver Bryant? The Kingsley butler?"

Jimmy and Jeff stared at her.

"How did you know?" said Jimmy.

"I went through Adam's files. Mr. Bryant's name came up in Donald Kingsley's will. So many Christian names, the initial O never registered. Guess he was counting on that anonymity to carry out his dirty deeds."

Jimmy broke into a sweat. "That explains a lot. Oliver used to talk about Gladys constantly. I thought he'd just met her there and was trying to get into her pants, like all the other ladies. He sounded so agitated whenever he mentioned her. He finally told me that even with his five-step plan, he couldn't get to first base with that green-eyed blondie. In the dining room, Gladys would only give him a curt nod. Wouldn't let him sit with her. He complained she liked younger men. But one day, he told me he'd come up with a new scheme." Jimmy shook his head. "I thought he'd meant stepping up the bait. What a fool I was."

"Wow," said Jeff. "Oliver could have been jealous enough to do her in."

"Hold on," said Marla. "Jimmy, didn't you bring a green sweater to Oliver the night of the fire?"

"Yeah, I sure did. Oliver said he had a hot date."

"Yeah, a hot date with the devil."

Could the devil's name have been Adam?

The minute she stepped into her parents' house, she was blasted with, "Do you want to get your head bashed in?" from one and, "Where's your common sense?" from the other.

"I already apologized. But let me do it again. Sorry." She twisted her neck. "Feels like I'm spiraling down a rabbit hole."

She picked at dinner, said little, then carried her dish to the sink.

"Go and rest," said her dad, "I'll clean up."

A few hours later, a gentle knock on the door interrupted Debussy's *Suite Bergamasque* as she lay in bed stewing. "Your mom's sleeping, honey. Can we talk?"

"Come on in. Should we assume our positions like the old days?"

"We did have some great debates, didn't we?" He turned her desk chair around, straddled it, and leaned his arms on the backrest. "Okay, Marla, what really happened today?"

Sitting cross-legged on the bed facing him, she blushed, thinking of the intimate feelings she'd had for Jimmy earlier.

Nope. Her dad didn't need to hear about that.

"After I dropped the girls off at camp, the police called to ask if I'd give Adam permission to pick up his things. I wanted to get it over with and said yes."

"Don't tell me you ran into him?"

"Not exactly. I saw Adam's Benz, a moving truck, and a police car leave my house."

"Did he see you?"

"Of course not. I'm not a cop's daughter for nothing. I got curious about where he was going and followed. Discovered a dirty little secret. Adam never sold his condo, Dad. He lied."

Her dad shifted in the chair.

"Turns out, I wasn't the only one interested in the move. I saw a young man taking photos, and shortly after, an old man went up to Adam's unit and started pacing at his window."

"Who were these guys?"

"I'll get back to that. Anyway, I left and met with Bob Wyllie on a work-related issue, then picked up some clothes from home."

"Your mom's right, what I say doesn't matter. Is there more?"

"Yes," Marla hesitated. "I stopped at Milt's to speak to Jimmy."

He slapped his forehead. "Tell me you're joking."

"Dad, I'm so glad I did. Wait till you hear. The man taking the photos was Jeff Snow, Jimmy's brother, doing detective work for Jimmy's law firm. And the old man in the Cadillac? William Michael Francis O. Bryant."

"Doesn't ring a bell."

"Remember I told you that Adam and the butler got Donald Kingsley's inheritance? They were both named in the will."

"Right, I did see that name in the file. That was Adam's butler?"

"Yes. The O in that name is for Oliver, the same Oliver that lived at Stoneham Manor. He was the one Jimmy went to see the night of the fire."

"Adam's butler, living under my nose? This information would have been crucial to Jimmy's case. Did you tell the Snow brothers about it?"

"Yes."

Her dad gritted his teeth. "An innocent man found guilty because of the inability to track names? That wouldn't happen today. A click of a button can trace a person's whole life history."

"Well, that computer click came too late for Jimmy," Marla said. "Now it's up to us to help clear him."

"I agree. Be discreet and give Jeff any help you can." He locked eyes with her. "That aside, Marla, what you did today scares me."

"I know, but look how much I learned."

"Get some sleep. We'll talk in the morning." As he walked to the door, his beeper went off. He used the bedroom phone to call the station back.

She watched the colour drain from his face as he set down the receiver and stare at her.

"Oliver ... Bryant," he stammered, "is ... dead. They found his Cadillac in a ditch just off the highway in the city. There was an empty bottle of scotch in the car."

"My God. I saw him alive and well this afternoon. How could this have happened?" She shivered. "Adam. Adam knows everything, Dad."

"I'm on it."

As soon as he left the room, she called Jimmy.

"Christ Almighty, I can't catch a break," Jimmy moaned. "I mean, I'm sorry for the guy, but Oliver's testimony could have been the key to exonerate me."

"Stay positive. What happened to that man was terrible, but it's a sure way of dragging Adam into an investigation. Several people saw them together, including the movers, Jeff, and me. Adam's luck is going to run out. I can feel it."

For a moment, Marla imagined herself safely in Jimmy's arms, cuddling under the stars at the ridge.

She flushed.

My family's falling apart and I'm thinking of him?

The vision disappeared in a mist.

Chapter 16

Adam carefully cleaned the Baccarat tumblers and placed the two dirty plates in the dishwasher. Now to fix the hole in the wall.

He really needed to control his temper.

Oh well. Nothing a Kandinsky abstract couldn't fix.

After sweeping the debris from the floor into a plastic bag and hiding it in a covered cooking pot, he hung a small painting he'd reserved for a client over the crack.

Perfect.

Adam patted a wad of money in his back pocket. The old codger sure wouldn't need it.

Not now—not ever.

Best to hide it as well, though.

As a matter of habit, he then opened the window next to the fireplace, dimmed the lights, and turned on his favourite Vivaldi *Four Seasons* track. The violins and violas of *Spring Concerto No. 1* in surround sound pulsated with the same energy now coursing through his veins—clear, strong, precise

It felt good to be free. No more attachments.

Poor Ollie.

Should have kept his mouth shut.

Adam looked at his watch before sitting down. He leaned back, ran his hands along the soft leather sofa, and could almost feel Marla beside him with her legs tucked under her. Mm, silky auburn hair, fresh lilac scent. A tingle went through him. If she'd only come back to him, he'd forgive her. They'd just have to get past her meddling parents and that damn new job of hers. It was a big mistake, letting Marla take that course. Oh well, he still had Sarah and Susan. They would never turn on him. Who else could he count on?

Nalin?

Eventually. After all, she had to sell her paintings somewhere.

Needy, greedy Gillian?

Damn sure. She had too much to lose for her allegiance to waver.

His best ally had been Oliver. History now, but Adam actually felt no remorse, just a vague sense of sadness and waste. He glanced at the bench where Ollie had left his fedora earlier and grinned.

Too bad. The hat would have made a nice memento.

Adam raised the imaginary bottle of scotch high in the air as a final gesture. The real bottle, swept of all fingerprints except Ollie's, was either still in the Cadillac, or in the hands of police by now.

"Nothing but the best, eh, Ollie?" said Adam. "Hope you enjoyed my parting gift."

He lowered his arm and gazed around his sophisticated urban suite.

Home, sweet home.

He and Marla had been happy here until the babies came along. The thought of kid clutter had terrified him. Twins needed a large house with plenty of room to spread out and he'd made sure they got it. Regardless of what he'd told Marla—sacrificing this condo, where his universe lay in perfect order? Never.

Adam glanced at the antique ginger jars above the bar and smiled. More than their artistic and monetary value, they served a higher purpose. He lifted one of the lids and stuck his hand inside. The *Iced Tea* audio-tape he'd made was still there.

Rummaging through the second jar, he pulled out a joint. At some point, cannabis would no doubt be legalized, but until then, his reputation demanded caution.

Adam lit it and sat back. The slow, fluid, adagio portion of Vivaldi's *Spring Movement* washed over him. He pictured the idyllic, pastoral meadow before him. His body and mind sunk with every draw.

Finally, down to its last embers, he stubbed it out and gave in to the blended waves of music. The quick, ascending pitch and trill of a solo violin, growing in tension, conjured up images of an uncertain and threatening sky.

Wait ... wait ... wait for it.

He lifted his finger to conduct the invisible orchestra of strings, their bows poised like soldiers at the ready.

Presto.

Virtuosity.

He could see the lightening and hear the thunder of a perfect storm.

Pure pleasure.

The sound of the elevator startled him.

Concierge hadn't even called up.

Adam jumped to his feet and raced to the bathroom to flush the incriminating ashes. Good thing he'd opened the window. He'd expected company, but so soon? He ruffled his hair to appear disheveled, opened the door and blinked. "Officers, what's going on?"

"Sorry to bother you, Mr. Mansfield. I'm Sergeant Wayne Purdy and this is Constable Sergio Bellino."

He ushered them in and turned off the music. "How do you know my name?"

"We have some bad news, sir. You may want to sit down," said Sergeant Purdy.

Adam remained standing and glanced from one officer to the other.

"Are you acquainted with Mr. Oliver Bryant?"

No point denying it.

"Yes. Has something happened to my friend? He was here today."

"I'm afraid to inform you that he had a fatal car accident."

"Fatal?" Adam reached for the wall. "He's dead?"

"Yes. We found a slip of paper in his pocket with your name and address. We assumed Mr. Bryant was either coming here or had already been. What's your relationship with him?"

"Come in," said Adam, lumbering towards the sofa.

The officers followed and sat across from him with their eyes glued.

Spotting for lies, no doubt. They'd never catch him.

Adam bent his head. "Oliver had worked for my late father. He and I remained friends.

What happened? I mean—where, how?"

"'Where' is in a nearby ravine. 'How' is what we want to find. What can you tell us about Mr. Bryant's visit?"

Adam rubbed his forehead. "My wife kicked me out for nothing. I moved into this place today. Truck was still here when Oliver arrived." Playing the poor husband sympathy card seemed to work. Both men raised their eyebrows.

"What time was that, Mr. Mansfield?" said the constable.

"Can't say for sure, but it had to be close to three."

"Why was Mr. Bryant here?"

"Ollie came to cheer me up," continued Adam. "We had a couple of drinks together."

"How many drinks did you have?"

He choked out the words he'd rehearsed. "Just a couple. He likes … *liked* … his scotch. I made us a couple of sandwiches. Ollie always enjoyed …" A painful, reflective look spread across his face. "My friend was a connoisseur and always insisted on pairing his drink with a bit of thinly sliced ham and some blue cheese. We chatted and I suggested he stay the night."

"Why didn't he? Did you have a falling out?"

"Fight? Never. Ollie was an easygoing guy. When he pulled his car into the underground, I thought he was going to stay." He stood up and paced in a circle as he continued, "I knew I shouldn't have let him leave. But as usual, Oliver got restless. He suddenly remembered a special event with a lady friend. Stubborn old man. I couldn't change his mind."

"What time was that?" said the sergeant.

"Around eight."

"Are you sure he only had a couple of drinks?"

"Yes."

"Mind if we go down to the parking garage and look around?"

"No problem." Adam walked them to the elevator. "P1."

"We'll be back to ask a few more questions."

He nodded and stood by the window, waiting for their return. It sounded as if the cops knew more than they were saying. They must have found the bottle. And what a shame that classic Cadillac Eldorado had ended up in the creek. It was likely a write-off now.

The tales that car could tell—especially about the night of the fire.

No one would have thought to search cars in the Stoneham Manor parking lot. Why would they? First responders had been rather busy that night, the fire and the safety of the residents a priority over motive. When the air had finally cleared and the crimes discovered, all the evidence had pointed to Jimmy.

Early the next morning, Adam had disposed of his clothing and picked up his Mustang at the service station. The mechanic had left the key for him in their mailbox—a small-town trust thing that had worked in his favour. He'd barely stepped back into his apartment when Marla had called, crying her eyes out and looking for a ride to town. He'd lied about not having his car yet. How could he have said yes? He had to transfer the goodies from Oliver's Caddy to his apartment upstairs before Mr. P returned from the market. As far as anyone could tell, the old guy standing beside the Eldorado was just a stranger, waiting for Mrs. P to open the diner.

With the job done, Ollie was likely on his second cup of coffee when Adam had clambered down the fire escape just as Mr. P arrived. "Hey, Mr. P. Are you okay?"

He'd felt the old man's eyes on him. "Sure, sure. What about you, Mr. Big Shot? You sleep good last night?"

"Not really. But I heard the fire department did a great job. Best thing I could do was stay out of their way and do my homework. Tough night, though. I need a coffee."

"Yah. Push pencil very difficult. You go in," said Mr. P, huffing as he struggled with a load of potatoes.

"Here, give me that," said Adam. "You're getting too old for this. Why don't you have it delivered?"

"You think I rich, like you? You must drive fancy car, four-wheels, not two-wheels like friend." Mr. P had pointed to Jimmy's bike leaning against the wall near the fire escape. *"You big show-off, no?"*

"That's right. The girls love me, Mr. P, and you love me too, no?" He'd pulled out his wallet and fanned some bills.

"Yah. You pay very good. You best boy I know."

Adam and Ollie had often laughed about that morning and how well they'd executed their plan. But, no more thrills for Ollie.

The elevator door opened.

"I've asked the concierge for the camera footage down there," said Sergeant Purdy before repeating his earlier question. "Mr. Mansfield, are you certain Mr. Bryant only had a couple of drinks?"

"Yes, he was definitely within the legal limit." Adam pulled out an open bottle. "Here it is. It's still about two-thirds full. No more than a couple of drinks each, see? And we drank it over several hours, with food. The plates are in the dishwasher. I wouldn't have let him drive a long distance on a highway if he was putting himself or, anyone else, at risk."

The officers strolled into the kitchen. He heard them open cupboards, the dishwasher, and the trash can. "Okay. Have you been home the whole night?" said the sergeant.

"No," Adam admitted. "After Ollie left, I remembered my car was on the street. I went out to park it underground and instead decided to grab a coffee and go back to my studio to take care of some paperwork."

"Any surveillance in your office?"

"Yes."

"We'll be in touch if we have any more questions. Sorry for your loss."

Mother of Christ. Think, think—only a matter of time before they check the police records and see his name. The charge for robbery had been dropped, but the domestic assault would still be outstanding. And now his link to a traffic fatality of a guy from Stoneham.

Stoneham! What next—Gladys?

Adam phased in and out of Marla's dreams. His deep-blue eyes had turned steely-black, and his razor-sharp teeth struck terror in her heart. Looming behind his ominous face, a fire raged and engulfed everything in its path. Adam's image grew larger as he inched towards her and the twins. They huddled together, unable to move, feet like concrete, while the heat from the flames became unbearable and the smoke suffocating.

In their struggle to escape, the twins finally loosened their grip and slowly distanced themselves from her and each other. "Hold on," Marla yelled, her agony beyond measure. But still, Sarah and Susan receded and faded, like phantoms. Her rubber arms stretched out to reach them. Then, snap, *she toppled over, sending her body into freefall. She woke with a jerk, just before the inevitable crash into the void.*

"Sarah, Susan!" Marla screamed—her body drenched in sweat.

Pepper, sleeping on the rug at the foot of her bed, woke yelping and barking, his hair standing on end.

The bedroom door flew open.

"Marla, what's wrong?" shouted her dad.

Cane in hand, her mother limped behind him. "Oh God, what now?"

"I have to call the girls," Marla moaned. "He's going after them, I know it."

"It's a dream, Marla," said her mother, with a dismissive flick of her hand.

Her dad stroked Marla's back. "You dropped the girls off on Monday and Adam's in the city. Honey, nothing has happened to Sarah and Susan."

She slithered to the floor. "No, no, no. I forgot to take Adam off the contact list."

"You can't do that without a court order," said her dad.

"But you have no idea what he's capable of. I have to call them."

"It's too early, Marla," said her mother. "If you call now, you'll frighten them. Clean up and I'll put the kettle on. You need to calm down."

Adam gazed at the young, sporty councillor in the camp office. He held out his hand to her. "I'm Adam Mansfield, Sarah and Susan's dad. I didn't get to see my daughters before they left yesterday. Any chance I can spend a few moments with them? Please."

His alluring eyes and killer smile had always been weapons of power over women. This one would crumble.

The young lady blushed at his touch. "We generally only allow visitors on designated days, Mr. Mansfield, but I'll check." She ran her finger down the list of names on her clipboard. "Cabin Eight, Athena Cabin," she said then picked up a second clipboard and scanned it. "Yes, Mr. Mansfield. I see your name is on the authorized list. No one is allowed to wander the property, but since the campers are still at breakfast, I'll call Sarah and Susan to the office, while you sign in. Activities start in twenty minutes." She used her walkie-talkie then flashed a demure grin.

Sarah and Susan came crashing into the office and pounced on him.

"Dad! I'm so glad to see you," said Sarah, "But what are you doing here?"

Susan tightened her grip. "Who cares? I miss you, Dad."

"That's why I came. Couldn't imagine three more weeks without you. We've only got a few minutes, though. Tell me what you've signed up for. Archery?" He pretended to draw back a bow. "I spent a lot of time at camps and mastered many sports as a kid, but bow and arrow? Loved it. Trick is to keep your eyes keenly on the target and let it rip. Same principles for a successful life, girls. Remember that."

"Oh, Dad. Always a lesson," said Susan.

"That's how *my* father was with me."

Susan hugged him again. "I think you're the best."

"Thank you," Adam laughed. "Everybody keeps telling me that."

He looked at his two beautiful daughters. "Will there be a parents' open house? I'll come back and visit."

Sarah frowned. "Dad, I don't understand. How come you drove all this way to ask these questions? You could have just asked Mom."

The Scent of Lilacs

He closed his eyes, preparing to tell them their mother was breaking up the family, that she didn't love him anymore. She loved someone else, her boss maybe. He'd wanted to tell them their mother was an evil woman and an ungrateful liar. That they shouldn't believe any bad things Mom might say about him.

Adam opened his mouth, but the girls seemed so content and bubbly. He'd have done anything to have this kind of relationship when he was a kid. No. He'd keep it from them for now. After all, the girls had yet to disappoint him. Unlike Marla.

Time to hatch another plan.

"Girls, I drove all this way because I have a surprise for you," he said. "When camp is over, we're going to take a daddy-daughter trip anywhere in the world. Where would you like to go?"

Sarah's eyes grew three sizes. "An African safari."

"Yeah," said Susan, bursting with excitement. "They have hot air ballooning. I read about it in *National Geographic*."

Africa would be a great place to get lost.

"Perfect. Promise you won't tell your mom ... or anyone else? I'll have to arrange for your passports without her knowing."

Adam saw them look at each other, shrug, then nod. "We trust you, Dad."

"I'll tell Mom all about it once we have the trip organized. Deal?"

High-fives sealed the new plan.

Damn, he was good.

He kissed Sarah and Susan on their foreheads and gave them each a squeeze. "Now, get out there and win. Remember—you're a Mansfield."

There. Adam didn't need Marla. She could rot in hell, for all he cared. But the girls? He could still find a way to hold onto them if he made a few concessions. Maybe he'd pretend remorse and plead guilty to those stupid assault charges. Tell the judge he'd had a bit too much to drink and would never do it again.

At Claire's insistence, Marla drank her tea. It did relax her a little. The radio had been tuned to a classical station instead of her mother's favourite oldies.

Thoughtful.

As soon as the hands of the clock hit eight, Marla called the camp office.

"What a coincidence—both parents on the same day."

"What do you mean?"

"Well, your husband literally just left."

Marla stiffened. "May I please speak with Sarah and Susan?"

"This is very unusual. Is there something we should be aware of?"

How could she tell this young councillor about the danger her children might be in without revealing the whole truth about her and Adam?

"To be honest, my husband and I have been trying to work out some things without alarming our daughters. Can I count on you to inform me if Mr. Mansfield contacts you again?"

"I have to go by the list."

"My lawyer will put it in writing immediately, but I need to talk to my kids right now."

"In the future, emergencies only, please, Mrs. Mansfield."

If she only knew!

Marla held her breath until she heard Sarah's voice. "Mom, what's going on?"

"Where's Susan?"

"Beside me. This is weird. Did you know Dad was just here? Don't you guys talk?"

"I'm in Stoneham and your dad's in the city. What did he say?"

The girls giggled.

"Everything's cool, Mom." Susan's voice this time. "Dad just wanted to give us a hug. Said he didn't have a chance to say goodbye on Sunday."

"Would you do me a favour? With so much going on, Dad and I aren't always together. He gets so busy he sometimes forgets to tell me things. Keep me posted if he visits or calls. Okay?"

"Sure, Mom. We will."

The Scent of Lilacs

With the phone on speaker, her parents had heard the whole conversation.

"See? Just your imagination, Marla."

"Mom, Adam was there. It wasn't just my imagination." Marla turned to her dad. "We have to move forward on this investigation as fast as possible. What did you find out about Oliver Bryant?"

Her dad sat down beside her and sighed. "I just heard from Sergeant Attard."

"I remember him. Read me the riot act when I barged into the station after Jimmy was arrested."

"That's him. After a quick autopsy, police confirmed the alcohol in Mr. Bryant's bloodstream had been lethal. Whether he'd slammed the car into drive or reverse wouldn't have mattered. Better in a ditch than the catastrophe he could have caused on the highway. Mr. Bryant had a massive contusion to his forehead from the steering wheel. No airbags in those old Caddies. He died instantly."

Marla bristled. "What was he doing at a ravine, anyway?"

"We'll probably never know. It could have been to relieve himself, or he may have preferred to drink and sleep it off there. They found an empty bottle of scotch in his car, almost fifty-five percent alcohol content. Easy to blow your mind with that stuff."

She shook her head. "Was it suicide or a tragic accident?"

"Likely the second."

"Dad, since Mr. Bryant was at Adam's, I can't help but connect him to the events."

"We can think what we want, but it's proof that matters."

"For Jimmy's sake, I hope the truth comes out."

Maybe Oliver was to blame. Otherwise, how could she and the girls live with ...

Chapter 17

Marla spread her drawings on the antique, oak dining table that her dad had inherited and buried herself in her work.

Her mother wandered in and glanced over Marla's shoulder. "Too many plants and they're too close together. They need room to grow."

A logical observation. Landscaping 101. She could have let it go.

"The goal is to achieve an instant, mature look," Marla snapped. "Can you give me a break and let me do my job?"

"More money than brains."

"Duly noted. Besides, didn't you tell me I was on my own if I got into this business? Where were you when I really needed you?"

"I'm an award-winning landscape designer, an entertainer, and a sought-after healer in this town," shouted Claire. "What do you have … a *foie gras* certificate and a broken marriage?"

"Goodie-goodie for you. Now that's the mother I remember."

Marla glanced in the full-length mirror—slacks, paisley shirt, blazer. Casual, but professional for her morning meeting at the tree farm. She tied a scarf around her neck and gulped back a lump in her throat before stepping into the kitchen. "Mom, I'm sorry about yesterday. My behaviour was uncalled for. I think I'm cracking."

"Middle shelf, first jar, far right. Steep it for three minutes," said her mother without looking up from her crossword.

"Thank you. I'll take it with me."

The phone rang as soon as she backed out of the driveway. "Hi, Bob. I'm on my way to the nursery to meet the owner. Can I call you afterwards?"

"Deadlines are coming, Marla. I'm just making sure you're on track."

Not like him to sound annoyed. "Are you having some doubts about me, Bob?"

"You didn't look well the last time I saw you. Don't mean to pry, but is there anything you want to tell me?" His tone softened. "You know I'm here to help."

"That's very considerate of you. This assignment means a lot to me. I know my absence and approach may be a little unorthodox, but I *will* deliver what I promised."

"It's not your work I'm worried about."

Hearing this made Marla wish she could unburden herself, tell him everything. But she couldn't. Yet, she did owe him some kind of explanation. She pulled over to the side of the road.

"You're quite right. There is something you should know." Marla had difficulty finding the words. Framing and speaking them out loud would make them real. "Adam and I have separated. My parents are helping me out while the girls are at camp. That's the reason I'm in Stoneham."

"Jeez, I'm sorry for you. What can I do?"

"You've already been really patient with me. Thank you. This project gives me a sense of purpose each day. I intend to give it my all." She stifled a sob. Why had she been such a blabbermouth? Well, she couldn't risk not telling him. What if Adam called the office fishing for information? He'd certainly be capable of it. No. Bob had to know at least that much. "I'll call you later."

"You bet."

She took a sip of tea, gripped the steering wheel, and drove off. *Music. She needed music.* A few bars of Samuel Barber's *Adagio* whisked her away.

Once she reached Main Street, it would only be a short distance. Too bad she'd have to drive by Andy's Diner, the fire station, and ... Stoneham Manor.

There was Andy's already. Since Mr. P's passing, the new owner had renovated the exterior. It now had a modern, inviting look to compete with some of the chain restaurants that had come to town. Hard to believe Adam had lived alone in that dumpy upstairs apartment back in '89. She dragged her eyes away from the bittersweet memories and continued on.

After turning right at the next corner, the mighty, unmistakable opening notes of the first movement of *Moonlight Sonata* sent a flutter through her. She raised the volume, anticipating the emotional journey Beethoven was about to take her on. It started with the soft, whispering *adagio sostenuto*, then changed to ascending and descending *arpeggios*. The goosebumps on her arms rose and fell as the notes built and twisted. The melody shifted from major to minor keys, giving the music a mysterious, almost haunting sound. It made her think of Adam again. They'd shared a love of music, especially this piece.

Their romantic interlude had begun in her university days, in a tiny apartment on Bretton Street. He'd shown up to break the news about Jimmy's conviction, courtesy of her mother's GPS signals of course. She'd wanted nothing to do with him at first. But Adam had been persistent and so smart, so cultured, so talented, and ... so interesting. With Jimmy gone, Marla finally couldn't resist Adam's advances.

Kindness and charm, along with their mutual love of music, art, and literature, had finally drawn them together.

Had he tricked her into marrying him? Did he even love her then?

The sonata came to a soft lingering end with two chords, spaced out with pauses and a low, delicate resonance. Six minutes of sheer bliss.

Marla looked up to see the iron gates of Stoneham Manor. A puzzling thought began to incubate.

The Scent of Lilacs

Could Adam have gone to the Manor that night in the length of time of a piece of music?

How? His car had been in for service.

She pulled over and dialed Jimmy's number.

"Marla, is everything okay?"

"I'm fine, thanks. Listen, I just passed Stoneham Manor on my way to Bud's Tree Farm. How long would it have taken you to ride your bike from the diner to Stoneham Manor back in high school?"

"You know I rode BMX. Remember my twenty-seven-gear racer?"

"I know, I know. You were a speed demon."

"I clocked that stretch so many times. Three-point-six kilometers, but fairly flat. With a good cadence, it would take me seven minutes, tops. Why?"

"How long would it have taken Adam back then?"

"On a bike like mine?"

"Yes."

"Adam may not have participated in team sports, but man, he was fit. Used to cream me on the tennis court. I could never win a set from him. So, with adrenaline kicking in and good weather, tack on a couple of minutes, he could have done it in about nine."

"Did you leave your bike at Adam's the day of the fire?"

"Yes, I did. How'd you know that?"

"A hunch. Remind me what happened that day, Jimmy?"

"It had started out as one of the happiest days of my life. I'd finally saved enough money to pay my uncle for the truck he'd fixed for me. Adam offered me a lift to pick it up before he took his car in for service. Told me to leave my bike by his fire escape and get it later."

Marla could almost hear the wheels of his bike spinning in Jimmy's head. "Are you suggesting Adam rode my bike to the Manor?" Another pause. "Adam's neighbours confirmed he'd been home all night, Marla. Even you spoke to him."

"I did, but it was at least a half hour after the fire started. I have a bad feeling. Did anyone report seeing a bike at the Manor that night?"

"My lawyers went through the police files carefully. They didn't find anything suspicious. The fire did attract lots of gawkers though. Some even on bikes."

"Jimmy, can you have Jeff look into the old reports? Call me back if something shows up. I'm a nervous wreck—flipping my lid, and barking at everyone, including my mother. It's a good thing the girls are away and I have my work to distract me."

"Adam's your husband, Marla. This must be tearing you apart."

Her stomach clenched. If only she had the strength to tell him about the adultery, the abuse, the fear for her life, and the worries about her children.

Jimmy could make her feel safe for a moment, couldn't he? But what good would a moment do?

Chapter 18

Manager's day off. Something to be said for routine. Adam arrived at his gallery, flipped the 'Welcome' sign over, and settled in front of his computer. The success of the June auction had left him low on inventory, and with Nalin gone, he needed to find a replacement. Someone as talented and prolific.

The door chimed.

Too early for a bona fide shopper.

He looked at his video screen.

Police officer! What now? Marla's doings? Can't be about Oliver, I executed my plan perfectly.

Adam quickly retraced his steps.

Same height and stature. Wore Ollie's hat and jacket. Parked Caddy in underground dead zone. Kept back to camera. Planted bottle of scotch. Snuck hat and jacket in condo while Ollie napped. Stopped for coffee. Drove to office. Sent Ollie to rendezvous point. Parked Benz a block from ravine—no tire marks at site. Wore grey hoodie—uniform of late-night walkers and stalkers everywhere.

He smirked. No, this visit wasn't about Ollie—and no time to ponder 'what if's'.

Adam's cellphone vibrated. He waved it in the air.

The officer took note and wandered around the gallery while he took the call.

"Hi, Susan. You're crying. What's wrong? Are you and Sarah, okay?"

"Yes, Dad, but ..."

Had to be serious, she could hardly speak.

"Pass the phone to your sister."

"Don't get mad," said Sarah, her voice catching with each breath. "Susan was so excited about the trip to Africa, she blurted it out to Miss Cindy. Then Miss Cindy called Mom."

"Okay, calm down."

"Mom started screaming at her. Told Miss Cindy she was calling the police. Why did Mom say we can't we see you anymore?"

"Take it easy, sweetheart. You know Daddy will fix everything, just like he always does. Be strong."

"Okay. But everyone's staring at us like we're freaks. Can we come home?"

"Stick together. Don't worry about anyone or anything. Others can only affect you if you *show* you're weak. Sarah, believe me, it'll all blow over."

The officer pointed to his watch.

"I'll call you later, Sarah." Adam hung up and walked towards the policeman. "Sorry. My kids."

"No problem, I have a couple of my own. The Benz with 'Gallry1' plates out front has been hit by a delivery truck. Yours?"

"Yes." Shaking his head, Adam followed him out to check the damage.

What next?

His phone rang again.

Durban and Associates. Finally.

The officer's patience looked tapped. He handed Adam a written report and nodded.

Adam saluted the officer and walked back inside.

"Mr. Wade. Good to hear from you."

"Call me Randy. Drew said to fast-track your defence. I can fit you in this afternoon."

So much for a relaxing day at the office. Low inventory. Smashed car. Girls traumatized. Wife out of control. And now he and his new lawyer had to figure out how to grovel in front of an omnipotent judge.

The Scent of Lilacs

Even with Adam's charm, good looks, and a week of apologies, Nalin had continued to ghost him. At least Dorian had remained loyal and ... he had leads on a couple of local artists. They'd have to wait, though. Today, he had a date. Some judge named Thelma D'Arcy.

"Oh God, not her," Randy had said on the telephone. "That woman is single-minded and tough. She only sees black and white. It'll be a tough one."

"I pay you plenty to do your job. See you there."

Adam met his lawyer in the parking lot. "I'm counting on you, Randy."

They reached the first set of double doors. Randy scanned Adam from head to toe then smoothed down his own, wrinkled tie. "Navy power suit, eh? You look more like a lawyer than I do, for Christ's sake. Why didn't you tell me you were going all GQ?"

"It's my pedigree," said Adam. He didn't care how pompous he sounded. "I was raised to dress for success."

Randy's nostrils flared.

Jealous streak, eh? He had that effect on most men.

Randy pressed the handle. "After you."

Adam walked forward and peeked through the glass reveals of the next set of doors. "Quite a crowd in there."

"More than one case is being heard."

"How long will it take?"

"Depends on how well-prepared the prosecutors are and the nature of the complaints."

Adam ran his fingers through his hair, buttoned his suit jacket, placed one hand in his pant pocket, and stepped inside.

Show time.

The hush in the room jarred him. Barely anyone glanced in his direction. He was used to all eyes on him.

Screw it. His only interest today was to take Marla's breath away—to remind her of the history between them, the nights reading poetry and making love in her plebeian little apartment.

That bloody woman should have been grateful. Hadn't he taken her out of that sleepy hick-town and gentrified her? Why couldn't she have been happy simply raising his children like a mother should?

Adam had a feeling he knew why. Bob Wyllie! Hired Marla for that city job. Made her think she was competent, relevant, a ... somebody. Bet that man had more than the job on his mind. Adam balled his fist in his pocket.

He'd only reached the third row when he noticed the auburn hair. Marla and her entourage in the front row of the gallery. Was that a cane in Claire's hand? And, of course ... Bill wearing his uniform to show off his authority for Ms. D'Arcy.

Adam's father-in-law turned and caught his eye, then immediately whispered something in Marla's ear.

When Adam saw her stiffen, he stopped to rest his hand on the nearby pew.

"What's up?" whispered Randy.

"Just checking out the opposition." Adam strained his head to look at a woman wearing business attire on Marla's right.

Someone from her counsel? And who was beside her? Evelyn Lam, Marla's friend and tennis partner. Can't believe she dragged her into this. By now, Philip must know, as well. Had they known when they came over for dinner a few weeks ago? Who else had Marla told?

A flurry of activity in the front corner of the courtroom caught his attention. A screen was being brought out.

Could Marla have gone to the trouble of providing proof? What did she have on him? He could explain away most of it as self-induced, although he had to admit he'd gotten a little sloppy last time. Jesus, after nagging him to death, what did she expect? Could he dance around accusations if Marla actually had photos or other evidence?

Adam bit the inside of his cheek. Bad habit lately.

No, some other poor sod had to be the victim, not him. What if Marla ambushed him like this at trial?

Ah, she had nothing. Besides, she'd never embarrass herself or Chief Slater.

"Let's get this over with, Randy."

The Scent of Lilacs

Adam was about to take a step forward when someone pushed past him. Someone tall, slim, with tawny skin and black hair tied in a bun. He recognized the peasant skirt, the loose, hand-knit sweater, and the boots. Nalin had worn that outfit the night of the Young Hands—Warm Art Show and was now heading straight towards Marla.

His stomach clamped just like the times Gladys had called him a bad boy when he was a child.

But he'd shown her, hadn't he?

For sure, Adam would figure out how to control Marla, Nalin, and this whole damn courtroom.

He glanced up and saw a lady in a pinstriped suit directly in front of them, someone who dressed for success like him. It had to be the barracuda for the Crown.

Adam shrugged and followed Randy to the front row of the gallery.

Imagine. He was in the same room with his wife, and he had to sit on the opposite side. And there beside her ... Evelyn and Nalin, both in court to tell a story ... a story to support Marla, not him.

Momma, this is all your fault!

Chapter 19

How dare Adam attempt to take Sarah and Susan away without Marla's knowledge! Thankfully, Susan had spilled the beans and today Marla was here to crucify her enemy—provided she avoided Adam's evil eyes—eyes that could shut her down in a blink.

The minute the facilitators completed their preparations and settled in their places the room became as silent as a confessional.

"All rise," said the court clerk.

Judge Thelma D'Arcy entered.

Marla gulped at the imposing, full-figured woman with greying, unruly curls that screamed, *just test me*. Whoever this judge sided with today, Marla perceived the other side was in serious trouble. Good thing Marla had a chance to watch the judge in action before her turn came up.

Third on the docket, Marla waited with discomfort—squirming and fidgeting till she heard, 'Mansfield Case'.

Her eyes swept over the gallery to the defendant's table, where Adam now stood beside his lawyer. Only Adam's profile was visible to her.

"State your name for the record," said the court clerk.

Head high, Adam spoke in a dignified voice as only *he* could.

Marla bristled.

"Thank you," said Judge D'Arcy. She glanced at her papers and looked up. "Madame Clerk, please read the charges."

Marla cringed at hearing her name and the word *assault* spoken in the same sentence. Her dad patted her knee.

After asking everyone to sit, the judge flipped a page in front of her and addressed the Crown Attorney.

"I've read Mrs. Mansfield's report. Is there anything further to add?"

"Your Honour, we have evidence that Mr. Mansfield intended to take their twin daughters, Sarah and Susan Mansfield, overseas without Mrs. Mansfield's knowledge," said the prosecutor.

This offence was bound to carry more teeth.

With her glasses balanced precariously on the tip of her nose, Judge D'Arcy carefully listened and jotted some notes. Then she peeked above the rims. "Has Mrs. Mansfield ever filed a complaint prior to this report?"

Still standing, the prosecutor said, "No, Your Honour."

Marla bit her lip, wishing she'd had the courage to report Adam much sooner.

"Have there been any other charges of this nature registered against Mr. Mansfield?"

"Subsequent to Mrs. Mansfield, another complainant, Miss Nalin Crawford, has come forward."

"Does Miss Crawford's case have bearing on the case before us?"

"Only that Miss Crawford will testify that Mrs. Mansfield's suspicions of adultery are substantiated. Miss Crawford has had sexual relations with the defendant. She also claims to have been assaulted by Mr. Mansfield, and has filed her own charges in accordance with the law."

"Is Miss Crawford present in the courtroom?"

"Yes," answered the Crown.

"Please stand, Miss Crawford," said the court clerk.

Nalin stood, erect and confident.

Marla saw Adam shift.

"Thank you, Miss Crawford. Please take your place."

Judge D'Arcy shuffled some papers. "Have there been any allegations of assault against the children?"

"None, Your Honour."

The judge turned her head to Adam's lawyer. "Mr. Wade, does Mr. Mansfield have any prior convictions? Is he in good standing with the courts otherwise?"

"No other convictions, Your Honour."

Ms. D'Arcy removed her reading glasses. "Mr. Mansfield, please stand." The judge looked straight at him. "Mr. Mansfield, do you understand the charges?

"Yes, Your Honour."

"Is there anything you'd like me to explain?"

"No, Your Honour."

She recognized Adam's tone. His intelligence had been insulted.

"Mr. Wade, how does your client plead?"

"Not guilty, Your Honour."

Marla dug her nails into her father's sleeve.

What? He actually thinks he'll beat this?

"Mr. Wade, please come forward to set the next court date," said Judge D'Arcy.

While those negotiations took place, Marla felt Adam's eyes on her. He'd turned his head and shoulders in her direction. That's when she saw it. A sprig of white lilacs on his lapel. The symbol of vows made and happy times shared.

Marla may have lived through twelve years upholding the sanctity of those vows, but he'd done nothing but make a mockery of them. She swallowed and gave Adam a bold, resolute glare.

Judge D'Arcy's voice broke their silent battle. "The recognizance of bail with all its conditions will remain in place. I've seen many of these performances before," she said. "Let's move on."

Judge D'Arcy may have inadvertently slipped out those last words, but their meaning had been clear to Adam. Behind them was another woman stabbing him in the back. He pressed his elbows against his sides.

If only the hotshot had given him a chance to speak, he'd have made a brilliant case for his side of the story.

Adam would have pointed out his wife had full knowledge of the nature of his business, a business that included social events. As a responsible husband and father, he had a driver on call and was careful not to disrupt his home-life. Unfortunately, his wife had a jealous streak and often needled him. Those were the times he'd simply lost control.

He'd have bowed his head before the judge while Marla listened and watched in shame. "I truly understand my wife's ambivalence and concerns, and ask for forgiveness and reconciliation. I'm prepared to do whatever is necessary to make my family whole again." Adam had even planned to wipe away a tear.

Could have had a captive audience today, if it hadn't been for Judge D'Arcy.

He wanted to do more than slam a door on a cat's tail!

Marla looked up and caught the eye of the woman wearing a robe of accomplishment. The woman with judicial wisdom and reserved neutrality. In that split second, an understanding passed between them.

Adam had met his match.

As soon as Thelma D'Arcy disappeared, the gallery was abuzz. Marla's row of supporters rose to leave. She turned to her dad. "I'm so worried. For Adam to plead not guilty, he must have a strong defence. I'll need a 'smoking gun' against him. Can I do it, or is this all for nothing?"

"One step at a time. The greater charge brings lots of jail time. If it's lowered to a misdemeanor, there are still serious consequences. You'll get justice one way or another. The important thing is you and the girls are safe and that bastard knows you mean business." He looked down at his pager. "I have to take this."

Standing and leaning on her cane, Marla's mother beamed. "I think you've lucked out with Nalin Crawford. She's my kind of woman."

What in hell had she meant by that?

"And," continued her mother, "Judge D'Arcy will go for the jugular. You can rest assured she understands the importance of a mother and her children."

This, coming from Claire?

Marla placed a hand on her mother's shoulder and marched her out in lockstep.

Evelyn waved them over to a bench under the shade of a locust tree. "Sit here, Claire. I'm sorry I have to go, Marla. But after what I saw today, you've got nothing to worry about. Everything will turn out fine."

They exchanged smiles and warm hugs.

When she turned around, her mother and ... *Nalin Crawford? Having a head-to-head?* Besides being promiscuous birds of a feather, what else could these two have in common? Marla gathered her courage and faced her husband's mistress. "Thank you, Miss Crawford. I won't forget what you've done for me today. Please stay safe. We both know Adam's still out there."

"Mrs. Mansfield, I can't change what's happened between Adam and me. It was a terrible misjudgment." Nalin snuck a peak at Claire, then back at Marla. "But there will be a reckoning. Life is like that."

She'd heard that comment several times lately. Marla wished *she* felt as certain as those two.

Nalin marched away, unpinning her bun and letting her long, black hair swing freely.

The photo in Adam's file!

Just for a moment, this young woman was the spitting image of Isabel Mansfield. No wonder the attraction.

Marla took a deep breath and sat beside her mother.

"Marla, that girl is powerful. She thinks like I do. Adam will never bully you again."

Her mother's words sounded like a manifesto. But how could she ever speak it into existence?

Marla shrugged and looked up, just as her dad came speeding towards them. "Something's about to happen," he whispered, as he sat beside her on the bench. "Be prepared, Marla."

"What is it, Dad?"

"Something to do with new evidence in Jimmy's case."

Chapter 20

Lost in thought, Marla heard a scuffle near the entrance of the courthouse.

"Get your bloody hands off me."

Adam?

Her dad jumped to his feet.

"Bill," shouted her mother, her face scrunched. "I've had enough. Take me to Marla's."

"No problem. I'll get an officer to drive you, honey. Marla, you wait right here."

Wait? And miss the action?

Marla inched forward, careful to stay hidden. Several police officers had swarmed Adam. They wrestled him to the ground and snapped handcuffs on him. Moments later, her dad returned and stood beside her. She laid her head on his shoulder and trembled.

Would this nightmare never end?

He stroked her back. "Marla, I knew this take-down would be big. Never expected it to happen here and now, though. Look, his lawyer's wiping his forehead. Doesn't know what to do."

"Dad, you said this was about Jimmy. What have they charged Adam with? Do you know?"

"Details were vague. Something about a bike."

Moonlight Sonata ... six minutes ... a trek racing bike ... and Adam in the middle of it!

Marla pulled her phone from her purse and put Jimmy on speaker.

"Where are you, Marla? I've been trying to get a hold of you for hours."

"Outside the courthouse."

"Courthouse? What are you doing there?"

"I'll tell you later. What did Jeff find out?"

"My lawyer and Jeff went through the old records of the interviews after the fire."

"And?"

"We have a witness, Marla."

She could hear the excitement in his voice. "Really? Great news!"

"Apparently one of the residents reported that she'd looked out her window shortly before the alarm went off. She saw something sticking out of a bush near the entrance. Metal, like a bike or something."

Marla's heart skipped a beat. She could hear Adam yelling in the background as Jimmy eked out the details. "Cut to the chase please, Jimmy."

"I'm trying. The old lady said she saw someone near the building, a man wearing light-coloured pants and a sweater with a hood. Then, just after her nightly news program came on, she heard a clunk, like a trunk closing. The alarm went off shortly after that. The police originally found no evidence of the bike and didn't believe the woman. She had a history of storytelling."

"So, what changed?"

"Jeff pressed her about the bike behind the bush. She said she'd never given it a second thought, and she couldn't understand the significance of dredging up such a silly thing after all this time."

Adam's lightning-speed mind made Jimmy sound painfully slow.

Patience. Twelve years in prison would affect anyone.

"Anyway," continued Jimmy, "they showed her a photo of a bike. Apparently, she stared at it for a long time and finally recognized the downward curve of the bar, the stripe, and even the orange colour. It was *my* bike."

Adam, taken down by something as simple as a bike? There had to be more.

"Why would the police believe that old lady now when they didn't before?"

"Because they now have Mrs. Pozinsky to back up her evidence."

"I'm confused. Mrs. P? What's she got to do with any of this?"

"Someone had obviously ridden my bike to Stoneham Manor that night. It wasn't me. I'd left my bike at the diner and picked you up with my new truck so we could celebrate. After driving you home, I went to the Manor to run errands."

"Yes, I recall all that."

"Anyway, Jeff and my lawyer started snooping around. Tracked down Mrs. Pozinsky living with her sister in a nearby town."

"She'd have to be in her late seventies now. Did she remember you or the bike?"

"Only because Adam used to tutor me in English so I could get my marks up for university. Since I spent so much time there, Mrs. P recognized the photo of the bike." He choked up. "I … I can't believe Adam would do me harm. We were friends."

"Adam is no one's friend," Marla snarled.

"I know that now." Jimmy paused, "But you are, Marla. Ever since you arrived on the scene, you've been like an angel on my shoulder."

Her dad's face pinched.

Was he embarrassed or did he feel guilty? Had the love lost between her and Jimmy suddenly occurred to him? Too late, Dad.

"Jimmy, I still don't get the connection. There has to be more."

"Well, it seems when Mr. and Mrs. P left the diner that night, they saw Adam riding my bike towards Elm Street. Mrs. P said her husband had made her laugh, saying, 'The big shot have no fancy car today. He wear hood and wait for night time to ride bicycle'."

"She saw him riding your bike that night?" shouted Marla. "I'm not your angel, Mrs. P is. Something really stinks. Okay, hang in there and keep me posted." She clicked the phone off.

"So, Dad—Adam's connection to Oliver and the Kingsley's. Elaine Parker the eye-witness. Mrs. P. And … a little help from Beethoven."

He gave her a puzzled look. "Beethoven?"

"Yes, Dad. Perfect timing!"

The Scent of Lilacs

Adam's head throbbed and his wrists burned from the handcuffs. He groaned. The cops had roughed him up, tossed him into the back seat, and slammed the door while all those people in front of the courthouse stared at him like a piece of dirt. His wife probably one of them. The voices of the cops still rang in his ears. "Hands behind your back ... under arrest ... murder of ..." At first, he thought they were going to say Oliver, but that couldn't be. Then he heard 'Gladys'."

Twelve years later? How? Adam's plan had been foolproof. This was a trick. He wasn't about to fall for it.

He leaned back against the seat. Pain shot through him from everywhere. Those bastards had come at him with a vengeance, shouting "Down ... down ... get him, boys." They punched, pushed, and pulled—over and over—till he was pinned to the ground. It played out like a movie scene, for Christ's sake. He closed his eyes and twisted his neck. Hell, it hurt. He'd make them pay for this. Adam broke into a bitter grin.

At least I managed a few good shots on those pigs.

As the cruiser pulled away from the curb, he bent forward and stared out the window. There she was, his wife—skulking with her self-righteous father. He frowned. Who in hell was she on the phone with? Was it Jimmy? They did this to him. Bloody Marla and Jailbird Jimmy. What were they up to?

Alone, they were both pushovers. But together?

The lilac, still pinned to Adam's lapel, filled him with rage. Unable to reach and tear it off, he kicked the back of the driver's seat with his heel.

Squealing to a stop, the officer jumped out, opened the back door, and delivered a volley of threats.

"Yeah, yeah."

As the cruiser sped off again, Adam snapped back against the seat. Thoughts of what lay ahead tormented him all the way to the police station. They yanked him out.

"Take it easy," he snarled. "Police brutality."

"Fragile, are you?" said one of the officers, forcing him up against the front desk.

He heard someone charging towards him.

"Adam, are you alright?" said Drew. "Randy called me. I came as fast as I could."

"Do I look alright? I'm bruised everywhere."

"Police said you resisted arrest. I checked the papers. They're in order. I can't stop them from processing you. This charge is serious, Adam."

He could feel his blood pressure rising again. "How incompetent can you get?"

"You know I'm not a criminal lawyer."

Randy arrived with a stunned look on his face.

"Useless bugger," snarled Adam. "You couldn't have helped me back there?" He gritted his teeth. "Just get me a telephone."

Within moments, Adam was dialing a number—his link to the only person he knew couldn't be intimidated. A problem-solver with a cool head. Someone whose intellect matched his own.

"Gillian, my love," he whispered. "Listen carefully. I can't explain right now, but I need a criminal lawyer."

Her gasp felt like a slap in the face.

"What kind of trouble are you in?"

"The worst."

Her silence unnerved him.

"Should I be worried? You didn't kill anyone, did you?" she said, with a little chuckle.

"That's what they say."

More silence.

"It's all lies, Gillian."

He heard a long, deep breath and could feel her slipping away. "You know I can't get involved with this, Adam."

"This isn't a debate. Send me the best damn lawyer money can buy, or else."

The Scent of Lilacs

He pictured her irritated scowl, like the day she threw the champagne in his face.

"I'll have to think about this," she said.

Okay, now she was really pissing him off. "Think? Think about how your face will look on the cover of *Forbes*. You've always wanted that, haven't you? But your headline won't be complimentary. Can you and Gregory afford a scandal? You know I can make it happen."

"Are you threatening me?" said Gillian, her voice ice cold.

"Just call it a friendly reminder."

"Leave it with me," she said. "I'll call for Gregory's jet. Be there shortly."

"That's more like it."

Wow, he couldn't believe Gillian was about to turn on him.

"Adam?"

She hadn't hung up yet. "Yeah?"

"Do my keys still work?"

"So far."

Shit! His condo! The cops would be sent to search it.

"What about the gallery?" she continued.

"Same key. You know what to do. And oh—the antique jars you love? You must take them. They're yours. Value added."

"Very generous of you."

He looked up to see Drew and Randy both mopping their foreheads.

"Randy, I won't need your services on this matter after all. Your job is to stick to the domestic. And Drew, you're safe ... for now. Take good care of my business or you'll have more to lose than your buddy here."

If anyone had spoken to him like that, he'd have told them where to go. Randy seemed relieved. But he knew Drew cared—too used to the big paycheques.

Adam lifted his chin. "Okay, officers. Let's get this over with."

He'd worn loafers—so, no shoelaces this time. They stripped him of his belt and tie, then more humiliating mug shots, fingerprints ... By the time they'd locked him in a holding cell, he was ready to tear someone apart.

179

Adam stared at the threadbare mattress and cringed at the thought of the filth that had lain on it. He forced himself to sit on the edge for a while. Slowly, he eased his back against the wall. Exhaustion set in. The moment he closed his eyes, the stench in the cell carried him away.

J. Jefferson Boarding School. Dirty socks, musty textbooks, and half-eaten chip bags—nauseating. He'd been the new boy at more than one school and had developed a solid strategy to establish chain of command. His full-length peacoat with an oversized inner pocket held lots of goodies, including Playboy magazines. Soon had all the guys drooling. Over time, he'd taught those preppy whiners to appreciate the more sophisticated activities in life. Drinking, smoking weed, graffiti—whatever crossed his mind that day.

The cell door rattled and jolted Adam awake. A barely conscious man reeking of alcohol was dropped on the cot in the corner.

"Put him somewhere else," yelled Adam. "Guy stinks."

"Enjoy the company," laughed the officers as they left and locked the gate behind them.

That click brought him back to St. James Clinic, where he'd battled his early demons. His photographic memory had become a curse.

"Adam," Dr. Volinoff had said, "you will be safe in here." He'd placed paper, crayons, and a pile of books on the little table beside the bed. "Draw some nice pictures and read. Be a good boy for the nurse and I'll come to visit you."

Adam might have been only eight at the time, but he knew his father and Dr. Volinoff had taken away his freedom—like the animals he'd seen at the zoo.

Did all boys without a mother, need to be caged in?

Two years staring at white walls and a tiny window. And that smell—that horrible medical disinfectant—had stayed with him throughout his life. It had become the smell of fear. The only thing that had kept him lucid had been Dickens, Twain, Greek and Roman mythology. In those books, Adam had learned to escape and live someone else's life.

His father's weekly visits (Professor Kingsley, as Adam was to call him) would inevitably be met with kicking, clawing, and biting. And each week, Adam's tirade would inevitably be met with the prick of a needle. He'd learned to welcome those pricks.

Could use one now.

Christ. He should never have gone to Brody's that night. None of this would be happening.

Hell, he'd only gone for a bit of fun, to reunite Marla and Jimmy. Instead, what did he get? Two nights' lockup. And if that place hadn't been bad enough, this dump was worse.

Sharing the same air with drunks and derelicts reeking of urine and vomit. He didn't belong with these lowlifes.

Marla. Nalin. Gladys. Professor Kingsley. Even his own mother.

They'd all betrayed him.

It was their fault.

Chapter 21

Marla sat with her head propped against the window as her dad drove home from the courthouse. She was fading fast.

"My life's a disaster," she said. "I wish I could wave a magic wand and make all this go away."

Her dad gave the steering wheel a slap. "Stop it, Marla! I'm right beside you and your kids need you."

After a moment's silence, he sighed. "I've got your mother on my mind, too. She's been so …"

Those were the last words Marla heard until her dad's gentle hand woke her.

They entered the house to the sound of the kettle whistling and melancholy music playing in the background. Disturbing.

Her dad strode past her and headed straight to the kitchen.

She was about to follow, but as Marla kicked off her heels and glanced around, she became transfixed. The layout, the furniture, the décor. Yes, definitely the Mansfield house. A chill went up her spine. Could she stay in this cold, empty, broken home? Her children had memories here, good ones. But soon, they'd become tainted. Living here could be painful.

She walked towards the den and pictured Adam at his computer going through his art inventory. Was she actually married to the man who ruined Jimmy's life—and hers, too?

The music got louder as she reached the kitchen. Her mother was sitting on a stool at the breakfast bar with her head on her hands, listening to Blossom Dearie's *Touch the Hand of Love*. Why had Claire picked this sad, lonely, haunting piece of jazz?

"What's going on? Not feeling well, Mom?"

"She's having a hard time right now," said her dad, who'd already taken over the tea-making.

"Well, this music can't be helping." Marla shut off the sound system.

Her mother snapped to attention. "I'll tell you what's going on, Marla. You, Adam, the kids, Jimmy. I can't take it."

"Wait. What do you mean, *you* can't take it?" She'd actually begun to feel sorry for her mother. But no, the evil witch was back.

"You heard me."

"Are you kidding?" shouted Marla.

Her dad came around the island. "Take it easy."

"No. She's not getting away with this, Dad."

"Your mother's overwhelmed. She needs rest."

"*She's* overwhelmed? What about *me*?" Marla stood face to face with her mother. "Guess what? I've been through hell *myself*."

"Yes, you have." Her mother folded her arms across her chest. "But up till now, you've lived a good life with Adam. More than me or most people."

Marla's eyes darted to her dad.

Would he just take that from her?

"Jesus Christ, Claire. I've given you everything. Bent to your every whim. You've gone too far."

Her mother ignored him, "I wanted to be a singer. Not a mother."

He slammed the counter. "Knock it off, Claire. You're being hurtful."

Her mother shrank back.

In her whole life, Marla had never seen her father angry at her mother like this. He'd always been able to soothe her, even if it meant giving in, and even if dad and daughter had to pay the price. The condition of their pinky promise—a promise that had been so wrong.

Was her dad finally going to put a stop to her mother's nonsense? And why today? Weren't their lives fragile enough?

"Goddamn it, Claire!" he said. "I survived your wild days. Thought you'd get it out of your system and finally settle down."

Her mother glared at him. "Seems to me I wasn't the only wild one, Bill."

"Yeah, but I came to my senses. You still had to go and screw around with Milt. In our own hometown, Claire. I managed to put a lid on the talk. But boy, it wasn't easy for me. Is there anything else I should know?"

"Of course not. Come on, Bill, I said I was sorry. You know the men in town think you're a lucky man. And the women all wish they *were* me. They're jealous. So, your reputation's intact."

How vain and self-absorbed could anyone be?

"Claire, have you lost your mind?" yelled her dad.

"I never meant to hurt you, Bill. You knew I was a free spirit. That's what you loved about me, isn't it? And I didn't take off and leave you, did I?"

Throughout this tense, intimate exchange, her parents hadn't even looked in Marla's direction.

Was she invisible to them?

"You've been the love of my life from our days in the church choir, Claire. But ... what am I ... to you?" He choked on his words.

"Bill, I hated being stuck in a small town. I wanted fun, excitement, freedom."

"Then why didn't you leave?"

Her mother rolled her eyes. "You know why."

"Yeah, I do. They'd find you strung out or dead in a back alley somewhere. You needed me. I think they call that love, Claire. I felt it. You felt it. We just fit together. Otherwise, I would never have stayed with you, either."

So much pain on her parents' faces—the truth between them dangling.

Why had it taken a horrific crisis in *her* life for her family to come undone?

The awkward silence only lasted a moment.

"Just cut the crap, Claire," said her dad, putting his hands on her mother's shoulders. "Let's talk about Marla, our daughter. We made her out of love. You and me. Look at her. She's beautiful inside and out. Our daughter didn't deserve this horrible life."

With her back against the wall, Marla slithered to the floor. If only her dad had been this honest from the beginning. She might have grown to be a strong, confident person. And her mother might have seen herself more clearly and lived up to her responsibility as a wife and mother. Then again, if he'd been tougher, would her mother have stayed? Therein lay the delicate balance.

"Who are you, Bill? I don't know you anymore."

"Too bad. All these years, your daughter—yes, *your* daughter—tried to live up to your standards. All she ever wanted was to be worthy of your love. And all you did was shut her out. 'Not good enough' is how Marla always told me she felt. Isn't that true, Marla?"

The tears blinded her now.

"Well, Marla and I didn't like the same things. She was all la-di-dah with books and French and Beethoven. What did we have in common?"

"Really, Mom?" Marla jumped up, shaking. "How could I compete with you? I *had* to find my own passions. Couldn't you have just been proud of who *I* was?"

Her mother turned to look at her and shrugged. "That's exactly what I did. I left you alone to do your thing. You had your dad in your corner."

"But I needed both of you!"

"Pull yourself together, Claire. Show some respect for me and Marla. Don't you see this poor girl is fighting for her life?"

"I know," shouted her mother, "why do you think I'm depressed? You want the truth? I'll give you truth, Marla. I wanted to end it when you came along. But for the sake of your father, I stuck it out. I tried to be a good mother. It just wasn't in me, even with help from Vera Volk, the reverend and those other mothers at the commune."

There it was again. Backstory from her childhood when her mother would hold court with her friends as they smoked and drank behind the beaded kitchen curtain. Marla had tried to escape it by hiding in her closet, but the pain of not being wanted had never really gone away.

"You think I'm selfish," continued her mother, "but I'm just being me. How was I supposed to know things would turn out this way? With everything that's going on now, maybe I should have tried harder. When Adam came to town, I figured you and Jimmy would outgrow each other and ... I didn't want you stuck in Stoneham like me. You and Adam had the same interests and he had the means to give you the world. Things I never had. In time, I thought you'd thank me for it."

Marla's lip quivered. "Mom, I wouldn't have been stuck. I loved everything about Jimmy. You may have thought we had nothing in common, but it was those differences that made our love stronger. We supported and cheered each other on. It's ancient history now, but Jimmy was such a good guy, and from what I've seen, he still is. Jimmy made me laugh. He made me proud. He made me happy. Jimmy would have been enough for me, Mom."

"Yeah, well, that's not what I had in mind for my kid."

Would Marla ever get through?

"How did I know Adam was so troubled?" shouted her mother.

The dam finally burst. There'd been signs of tears the night the officers drove Marla home from the police station in '89, and her mother had definitely shed them when she'd exposed the bruises on her back. But never like this. The depression her mother felt today had nothing to do with her singing career or being tied down. It came from guilt. Guilt for hurting Bill. Guilt that she'd pushed Adam onto Marla, and that indirectly, she'd sabotaged Marla's life and Jimmy's.

As hard as Marla tried to fight it, her pinky finger twitched. She put her arms around her mother. For the first time, her mother hugged her back. A grip so tight she could barely breathe.

"Mom," Marla whispered, "what's happened is not your fault. You may have thought you pushed Adam onto me, but *I* fell for him," she said. "We were good together for a while, had some great times. And he's been a wonderful father. I'd always thought his mother's death and the unorthodox way he was brought up made him different. It was a choice I made. And as long as we loved each other and he was good to me and the kids, nothing else mattered. I didn't know Adam had had therapy until I came across Dr. Volinoff's reports. He's never taken medication in my presence."

She shivered as her mind wandered back to the day Adam had picked her up to take her to the police station after Jimmy's arrest. They'd had an emotional discussion about the effects of their mothers on them. She'd said she'd eventually need therapy and Adam had said he'd already had plenty. At the time, she thought he'd meant bereavement counselling.

Marla sighed. "There's no one to blame. You don't expect someone who says they love you to take advantage. And let's not forget Adam is also an accomplished actor. He could charm anyone. He sure had me fooled. I'm a different person today and I'd like to think I'm wiser. I can see through him now." She paused. "I'm safe. Sarah and Susan are safe. Somehow, we'll rebuild our lives." She wasn't sure she believed it, but she had to hope a better future would arrive.

As the sobbing subsided, her mother reached for her dad's hand and locked eyes with him. "Are *we* good?"

"You know it, babe."

A love so strong, nothing could tear those two apart.

"Bill, let's go home," said her mother.

"Only if Marla thinks she can handle things on her own."

"I'll be fine, Dad. Besides I want to be alone with the girls when I break the news. "

"You did a good job with our daughter, Bill. She's strong, logical, and independent. She'll get by."

Chapter 22

A clang on the metal bars jolted Adam. He opened his eyes, sat up, and brushed the greasy hair off his forehead. "What now? A guy can't catch a wink of sleep around here."

"Move it, Mansfield. Someone in the interrogation room for you."

"About time." Adam smoothed the front of his shirt and tucked it into his sagging trousers.

"Hands in the slot," said the officer.

"Yeah, I know the drill."

The officer snapped on the shackles and nudged him forward.

He checked himself in the glass panel of the interrogation room door. Christ, who was that man? Chin stubble, bloodshot eyes, drooping face. How could he let himself get this way?

The officer poked his head in. "Cuffs on or off, Miss?"

Miss? No, no, no!

A firm but gentle voice said, "Off, please."

Adam rubbed his wrists as he entered.

A petite young woman stood to greet him.

You've got to be kidding. Was this the best Gillian could do?

She extended her hand. "Heather Holden. I'm here to represent you, Mr. Mansfield."

He shook it.

Manly.

"How's it going?"

"I've been better."

Heather handed him a sheet as if she'd anticipated his hesitation. "Review this. If you're satisfied, we can proceed."

Adam scanned the list of high-profile homicide cases she'd won. Her credentials seemed solid and she'd made partner in record time. Despite her diminutive size, she had an air of confidence that made him pay attention. Maybe that was her *MO*. No one would expect her to be tough and resolute. Heather Holden might be just the winner he needed.

"Okay. Phenomenal resumé. Let's do it."

"Good," she said, passing him a pen and paper. "A signature on the contract, please."

A professional with no time to waste. Well, neither did he.

He scribbled his name and sat across from her.

"Okay, first names and down to business," Heather said, as she picked up a bankers' box from the chair beside her and placed it on the table.

He blanched. Was this *his* bankers' box?

He took a closer look. No, not his.

"Your case is intriguing and challenging. Right up my alley." She smiled a cold, ruthless smile. He wouldn't want to be on the other side of it. "I believe we can win this case."

Finally, a lawyer with a brain and the guts to go with it. He leaned forward and opened his mouth to speak.

She stuck out her finger. "I'll do the talking. The detectives are going to question you. I need you to trust me. Do and say exactly what I tell you."

Man, taking a back seat wasn't going to be easy.

An officer knocked then entered and handed Heather a folder. She skimmed it. "Search warrant. Your car, your condo. Normal police procedure. It says they already checked your marital home. It's clean. No need to go back there."

Of course. His damn wife had let the cops take everything he valued.

Heather put her elbows on the table, interlaced her fingers, and looked him in the eyes.

"Anything else I should know, Adam?"

"No. Nothing," he said, with a straight face.

Only a ginger jar you'll never get your hands on!

No big deal if cops discovered the weed, but that cassette tape? Dangerous! Ah, no worries. By now, Gillian had removed the jars and trashed the tape in her hotel, thinking it was just another crappy piece of symphony music. She'd never even bother to listen to it. So, no ginger jars—no *Iced Tea*.

"Good," said Heather. "First question. Did you kill Gladys Kingsley?"

"No."

"Did you kill Gladys Kingsley?" Louder this time.

Was she deaf?

"I said no."

"Did you kill Gladys Kingsley?"

He slammed his fist on the table. "No. What the hell's wrong with you?"

"Control your temper, Adam. You think this is bad, wait until the detectives start on you. When they do, keep your answers short, facts only. Use 'yes', 'no', or 'I don't recall' as much as you can."

"Did you see Gladys Kingsley the night of the fire, Wednesday, March eighth, 1989?"

Was she tricking him?

Heather showed no signs of emotion or letting up as she grilled him. She'd said, "Control your temper," but Adam had to restrain himself from putting his fist through her face several times.

She finally sat back and folded her arms.

"We finished?"

"Just a pause." Heather picked up another piece of paper and stood up. "Let's talk about the new evidence from Mrs. Pozinsky, the wife of the deceased owner of Andy's Diner."

Adam waved his hand dismissively. "The nonsense from good old Mrs. P? Rubbish."

"Mrs. Pozinsky—or Mrs. P, as you call her, stated that at approximately nine thirty-five p.m. of the night of March eighth, 1989, she saw you riding the bicycle belonging to James Snow."

Bloody hell. How could he have known the old lady would check her rearview mirror when she left for the night? "Yeah, so what? Can't a guy go out for a ride?"

"This evidence would have been irrelevant at the time, since Mrs. P had no way of knowing where you were going, just in the general direction of Stoneham Manor." Heather tapped her pen on the table. "The problem is Witness Number Two. A resident at the Manor, Elaine Parker, saw someone matching your description and identified the racing bike behind a bush on the property at about nine-fifty p.m. She was certain, because she was waiting for the news to come on. Based on these two ladies, you could have feasibly ridden there within that timeframe. Were you there?"

The possibility was hard to disprove and he had to keep Heather's trust. Even though the new evidence from these old biddies was nasty, if Heather was any good, she'd toss them out as circumstantial. "Yeah, so what?"

"Why were you there, Adam? Remember, prosecution is looking for motive."

Adam drummed his fingers on the table.

What to do? Tell the truth or stick to the story he gave the cops?

"I repeat, what were you doing at Stoneham Manor at nine forty-five p.m. on March eighth, 1989?"

He met Heather's gaze. "I went for a bike ride. Oliver called my cell and told me Gladys wanted to speak to me face to face about my mother's belongings."

"Oh yes, William Michael Francis O. Bryant—the butler, according to your files?"

She didn't miss a thing.

"And you agreed?"

"Since I had a big assignment due the next day and important meetings planned in the city over March break, there was only a small window. Figured since I was almost there anyway, I might as well."

"There's no record of you signing in as a guest. Can you explain that?"

"Oliver suggested I go straight to her patio door, since she lived in the end unit on the main floor. Easy and no protocol."

Good thing that mouthpiece was gone.

"Back to the night of the eighth. What belongings was Gladys talking about?"

"My mother's journal, a briefcase with my father's notebooks, and some jewellery."

"Okay. So, you hid the bike under a bush near the entrance, where Elaine Parker saw it. Why'd you hide your bike—correction—Jimmy's bike? Did you set Jimmy up to get caught?"

"*Placed* the bike, Heather. I placed it near the bush at the entrance so it wouldn't get stolen, and I didn't want to make noise. I know old people like to go to bed early."

Why couldn't the Parker lady have been one of those bloody early birds?

"What happened next, Adam?"

"The patio curtains had been left open. I saw Gladys sitting near the door, smoking."

Well, he couldn't tell her the truth.

Everything had gone to plan. He'd arrived to see Oliver wearing white servants' gloves and the green sweater Jimmy had delivered—both to please green-eyed Gladys. Clever ... the gloves would also leave no fingerprints. To avoid cameras and run-ins, Oliver had used the back stairs instead of the elevator. He'd hidden and watched Jimmy return the borrowed notebook to Gladys and leave with the pearl necklace and some money—Ollie had suggested she let Jimmy take it to the jeweller to get the clasp fixed. After that, Oliver could start his date with blondie. He'd entered, zip ties in his back pocket, same kind Jimmy used for bike repairs. As instructed, Oliver had then closed the curtains. Funny how the old guy hadn't needed anyone to tell him how much gin to pour down Gladys's greedy throat. Worked like a charm, too. Gladys signed the Bill of Sale, back-dated, of course—although, according to Oliver, she'd needed a little help to steady the one free hand. As soon as all but a table lamp had been turned off, Adam put on his gloves and slipped through the open patio door.

The Scent of Lilacs

All the planning and execution had come down to that moment. His adrenaline had soared as he'd stared at his stepmother, propped up on an armchair near the curtain. "Remember what you said to Dad?" *he'd whispered in her ear.* "'There, there, Darling. I have money. I'll make this little problem go away.' Guess what, Gladys? Now I have the money and you're the little problem." *Her eyes had bulged in horror.*

Adam had checked his watch and peeked outside. Okay, Jimmy. Go back to the rear entrance, check the duty roster for the March break schedule and sign yourself out. Three, two, one. Jimmy's headlights shone from the parking lot. Perfect. Now, go home, Jimmy. I know you have a heavy foot. By the time the alarm goes off, you'll be long gone. Too bad all the evidence will point to you, buddy. When you arrive home, Marla will be expecting your goodnight call. Enjoy—it'll be your last.

It had been pure pleasure to light the cigarette for the blob on the chair.

Adam had waited so long to settle the score with the witch, and from all the reading he'd done, witches were meant to burn.

"Hey." Heather's fingers snapped in front of him. "I'm talking to you."

How long had she been doing that?

"Sorry, Heather. You were asking about Gladys? We had a brief discussion. She said she was getting on in years and I had a right to the jewellery, whatever had belonged to my mother, and anything else in my dad's will. She promised Oliver would deliver everything to me the next day. I thanked her and left."

Curtains make great kindling. As her hair began to sizzle, she blanked. He picked up his belongings to throw into Ollie's unlocked trunk and was gone before the alarm went off.

"Look Heather, with school on my mind, I was there ... four, five minutes, tops."

"So, she was fine before you left."

"Of course. Like I said, Gladys was smoking a cigarette on the patio and was waiting for Oliver to come down for a nightcap. I didn't even go in."

He frowned and looked away, hoping eagle-eyes would notice him.

She did.

"Have you just remembered something, Adam?"

"You know, Oliver had been madly in love with Gladys for years. I think that's why he stuck with her. But it appeared to me she didn't have the same feelings for him. He could have decided to do her in."

Heather scribbled some notes. "Let's stay on track. What time did you get back to your apartment?"

"Just after ten."

"You must have been flying. Did you hear the alarm?"

"No. I plugged in my earpiece to listen to music and pedalled home."

"Now answer this. Why didn't you tell the police this before?"

"Cops only wanted to know if I'd seen Jimmy that day. I told them I'd driven him to his uncle's farm to pick up his truck that morning, then took my car in for service. Jimmy had made plans to go to the diner with Marla Slater after school and then run some errands, so, I walked home, had dinner at Andy's, and went up to do my assignment. Guy across the hall vouched for me."

"Did you tell the detectives you'd been out?"

"Yeah, I said I went for a short bike ride to clear my head from all the homework. Didn't think the rest was important, especially because I was only there a few minutes."

"Okay. What time did you get home from the Manor?"

"Christ, Heather, how many times are you going to ask me the same damn question? Somewhere around five, ten after ten."

Heather jotted some notes again.

"Now are we done?"

"Almost," said Heather. "Your story creates compelling suspicion, but also reasonable doubt. In light of all this, chances are, they'll reopen Jimmy's case. If he's found wrongly accused, he'll be exonerated by the Court of Appeal. As for you, I expect it'll be about circumstantial evidence, since Oliver is no longer alive to testify. This case will take a little time, and I can't promise bail, but," she grinned, "don't get too comfortable in here, Adam."

With winners like Heather and Gillian on his side—home free!

Chapter 23

Marla took one last look around the kitchen before picking up the keys and Pepper's leash. Phew, it was nice to be alone again. No more of her mother's smelly tea and histrionics. Mind you, her mother's guilty-conscience confession had been cathartic, even though the intimate revelations had traumatized her.

What she faced today would be even worse. It was a wonder she hadn't cracked yet. Where was the strength in Marla coming from? Had to be the girls. They depended on her.

As David Foster Wallace said, "The truth will set you free. But not until it is finished with you."

No truer words.

Marla headed to sports camp. "Pepper, I'm so glad I've got you to comfort me. Today's the day I tell Sarah and Susan about their father. How about I practice on you? Do you mind?"

If only she could be sure the kids would react with calmness and empathy, the way Pepper had for the past hour and … oh … was she here already? Marla pulled up to the curb.

Sarah and Susan rushed from the crowd of campers and threw their arms around her and Pepper.

"Toss your bags in and I'll thank your councillor. Then I want to hear everything."

As they buckled into their seats, Sarah sighed, "Three weeks is too long, Mom."

"Yeah, I can't wait to see Dad," said Susan.

Any mention of Adam had Marla quaking. She drove off.

"Mom," continued Susan, "I'm sorry about all the secret stuff with Dad."

"Not your fault. Let it go."

"Dad told us to be strong. He was right. Everybody forgot about it. Camp turned out to be a lot of fun."

"Now we just want to get back to normal," said Sarah.

Normal?

"Will Dad be home for dinner tonight?"

"No, not tonight," Marla said. "Come on, girls, you know I'm dying to hear about your adventures. Give me the long version."

Anything to delay the fireworks.

She'd managed to keep the girls distracted until they rolled into the driveway, emptied the car, and entered the house.

"Feels weird in here," said Sarah.

"I'll fix that." Marla turned on lights and music. "After I make a special dinner, you'll feel right at home again."

Sarah touched her arm. "Mom, we don't want all that. We want to know where Dad is."

"Girls, come and sit on the sofa."

She pulled the armchair over to face them.

"What's going on?" said Susan. "Is someone sick?"

"No, nothing like that, honey."

Nothing that easy.

"Every time we mention Dad, you change the subject. Are … are you and Dad getting a divorce or something?" said Susan.

"Yes."

The shrieks that followed would haunt Marla forever.

After a few long, painful moments, Sarah put her elbows on her knees and stared at her. Tears streamed down her face. "Don't you love him anymore, Mom?"

Marla swallowed. "It's more complicated than that. Your dad's different when we're alone."

Sarah reached forward, brushed Marla's bangs to the side, then gently pressed her fingers where the last bruise had been. "Is that why?"

"Yes. Your dad can't come home."

Susan jumped up. "What do you mean, he can't come home?"

"Shut up, Susan. Mom, we saw bruises before, but when you told us how you got them, we believed you. Are you saying Dad did that?"

"No way," said Susan, glaring at her as if she was spewing nonsense. "Dad would never do something like that. He's kind and gentle. You're making all this up."

The girls had a right to question the accusations. After all, they loved their dad, too.

"No, I'm not. Look, Dad would never hurt either of you. He loves you both deeply. And I think he loves me too, but I can't keep letting him hurt me. When your dad said he wanted to take you to Africa, I was petrified I'd never see you again. That's why I made that fuss with Miss Cindy. I love you, and I never want to lose you."

Pepper jumped onto the sofa between the girls, his chin on his paws. Marla bit down on her lip as she watched the three of them huddled together.

"Susan, you saw Mom's bruises. She can't be making it up," said Sarah.

Susan sobbed. "I don't *want* to believe it."

"I tried for so many years not to involve you, hoping Dad would get help. But he refuses to." Marla knelt in front of them and held their hands. "This is going to be hard. I have something more to tell you, but you need to be strong."

They held hands and stared at her.

"Your dad's been arrested."

"Why?" yelled Sarah.

"He may have done something bad when he was younger. The police just found out about it. It's serious. He might go to jail."

"What did he do?" shouted Susan.

"It has to do with an old fire that happened in Stoneham when we were in high school. Someone died. You may not see your dad for a long time, girls. He's not allowed contact with any of us."

She lifted Pepper onto her lap and sat between the girls, then gave herself permission to cry along with them. If only she could have kept them innocent forever. "I'm so sorry," she finally said, the salty tears dripping onto her tongue. "Your dad's trial will be hard on all of us, but we have to stick together."

They'd never be the same again. How could they? How could she? Would they ever get back to a normal life? And what would normal look like? All she could do was help Sarah and Susan navigate through their daily lives and hope ... just hope that they'd eventually heal.

Chapter 24

Adam stepped into the communal showers. As he slathered on the soap, pain shot up and down his arms, chest, and back. "Ow," he groaned. Even the spray of water hurt. He stepped out and towel-dried, careful not to press the bruises. The cops really worked him over the morning of his arrest, kept him awake all night. He looked at himself in the mirror. A few greys he hadn't noticed before and his eyes looked more bloodshot and puffier than yesterday. Between no sleep and the relentless questioning, he hardly recognized himself.

From the corner of his eye, he caught a glimpse of a naked, burly inmate leaning against the adjacent shower wall, watching him pull his pants on.

"Hey, man, what are you staring at?" said Adam.

"You, pretty boy. Thinking we might have some good times together. Soon as you heal, of course."

"Over my dead body." Adam gave him the finger, picked up his towel, and bolted out. Man, he'd better not be convicted. He couldn't take it. Being locked up in this deplorable, lowlife hotel, waiting for his lawyer, was already hell.

No sooner had the door to his cell snapped shut than he heard voices and footsteps. Adam placed his hands on the cold metal bars—bars that separated him from freedom.

"Mansfield. Hands in the slot. Your lawyer's here."

What in hell had been Heather's hold-up? She'd said 'circumstantial'.

As they reached the interrogation room, the guard uncuffed him. He was at least grateful for that. Adam walked into the dingy room. There was nothing in it but an old wooden table, four chairs, and a dim, overhanging light. Heather glared at him through thick glasses and tapped something on her lap.

Why did she look like a sourpuss?

"Privacy, please," Heather said to the guard.

Adam placed his hands on the table and leaned in. "What's up?"

"You tell me." She held up an old cassette and waved it in the air. "*Iced Tea?*"

He made to grab it.

"Oh, no, you don't." She tossed it in the air and caught it. "This is just a copy, courtesy of a friend of mine. The real deal is in the hands of the District Attorney."

Gillian had let the cops get to it! Had she even gotten on that plane?

His brain was exploding, but he kept his face deadpan.

"You ever heard of 'pre-meditated'?" said Heather. "Are you familiar with the fine prison-palaces in our neighbourhoods?" She placed the tape in the recorder and dangled her finger over play. "I managed to get my hands on one of these dinosaurs. Works quite well. I've heard both sides, but why don't we listen to side two together? Might jog your memory."

Even though the inside of his cheek had become raw, Adam bit hard. "No need."

Side one had a loud symphony, telephone conversations, a kettle whistling, taps running, toilets flushing, and doors opening and closing—all for the benefit of the tenant across the hall. That alone could never get him convicted, but ... side two? The part recapping the timing and plan in precise detail with Oliver?

Well, he wasn't about to go down alone. Needed leverage just in case his buddy got cold feet or turned on him.

The mistake was not getting rid of the cassette along *with* Oliver. His goddamned wife accusing him of assault had taken his mind off it. Too late for all that now. He needed a chess move.

By Heather's judging eyes, she'd already made up her mind about his guilt. Adam stared at her. "You're an accomplished defence attorney, Heather. Ever heard of 'plausible deniability'?"

She waved him away like a child.

How much could he take from Heather, Gillian, his wife—all these vicious women messing with him? He kicked a nearby chair and sent it flying across the room. "So, are you saying that's the end of the 'not-guilty' plea?"

The guard rushed in and jangled the handcuffs.

Heather barely flinched. "No need at the moment," she assured the guard.

Righting the toppled chair, the guard threw Adam a steely-eyed glance, then positioned himself outside the door, one eye trained on him.

"Adam, 'not guilty' is definitely off the table," said Heather.

He sat down again, thinking about the awful but necessary things he'd done to assert his power in life. The biggest lesson he'd learned from his late father and Gladys was that life was what you made it. He'd managed to get Jimmy to take the rap. He'd eliminated the threat of Oliver's big mouth. Mrs. P and the Parker lady's crap about the bike would be easy to deflect. But ... this tape?

Adam could almost see steam billowing from Heather's ears.

"Knock off the attitude, Adam. And don't you ever withhold information from me again. If you think you've had it rough, think again. You're lucky Canada has no death penalty."

Was this woman trying to scare him? To hell with that. Even though he needed her, he wasn't bowing down to anyone, including her. She'd have to dish it out and take it too.

"What happened to 'We can win this case'?" Adam mocked. "Lost your appetite, Miss Holden? I told you I didn't kill Gladys Kingsley. The tape might show I was there, but that's about it."

"Keep your voice down."

"Are you sure you *earned* those accolades you were showing off? Cause maybe you need to reflect on the real killer. It wasn't me. And if it turns out it wasn't Jimmy, it must have been Oliver. Or maybe Walter, the maintenance man? Apparently, he liked money and … spent some time with the old lady."

"All those possibilities will be re-examined. My job is to keep *you* out of prison," she rolled her eyes. "Or at least, minimize it now. So, let's go over the options."

Adam slouched back in the chair and laced his fingers. "That's more like it. I'm all ears."

Heather tapped the *Iced Tea* tape again. "This evidence is incriminating. It shows you planned to make others believe you were home at the time of the fire and the murder. You say Gladys was expecting you. Then why did you tape the plan of entry with Oliver? It sounds as if you colluded with Oliver to let you in, in order to surprise Mrs. Kingsley."

"That's your interpretation."

Heather held up the tape and shook it, "I plan to pull this audio apart thoroughly, but on my first run, I thought I heard something about Oliver making a very tall drink to make … did you say Bon … Blon … Blondie docile?"

Adam sat motionless and tasted blood in his mouth.

"All right, what do we have so far?" She itemized each point with her fingers. "The *Iced Tea* tape and two witnesses that have come forward to identify you. You had means of transportation and the timeline was spot on. Besides all that, you had motive to retrieve your belongings and a perceived hatred for the lady in question. By the way, your wife's domestic assault charges, and, oh, who was that other one?" She sorted through her papers. "I'm running out of fingers. Oh, yes, here it is, Nalin Crawford."

If he could only shut her up.

"I read through some of your files, Adam. You show a propensity for violence."

"Why, because I kicked a chair over?"

Heather frowned. "Not just the chair. Your school reports indicate brilliance, but 'unacceptable behaviour' leading to expulsions."

Did she have to bring back those blasted memories?

The Scent of Lilacs

Those nerds had followed him around like a god. He'd been proud to slip some excitement into their boring lives. Goddamned parents, always interfering in a kid's real education.

Heather slapped the table. "Are you daydreaming? Your life's on the line here. Pay attention." She fanned another sheaf of paper. "These are copies of your doctor's reports. They indicate Conduct Disorder and antisocial tendencies that, if not addressed, would likely develop into Antisocial, Personality Disorder in adulthood. Things like breaking precious artifacts and killing your stepmother's cat. Those events sent you back for further treatment, didn't—"

"I was a kid. They were accidents."

"On the night of the fire, did something trigger you to lose control? Did the doctor's prediction become a reality?"

Adam clenched his fists, aware that, even now, he was showing aggression. Was she pushing him to get mad? *Of course.* Heather wanted him to come to the conclusion that he may have been dealing with mental health issues at the time the crimes were committed.

"Adam, the report also recommended a mood stabilizer. Did you follow the recommendation?"

"For a while—I had an ongoing prescription refill with the pharmacy, subject to Dr. V's approval and any deemed changes."

"Were you on them the night of the fire?"

"Don't remember."

He couldn't very well tell her he'd switched to pot. Man ... he could use some now.

"Think about this," said Heather, "If you plead not guilty and the courts disagree, it means a life sentence."

"What about bail?"

"Hearing is tomorrow, but don't expect leniency."

"Why?"

"Adam, in first degree murder cases, the necessary elements are planning and deliberation. There's *actus reus*, 'guilty act' and *mens rea*, 'guilty mind.'" Heather frowned and walked around the table as she talked. "We've been through this. Maybe now it'll mean more."

Just like his sanctimonious father, preaching and delivering lectures to him.

"Individuals are held responsible for their actions and liable to be tried, convicted, and punished," she continued. "However, the chief exceptions are drunkenness or legal insanity—circumstances when the 'guilty mind' is not present, and, therefore, individuals are not responsible for their actions. There are also shades of stability, that of partial or diminished responsibility, which is like pleading to a lesser crime."

"What are you saying?"

"Okay, here's what I want you to think about. The common defences are: justifiable homicide where there's perfect self-defence, reacting to an aggressor—someone shoots, you defend yourself. Rule that one out, Adam. Next one is inability to intentionally kill, which means an individual is not of sound mind to know the difference. In these cases, it's a non-guilty plea and the defendant is sent to an institution instead of jail."

Dealing with shrinks had never been a problem for Adam. He'd take the chance.

"Any more options?" he demanded.

"Diminished capacity, also known as provocation when a defendant acts under extreme stress. Hard to prove to a jury, but charges usually get reduced to voluntary manslaughter—roughly ten, eleven years in penitentiary."

Him locked up with real criminals, like that guy in the shower? No way.

"I hired you to get me off, Heather. What are you going to do about it?"

"Adam, if after your hearing tomorrow," she said, "bail is not granted, you're being remanded to a detention centre to await trial. While you're there, the Crown and Defence will seek independent, psychiatric assessments."

Dr. Volinoff? Perfect!

Chapter 25

Marla's eyelids fluttered as the sun filtered through the chinks in the blinds. She felt a warm body beside her and turned her head to see her precious daughters, swollen with tears and sleep, and good old Pepper at the foot of the bed.

She slid off and tread softly into her dressing room. After throwing on a track suit and tucking her hair into a clip, she gathered Pepper in her arms and crept out.

Her dad's advice had been to find joy in little things each day. Would laundering the girls' smelly sports clothes be deemed joyful? No, but at least it would keep her busy.

The doorbell rang as she swallowed the last trickle of coffee.

Evelyn and Amy? Pizza, wine, and doughnuts? No, no, no. Too soon for visitors. The girls' pain was still raw. But how could Marla turn them away? The twins would have to confront their friends eventually, wouldn't they? Better at home and now.

"Hi. I must be losing it. Did you say you were coming, Ev?"

"Didn't know I had to. Are you letting us in?"

Marla forced a smile. "Of course. Sarah and Susan slept in my bedroom last night, Amy. Go ahead and take the treats up. Thanks for the lunch, Ev."

They walked to the kitchen.

"Out with it," said Evelyn. "I can see you've been crying. Is your mother sick, or has that schmuck done something else?"

She led Evelyn into the den, closed the door and collapsed on her friend's shoulder. "Sorry I haven't called you. I've been confused and ashamed."

"Why?"

"It's not easy for me to tell you this, but right after you left the courthouse, the police arrested Adam."

"Why?"

"There's no way to soften this. He's been charged with murder."

Evelyn gasped.

Marla trembled and looked away. "If you want to walk out of here and never come back, I wouldn't blame you. It sounds like an episode of *CSI*, even to me." She burst into tears.

Evelyn threw her arms around her. "Stop it. You're not the criminal here and I'm not going anywhere."

Footsteps.

In poked three tear-stained faces.

"Mom, we need some air," said Susan. "We're going to take Pepper for a walk."

"Good idea. I'll warm the pizza."

No one would be hungry, but they'd go through the motions anyway.

"How much do the girls know, Marla?"

"I struggled with what to tell them. When they came home to an empty house yesterday, I couldn't hold off any longer. Hardest thing I've ever had to do. It's going to be a tough year for the girls. I have no idea how to handle it. We'll need some counselling."

"Smart. No one could be prepared for something like this. I knew that man was too good to be true." Evelyn balled her fists. "The abuse, the cheating, and now…?"

"Evelyn, before the girls come back, I have to ask you for a favour." Marla flushed. "I have to drive to Stoneham on Thursday. Just for the day. I know it's a big ask, but could you …"

Evelyn held up her finger. "I'm here for you. Whatever you need."

The Scent of Lilacs

Marla had arrived early for her meeting at Mr. P's old diner. She squirmed as she sipped her coffee, hoping no one she recognized would come in. Regardless of the risk of being spotted—she had to tell Jimmy goodbye. This time, *she'd* be the one to cut the ties.

She peered outside and caught her reflection in the window pane. Good, her shoulder-length curls had behaved that day. Adjusting her scarf, she looked up as the door opened.

Jimmy smiled and waved as if time had stood still. He approached their familiar corner booth and gave her a hug and kiss on the cheek. "Marla, you're so beautiful, you take my breath away."

"Thank you, Jimmy."

He sat across from her and for a moment they just stared at each other, letting those old feelings settle.

"We sure spent a lot of time here," she finally said.

"Here and under that old oak at Clarence Creek, remember?"

"Sure do. You shocked the hell out of me when you started reciting poetry. Most romantic motorhead I'd ever met."

They laughed.

"It's a bittersweet memory, though. I owe my academic achievements to Adam. Seemed he knew us better than we knew ourselves."

"Come on, Jimmy. Yes, I liked that you went all dreamy on me. But don't ever think that's what made me care for you. You had me way before Adam came into the picture."

Jimmy nodded. "You know, the more poetry I read, the more meaning I discovered. I found myself *wanting* to share it with you."

Marla blinked back the tears. Oh hell, she'd come to say something. If this kept up, she'd break down and lose her nerve. A smile crept over her face. "How could I not have loved a guy with a spastic, slathering Dane named Duke?"

"Oh, so my dog attracted you?" he laughed, then met her gaze. "*Had*, Marla?"

She bit her lip. "Jimmy, I was so in love with you." For a second, she imagined his arms around her. They'd belonged together then. "I would have waited for you forever if it hadn't been for that devil. Now, with all that's happened, how can we ever go back? Things aren't the same anymore. Adam will always come between us. I have two daughters—Adam's daughters. I have to do what's best for them." She touched Jimmy's hands. "It's going to be hard for me, for you, for everyone, till the trial is over. But you deserve the truth and a good life."

"I want that too." He leaned in closer. "But I want it with you."

She pulled away. "Jimmy, I can't. It's time to let go. Our memories are ours alone. No one can take them away from us. I'll always think of you the way you were. All sporty, kind, and caring. You'll always be a part of me. A good part."

Tears trickled down Jimmy's cheeks. He wiped them away with his fists. "Funny how life has its own plans for us. Marla, you're the one who kept me going when I was in prison even though I knew you were with Adam. Staying in contact with him helped me to stay close to you. I know us being together is impossible. Just answer this. Can I still count on your friendship?"

"Always, Jimmy. My gut tells me you'll be exonerated."

She squeezed her eyes shut.

But would Adam—her husband—be found guilty instead?

Chapter 26

No bail had come as no surprise after Heather's warning. Adam stretched out on the mattress in his tiny room at the detention centre. He laced his fingers behind his head and looked around. At least it wasn't a stinky dump like he'd just been in. Even had a proper bathroom.

Place was quiet, too. They'd given him some old *National Geographic* magazines and worn-out copies of *Catcher in the Rye* and *Of Mice and Men*. High school re-reads, but better than nothing.

His mind drifted to the Crown shrink he'd been seeing—as easy to manipulate as Dr. Volinoff.

Adam rubbed his chin with both hands. *No shaving today.* Being foul-mouthed, grimy, and dishevelled would ramp up Dr. V's compassion, humanity, and ... blindness. Imagine the doctor thinking *he* could be saved? Full marks for trying, but Adam Mansfield had standards to uphold—and not the saintly ones. Saved, he'd never be.

Heather arrived first. "You look terrible, Adam. Why didn't you clean up? She's going to be put off."

She? No way!

"I thought I told you to call Dr. Volinoff?"

"I did. Dr. Fayina Volinoff." She gave him a quizzical look. "What's the problem?"

"Where's Dr. Fyodor Volinoff?" His heart raced.

Who was this new person? He enjoyed being the deceiver, but what right did Heather have to sneak one on him? How would he be able to hold on to his edge if he didn't know who he was dealing with?

"Fayina's father died several years ago," said Heather.

Daughter? Perhaps he should have shaved.

"Don't worry. You're in good hands, Adam."

The guard stuck his head in. "Doctor has arrived."

"Okay, Adam. This is where I leave you. Stay calm. You've got this."

He heard high heels clicking before he saw the tall, willowy, sophisticated brunette.

"Mr. Mansfield. I'm Dr. Fayina Volinoff." No handshake. She simply nodded.

Cold. Whose side was she on, anyway?

"Sorry to hear about your father's passing," Adam said. "He was a kind man and very good to me."

"Thank you. Please sit down, Mr. Mansfield." She fished reading glasses out of her purse. "I joined my father's practice before he'd taken ill, so I'm quite familiar with your file."

Is that what he'd been reduced to? A file? He'd sit whenever he damn-well pleased.

"You were so young when my father began treating you. He felt especially responsible for your welfare."

Pity?

He gritted his teeth. "Yes, we had a long history together."

Fayina flipped through her notes then peered at him over her glasses. "Please, do sit."

Christ. He might as well concede ... but just a little.

"The journal entries show my father tried to contact you many times, with no success. Miss Holden's call came as a surprise." She paused and tapped her clipboard as if it held special insight. "A shame."

Insensitive snake—pretending to see through him.

"May I call you Adam?"

New strategy, huh? Casual first-name basis? Make me open up? Two can play this game.

"Sure. Everyone else does, Fayina."

"Adam, I've discussed the Crown psychiatrist's report with your lawyer. I'll go over it with you in layman's terms."

Now she thinks I'm a moron.

"Yes, please keep it simple. I'm not a doctor."

With a hidden smirk, Adam listened to her rattle off the same spiel Heather had given him.

Good. With the non-guilty plea he was sure they'd hand him, he'd see hospital, not jail time. And just like the past, he'd miraculously be cured and get his family and business back on track. Adam pictured the family photo on his fireplace, Marla's fireplace now. He held back the impulse to ball his fists.

"Ahem. Adam."

Christ, the doc was talking and he'd zoned out.

She scribbled on her clipboard.

"So, Dr. V, what do you think? Do you agree with the Crown doctor?"

"You know, my father believed you were resilient. With supervision, medication, and therapy, you could control your episodes. They'd have a steeling effect to allow you to function. Without them, your actions may very well have been beyond your control."

"You didn't answer my question."

"I'll reserve judgment until I've spent time with you, Adam. I'm going to recommend that you be transferred to a another clinic where you'll be more comfortable. I'm also planning to interview Mrs. Mansfield."

"My wife?" He slammed his fist on the table. "What for?"

"I'd like her observations over the course of your lives together."

"That woman put me in here," Adam yelled. "You'd believe her over me? Anything she says is a lie. And you expect me to trust you?"

How had he gotten stuck with Fayina Volinoff?

Would he always be at the mercy of women?

Chapter 27

Marla didn't know what the final plea would be, but at least Adam was locked up for now. Her father had just called to update her. "Under court order, Adam's been transferred to a Forensic Services Unit."

"How long will they keep him, Dad?"

"It's a small unit, only a few beds. They'll determine if he's fit to stand trial. Turnover is quick. Then he'll be transferred to a more permanent facility. No need to worry. Adam's not going anywhere without a police sidekick."

"If you say so."

Marla had barely hung up when the phone rang again.

"Mrs. Mansfield, this is Dr. Volinoff's office calling."

Adam's psychiatrist? Wasn't he working for the defence?

"Yes ... what's this about?" she stammered.

"Sorry for the short notice. Dr. Volinoff asked me to arrange an urgent meeting with you today."

"I'll have to call you back on that."

She frowned. Were they trying to coerce her into helping the enemy? She called her dad back. "Should I go?"

"They'll subpoena you anyway. Just tell the truth and bring some of your prize photos. Tell them about the lying, cheating, turning the girls against you, and anything else you've endured throughout your marriage. They'll realize you can do their case more harm than good."

"Now I'm pumped. I'll call you later."

Marla changed into business attire and maneuvered through town.

There. The sign on the Brownstone read *Dr. F. Volinoff.*

"I'm here to see Dr. Fyodor Volinoff."

"I'm sorry, Fyodor passed away some time ago," said the receptionist. "His daughter Fayina has since taken over the practice."

That explained the signage remaining the same.

An attractive woman her own age walked towards her.

"Thank you for coming on such short notice, Mrs. Mansfield."

Marla followed her down the corridor and accepted a glass of water before she sat down. "Why am I here, Doctor?"

"Mrs. Mansfield, I simply want to get your perspective. You know Adam best. Who better to talk to about him? Do I have your permission to record our conversation?"

Adam's file had to be thick and this woman likely knew everything about him already. But what Fayina Volinoff didn't know was what Adam was trying to get away with.

Could Marla bare her secrets to this stranger? She had to.

"You want to know about my husband? Go ahead and put this on record." She started with Paris and after blurting out Adam's offenses, including Adam's attempt to take the girls to Africa, she opened her purse and fanned the photos she'd brought. "Take a look at these. In court, Judge D'Arcy believed me. Maybe you will too."

Dr. Volinoff studied each one. "Why didn't you tell someone?"

"Lots of reasons. My dad's a police chief. I didn't want to embarrass him. According to my mother, Adam could do no wrong. And the biggest reason is our twin daughters. They adore their father."

"So, Adam is a good parent, then?"

"The best." She shifted in the chair. "That's why I stayed."

"What finally made you go to the police?"

Marla wasn't sure how much to tell this doctor, in light of the ongoing investigation. She'd tread carefully. "In June, my parents came to stay with us here in the city while Adam was away. My father needed to borrow cufflinks from Adam for an event. We discovered some jewellery in Adam's closet that seemed suspicious. Turned out the jewellery was connected to the crimes that occurred twelve years ago in Stoneham—the fire and murder my old boyfriend, Jimmy Snow, had been convicted of."

"Are you referring to the crimes that Adam is now being accused of?"

"Yes. The charge of possession of stolen property didn't stick, but we found more incriminating evidence—files dealing with his family, his estate, his mother's suicide, schools he was expelled from, even your late father's reports from St. James Clinic. Details that linked him to the alleged charges."

"Thank you for that valuable information. Let's get back to you and Adam for a moment. When Adam was at home, did he frighten you?"

Marla looked away. "Have you met Adam?"

"Yes."

"So, you know how handsome and charming he is?"

"Without a doubt, Adam is very good-looking. But of course, there's more to a man than looks."

"Oh, he has more than looks, Doctor. He's brilliant, well-read, cultured, thoughtful, generous. A perfect ten to most people. But no one sees the monster at night. The next morning, he acts as if nothing ever happened. Do you have any idea how he made me feel? Ashamed of even thinking the way I did. As if I was in the wrong. As painful and humiliating as it was, it had never amounted to anything life-threatening. So, I made the choice to continue. Of course, that's impossible now. If he's guilty of murder, you bet I'm scared."

"Please go on, Mrs. Mansfield."

"Recently I learned Adam had been visiting Jimmy in jail all these years. He told me he'd convinced Jimmy it was only fair to let me go. Then he asked for Jimmy's blessing to date me—like passing a relay baton." Marla locked eyes with the doctor. "I now believe Adam planned it."

"Do you have any idea why he'd do that?"

"I take commitment seriously. My nature is to be trusting and loyal. I don't pretend to be a psychologist, but is it possible that Adam used me to create the perfect family he'd been denied?"

"That warrants valid consideration. Now, Mrs. Mansfield, did you ever see Adam take medication?"

"No." She frowned. "I now know from Adam's files, that your father prescribed it for him since childhood. Would it have made a difference?"

"Excellent question. The answer will be part of my findings."

Dr. Volinoff scribbled some notes.

"What else can you tell me about Adam's personality, Mrs. Mansfield?"

"You mean like possessiveness, his staged perfectionism, and the mirror being his best friend? Or, how about this. Ever since I met Adam, he's had these blackouts. They only last a few seconds, but he disappears. I've gotten used to it over the years."

"How often do they occur?"

"Seems like anytime his mother or father are mentioned."

"I see."

Marla answered a few more questions before Dr. Volinoff closed the file.

She was glad it was over, but couldn't hold herself back. "Frankly, Dr. Volinoff, I don't know how you can defend him."

Chapter 28

Coming through the doors of the Forensic Services Unit, Adam had realized how serious this phase of his scrutiny would be—last chance to fight for his freedom.

He appreciated the clean, private room they'd given him … civilized. But after ten days, it had become another sterile shithole. Might as well have been a cell. Revolting medicinal odours instead of urine and sweat.

He knew Heather wouldn't show her face here—not since that first day she'd come to see that he was settled. He'd pumped her for the doctor's results.

"Sorry. Nothing to report. Try to stay calm and focused. You'll get through this."

"Come on, Heather. I'm suffering."

She'd sucked in her cheeks and cast her eyes downward.

Jesus Christ, she couldn't care less!

Wild-eyed, Adam leaped to her side of the table with his fists clenched.

"Back away," she yelled, "or I'll call for help. Wouldn't look good on your record."

He could see the guard's head in the window.

Too bad. He wanted nothing more than to teach Heather Holden a lesson.

Since that episode, his lawyer had only reached him by telephone.

Today Adam would stay composed for Dr. V.

The Scent of Lilacs

After exchanging greetings, the doctor folded her arms and squared her shoulders. A shadow seemed to cross her face.

"What's up with you?" he said.

"Let me ask you that. Is something bothering you, Adam?"

So many questions. He was getting sick and tired of this dance and moved to the edge of his chair. "What did my wife have to say?"

"I'll get to that. How do you feel, Adam? Are you tired or hungry?"

"Don't worry about me," he blurted, "no one else ever has."

"What about your mother? She cared about you, didn't she? Do you remember her?"

Adam rolled his eyes. How Freudian could she get? And why did she have to pick at his scab? As much as he fought to push thoughts of his mother out of his mind, Isabel Mansfield's power overtook him.

Of course, his mother had cared for him—while he had her, goddamn it. He loved her so much. Without her journal, she'd begun to slip further and further away. What was that first baby poem she'd written for him?

> *A cuddle and a peep*
> *From your fuzzy bear and sheep*
> *A whistle and a toot*
> *Comes the magic from your flute*
> *A block, a book, a train, a plane*
> *All invented—a child to gain*
> *Play and grow*
> *The world to know*
> *Be free—enjoy*
> *My precious little boy.*

She'd illustrated the poem with pastels and even signed it with a red lipstick kiss. *Well, Momma, I did grow to know the world. And without you, life has been shitty!*

Adam could feel his eyes fill up. And just like that, the anger set in.

You left me. You bitch. You chose that asshole professor. Your note said you just couldn't live without him. Well, what about me?

His stomach heaved.

His so-called father had latched onto that witch, Gladys, who acted like she was his mother. Woman had no clue about kids. All she knew was money and cats. Good riddance. He didn't need them.

He blinked.

Was someone calling his name?

"Adam, Adam ... Come back."

"I'm right here. What are you yelling for?"

"To get your attention. What were you just thinking about? Was it your mother?"

"Yeah, so what's it to you?"

"Adam," said Dr. Volinoff.

More pity?

"Don't look at me like that." He slapped the table.

"Your mother's death still haunts you, doesn't it?" Dr. Volinoff stood up. "I'll submit my report tomorrow. Your lawyer will be in touch."

"Never mind about reports. I want to know what my wife said."

"Your wife said some very positive things about you, but she also shared her fears."

"What? What did she say?"

"I'm not at liberty to discuss it."

Adam threw his hands in the air. What did Marla have to be afraid of? That woman had everything. He slammed the table again as he locked eyes with Dr. Volinoff. "You and this legal system are screwing up my life. I want to see my wife and children." He jumped to his feet and stomped around the room. Like a wounded animal, he let out a deep cry, then smashed his fist against the wall. Blood dripped from his knuckles—leaving the wall stained with a sticky mixture of blood and skin.

Dr. Volinoff backed up towards the door and pressed the buzzer.

The guard rushed in with a male nurse. Adam's knees buckled the minute the needle pricked his arm.

God, he was so tired. No one cared about him. His body felt like a bag of lard as they shoved him onto the bed and strapped him down.

The Scent of Lilacs

Adam woke up screaming, "Volinoff? Where are you?"

The nurse came in, holding another syringe. "Be quiet. She'll be here when she gets here."

He continued to thrash and yell. "Go ahead, poke me." He longed for the blackout ... to escape this hellhole and the reality of his life.

The next morning, the attendant came into Adam's room and after completing routines, he looked at Adam with sad eyes, "Don't even think of acting up, buddy. No drugs today. Doctor's orders."

"What? How else am I going to survive in here?"

"She wants you alert. They're shipping you back to Detention in a couple of days. Might as well throw in the towel, man. It'll go easier on you."

He hadn't met many, but maybe this was one of the good guys. Adam shrugged. "I'll think about it."

Heather didn't show up until the third day after he was transferred to the detention centre. She had Fayina Volinoff's report in her hand. He looked at his lawyer, then checked through the glass pane of the door.

Yup. The woman was scared. She'd posted a guard.

They'd weaned Adam off the meds, but a clear mind hadn't taken away his anger.

"Okay, what did the doc say?"

"Dr. Volinoff has determined that you have excellent cognitive abilities and has convinced the Crown that, under proper treatment and therapy, you are able to function as normal. That makes you ... responsible for your actions, Adam." Heather shifted her eyes to the door. "It boils down to a guilty plea."

"No way!" he yelled.

"Stay put," she said with her arms stretched in front. "Hear me out."

Adam backed away, dropped onto the chair, and laced his fingers together. "Sorry. Go ahead, I'm listening."

219

She sat on the edge of her chair. "Adam, it means you were responsible for the crimes, but were driven to commit them because of your state of mind at the time. You most likely were not on your meds. Diminished capacity is our best defence."

"But it means jail time."

Where did he go wrong? Why had he failed to sway Dr. V? Her and that goddamn Marla.

"We'll go for a reduced charge, Adam. With leniency, you'll likely get ten or eleven. With appeals and good behaviour, you'll be out in less."

"Well, yippee. So much for getting me off." He took a deep breath.

"Consider yourself lucky, Adam."

Lucky? Man, she was asking for it!

"As I've said before, the diminished capacity plea wouldn't get you out any faster."

If the shrinks were like old Dr. V, he'd be out in no time. What choice did he have now? Adam didn't believe in luck. That was for dreamers. But things were definitely not going his way. Would he even make it in jail? His mind went back to the showers in the first prison. He knew what to expect. Logic and critical thinking weren't how those guys operated. They didn't play nice. How in hell did Jimmy do it, and all the while being an innocent man? At least he knew he was guilty.

Adam's eyes sank deeper into their sockets. "Look, lady," he croaked. "Do what you have to do."

Trapped again!

Meanwhile, his wife, Sarah, Susan, and Pepper were comfortable and carrying on without him. Or ... could Marla now be with ...?

No! He had to take care of this! He had a reason to live.

New plan!

Chapter 29

Marla had been crossing off the days and events on her calendar. Today's date, November thirtieth, had an X marked on it. More than a year had already gone by. A year filled with court dates. So many anxious moments—wins, losses, and compromises—as lawyers settled the affairs between her and Adam.

She cleared away the breakfast dishes and began her new landscaping assignment just as the phone rang.

"Marla," shouted her father. "Jimmy's been exonerated."

"That's great news, Dad! I'm so relieved. It finally restores my faith in the system."

"I feel the same way. What a screw-up. I let you and Jimmy down."

"I don't hold it against you, Dad. And I don't believe Jimmy does, either. He knows you had nothing to do with his conviction."

"That's what he said. I saw him this morning." Her dad's voice broke. "He shook my hand."

"That's the Jimmy I knew. I hope he finds happiness."

"Me, too. By the way, Marla. Your mother and I have started cleaning up the crawl space in the basement. Is it all right if we have some of your old things delivered to you?"

"Can't it just wait for my next trip out there? I have my hands full right now."

"You know your mother when she gets something in her head."

"Say no more," Marla laughed.

"I was counting on that. The truck will be at your place later today."

The next call came as no surprise.

"Marla. It's over."

"I know, Jimmy. I just got off the phone with my dad. I'm so happy for you." She wiped the corners of her eyes.

"I have some more good news," he said. "I've landed a job with a car company."

His dream had come true.

Marla wished him well, hung up, and burst into tears. A huge weight had lifted. Her heart felt easy as she prepped the chicken for the evening meal and waited for the doorbell.

A uniformed man held a bundle of plastic and blankets. "Mrs. Mansfield, we have a delivery from the Slaters in Stoneham. While my partner unpacks the piano, I'll cover your floors."

"A ... a piano? I ... I had no idea." She'd never wanted one in this house, too painful a reminder of the past. But so much had changed. A warm feeling now swept over her. Marla walked around the living room trying to visualize it. What kind would it be? Her childhood piano was gone, thanks to her temper. Whatever it was, she'd graciously accept it. "I'm afraid I'll need your help moving furniture."

"We're prepared for that, Mrs. Mansfield." He handed her a room design and a photo.

The antique Mason and Risch upright! Her piano!

She studied the layout.

Marla couldn't have preplanned the space better herself.

Her excitement was off the chart as the men maneuvered it into place.

"Looks great," said the lead hand. He pulled an envelope with her name on it from his breast pocket.

Her mother's handwriting.

The minute they left Marla ripped it open. A lump formed in her throat.

To my dear daughter.

Okay, now she was really going to lose it.

Marla, because of me, you destroyed your beloved piano and gave up on something that gave you so much pleasure. How could I have

The Scent of Lilacs

expected you to follow in my footsteps? I should have seen the uniqueness in you. Your talents, your wishes, your dreams. It's a little late, but maybe not. You've always been a kind and forgiving angel.

Your dad suggested we store the old piano, hoping someday you'd change your mind about it. I agreed. After all you've been through and all you've lost, we thought you might want to rekindle the passion you used to have. The piano has been restored to its original glory. Enjoy. (Even though music created by those old, dead guys is not my cup of tea.) Love, Mom.

Love? She'd waited so long to hear those words!

Marla held the note against her chest, wiped her eyes, and stared at the piano. Would she even remember how? She feathered her hand along the curve of the lid and lifted it. Her heart skipped. She pulled back the bench to sit down. Not quite right. She moved the bench back and forth until it felt comfortable, then stretched and curled her fingers in and out a few times before letting them rest on the keys, her thumb on middle C. CDEFG—C major scale, D major, F#, intervals, chords. Her left hand was a bit stiff, unfamiliar, but it was still there. Warm, happy memories dictated where Marla's fingers should go next. She began to lose herself, unaware the front door had opened.

"Mom?" squealed Sarah as she ran to the room. "You're playing the piano."

Her sister arrived steps behind her. "Where did that come from?" said Susan.

"Grandma and Grandpa."

The girls ran their hands along the veneer.

"It's beautiful. We didn't know you could play," continued Susan.

"It was a long time ago."

"We want to hear you, Mom," urged Sarah and Susan.

"Maybe." Marla lifted the lid of the bench and was amazed to see the sheet music she'd left on top. Clefs, key and time signatures, accidentals, reps and codas, accents, and ornaments. So much to remember.

"Okay. I'm rusty, but I'll do my best." She arched her fingers and planted the tips on the appropriate notes.

Could she really play something complicated after such a long hiatus?

She fumbled a bit with the first few bars, but it soon took shape. Her fingers began to dance, the "dah-dah-dah-dahs" bursting from her fingers.

This had been the last piece she'd practiced on the day of the fire. It had seared into her brain. Then it hit her. The irony. That famous, four-note musical motif that emitted terror and pain was said to represent fate knocking on the door. Her door?

Such hocus-pocus.

She dropped her shoulders and took a deep breath, reminding herself that Beethoven's Fifth moved from dark to light, tragedy to … triumph.

Marla bit her lip and buried her head in the pillow that night. So much had changed. Sure, she was safe in this big house and she had so much to be grateful for. Her girls, Pepper, her work, loving parents, and now even her old piano. But there was still an empty, supermassive hole in her heart.

Lying in this king-sized bed, she could almost smell Adam's cologne and feel his arms around her. She caught herself reaching out to touch him. Was this real? Marla thrashed from side to side and finally woke in a cold sweat, her breath coming in spasms.

Not this dream again. Adam had taken up so much room inside her, would she ever get him out? She could have lived with his eccentricities and indiscretions like many before her had. But Adam the conman, the misogynist, the murderer? She sluffed his imaginary touch from her arms, then jumped out of bed and splashed cold water on her face.

Pepper eyed her from the bathroom doorway. "Come here, boy," she said, reaching down to pet him. "What do you think, old friend? Will we be, okay?"

Pepper gave her a cloudy stare. Not the answer she'd hoped for.

Was life as nebulous as her dog's vague gaze? Would she live like this forever? Could she live like this forever?

'Even the darkest night gives way to dawn.'

Who'd said that? She couldn't remember, but she had to get it together, stop feeling sorry for herself. She marched to her closet. "Okay, sport. What to wear? One by one, she slid the hangers aside. Blue tailored blouse, navy pencil skirt, wide belt and … she slipped her feet into a pair of three-inch heels.

Pepper padded behind her to the kitchen. She pressed the volume button on the radio to full blast, tied on a Christmas apron, and with the recipe binder open, shouted, "Hello, Julia. I'm back."

She banged pots and pans, whizzed the blender, and put the griddle on sizzle, giving no consideration to sleeping children.

Sure enough, the girls came bounding down the stairs and into the kitchen, their mouths gaping.

"Mom, what's gotten into you?" shouted Susan.

"Yeah, how come you're all dressed up to make breakfast?" said Sarah.

"I've decided to look my best, stop feeling sorry for myself, and just live. Want to join me?" Marla flipped some finished pancakes onto a plate and poured on enough syrup to drown them. "Get the whipped cream, girls."

"Mom. I don't know what's up with you," laughed Sarah, "but I like it."

Marla speared a piece. "I can't change what's happened to our family, but together we can shape what's to come." She smacked her lips. "Sarah, I'm so glad you've found a love for gymnastics. I knew you would. And Susan, dance your heart out."

The oven beeped. "Okay girls, wash your hands and roll up your sleeves. We're going to make strudel." Wasn't long before the counter was covered in flour, sugar, spices, bowls, and it seemed, every utensil in the house.

The telephone buzzed. Marla looked at the display—*Bob*.

"Girls, please start the cleanup." Marla picked up the telephone, walked to the den, and almost sang 'good morning'.

"Great news," said Bob, "our park project won the Urban Design Award."

She grabbed the edge of the desk. "I can't believe it."

"You put us on the map, Marla. And your mother's recommendation to use Bud's was brilliant. I might have to hire her."

Marla cringed. "It's either me or her." She paused. "On second thought, I guarantee she'd say no. In Stoneham, she's a legend. Still singing at Brody's. She and my dad are a tag team."

"Well let's leave them to it, then. Marla, how about dinner tonight to celebrate?"

"I'd love to," she said, without a second thought.

The girls eyed her as she slinked back into the kitchen.

"Mom, you look like the cat that swallowed the canary," said Susan.

"Call Amy and your teenage friend Debbie for a pizza party, because I'm going out with my boss tonight. It's a celebration dinner. We won the award for park project of the year." Marla bowed as they clapped. "Couldn't have done it without your patience and understanding, my lovelies."

Well, that wasn't entirely true. No point dredging up the past, though. After all, they were only kids and ... why wouldn't they have trusted and obeyed their father?

Her words must have struck a nerve.

"Mom, Sarah and I are ashamed for taking Dad's side back then," said Susan.

She gave them each a hug. "Let's forget it."

The girls burst into tears.

"We miss Dad so much. The old Dad," said Sarah. "The one who laughed and played with us. Why did he have to do it? Didn't he love us?"

Marla clutched their hands. "You have no idea how much you father loves you. It's probably killing him not to see you."

"Then why, Mom?"

"We have an appointment with Dr. Barrett next week. She's going to help us sort it out. All I know is he had a terrible childhood because his mother took her own life and abandoned her little boy.

It made him so angry that he blamed his dad and his stepmother and took it out on everyone around him, including me."

"He wasn't mean to us," said Susan. "He was smart and funny and kind."

"You girls were special. He brought you up the way he wished he'd been brought up." She really wanted to believe that. "Let's save our questions for the doctor."

Did she still believe in redemption?

Marla wouldn't hold herself to any promises, but for the sake of her daughters, she'd ask the therapist if they might someday visit their dad.

Seven on the dot. Marla tossed her shawl and evening bag over her shoulder, checked her lipstick, and opened the door. "Don't you look spiffy, Mr. Wyllie," she said, giving him a wolf-whistle.

A decade older than her; full, silver-streaked head of hair; and fit and tanned from outdoor, work-related activities—her boss was handsome and distinguished-looking. The touch of burgundy in his paisley tie gave him extra pizzazz tonight.

"As I recall, Bob, you never wear a jacket and tie unless there's a major client to impress."

From the first day they'd met, she'd allowed herself to be casual with him—like the old Marla who used to tease, joke, and laugh with Jimmy. Adam had been attracted to her for that reason as well. She'd been the funny redhead. Adam had even nicknamed her Red.

"Jeez, Marla. You're stealing my fire. You look terrific. I ... I'm the one who's supposed to do the whistling. And the jacket is because an award like this *is* a big deal."

"Well, thank you. Bob, why are you standing at attention? What's behind your back?"

"For the twins. Just something little. You know I don't have anyone to spoil. And oh, flowers for you." He revealed two gift bags in one hand and a wrapped bouquet in the other.

"How sweet. Anyone who can sit through a children's version of *Swan Lake* is already in their good books." She peeked under the flap of the bouquet. "Purple lisianthus. My favourite." She'd sure had enough of lilacs for a while. "How did you know?"

"Well, they're in season. And besides, I didn't see you as a 'roses' kind of lady."

"Correct. Roses are the show-offs of the world, too perfect. I no longer trust perfect." Marla bent her head to smell the lisianthus. "These, on the other hand, are true to life. Delicate, fragile, and random. Thank you."

"After what you've been through, you're still able to find beauty all around you. Marla, you're the strongest, most resilient person I've ever met."

Had Bob just said she was strong?

She'd gone through life feeling weak and insecure. Feelings that caused anxiety, doubt, and pain. Her mother's words after her parents' big blow-up had touched her and given her hope, but had her mother really meant them? She wasn't sure.

And Adam ... well, he'd never wanted a strong woman, just someone to control. Yet he'd surrounded himself with powerful women like Gillian and Nalin. He truly was a study in contrasts.

Marla fought back a tear. "Bob, that means so much to me. Come in while I put the flowers in water."

"Mm, this place smells like my granny's did, cinnamon and apples."

"Good nose. We baked strudel today."

"Any for me?"

"How about we have coffee and dessert here afterwards? The girls will want to thank you for the gifts."

"Sounds great."

"I want to hear all about the award, Bob," she said, as she slid into his car. "Who, what, where, when, how? Is there a trophy or a plaque? Come on, tell me everything. By the way, where are we going?"

"You're quite the chatterbox," Bob said, smiling as he backed out of the driveway. "It's the new Spanish tapas place."

The Scent of Lilacs

"I know the one. Great reviews. Evelyn and I have been meaning to go."

When they reached the corner, he turned in the opposite direction she'd expected. "Marla, I have to make a stop at the office first. Won't take long. Come up with me."

"Sure. Might as well check my messages."

He held the door open for her.

Something on the lobby wall caught her eye. "It's the Central Park scene I told you about," shouted Marla as she ran over to examine the signature. "Where did you get this?"

"When you told me this piece inspired your vision for the city project way back before the ballet recital, I took a drive over to Gallery One."

"You bought it from Adam?"

"No, it was a young lady with black hair."

"Nalin Crawford?"

"Yup, that's her. I really liked the painting and made her a generous offer. Didn't give my name until after she'd called her boss. He agreed. Said he couldn't have done better at auction. I've been enjoying it in my home until now. But since we won the award, I thought it should hang here to inspire you again—you know, to keep the awards coming. And ... I have another surprise. Follow me."

They passed her office and down another corridor to a room with a modern etched-glass door. On the wall to the right of it, a brushed nickel plate held her name in large letters and below it the word *Partner*.

Marla's chest swelled. That massive hole in her heart had only been empty to make room for what was to come next. A future maybe brighter than she'd hoped for.

Tonight, everything was exactly where it was supposed to be—in her own hands.

Chapter 30

Adam watched Jimmy hand three books to the guard for inspection.

"So, planning to read, or are you using them for weight-lifting?" said Jimmy as he sat on the visitor side of the booth.

"You never did understand poetry or literature. I recall spending a lot of time tutoring your ass in high school."

Jimmy snarled. "You think that makes up for what you did to me?"

"We do what we have to do, buddy."

"And if you think I'm your buddy, you must be smoking some bad stuff."

Adam knew that, but whatever reason Jimmy had for regularly coming to the Correctional Centre was okay with him.

The guard placed the books in front of him. He pushed his glasses further back on the bridge of his nose. In the past, the glasses had been a ruse. Now the words on the pages blurred without them. Adam checked the spines. Proust's *In Search of Lost Time*. And *Ulysses* and *The Odyssey* by James Joyce. Books with substance. "Yup, you got them right. Thanks. There's a whole cast of characters on these pages. They're all I need."

At least that's he wanted Jimmy to believe.

"So, what's going on in the world?"

"I've invited Marla and your girls to come to my car race."

"Ouch. Did you come to hurt me, Jimmy?"

"Why else? I want my face stamped in your memory." Jimmy moved closer to the glass, his eyes like lasers. "Cause I never want you to forget me."

"Aw, and here I thought you really cared."

"I care enough to watch you rot."

Unlikely.

Jimmy was incapable of true hatred and would never stoop to revenge. Unlike him. Even now it warmed Adam's heart thinking about his father and that puff-faced Gladys—watching the fear in their eyes as they were about to die at his hands. He'd felt differently about Oliver, and had even said 'sorry' as he'd slipped the gear into drive with Oliver drunk and oblivious behind the wheel. Oh well, it had to be done. But he did miss Oliver's antics and … that white fedora.

"You're full of it," said Adam. "You're too much like your mother."

Jimmy scraped his chair back. "I'm out of here. I'll bring *The Divine Comedy* next time I come. You can read about the Inferno—a place I hope you'll burn in."

"I was weaned on that book. Doesn't scare me a bit."

Jimmy gave him the finger and turned his back.

"Hey, sorry, man. Don't go yet, please. I thought you had photos of my family to show me?"

Please. Thanks. Sorry.

All in one day?

Fayina Volinoff's bloody medication!

Adam drummed the table while Drew shuffled the papers Randy Wade had drafted. Since his transfer to this prison, Drew's visits had gotten more frequent. Seemed like all he did was sign papers.

As he initialed the documents, his thoughts flashed back to the events that had led him to this place. Except for Gillian's cruelty, he would have gotten off on circumstantial evidence—he was certain of that. He wanted to strangle that woman, and he would someday, but right now he still needed her. He put the pen down. "Drew, my old staff is withering away, and so is my business. I want to keep Gallery One going. Negotiate with Gillian to take over till I get out. Just keep her away from the Kingsley paintings."

"I've already protected those from anyone but you." Drew grunted. "Are you sure you want Gillian to take over the shop? And, why would she even bother?"

"I'm not asking."

"Okay, okay."

"One more thing. Gillian must sever ties with Nalin Crawford."

Four days later, Drew faced him again. "I don't get it. Gillian said yes."

"Trust me—I had a chess move." Adam grinned. *And, he always would.*

"Here's the deal. Gillian agreed to hire a manager, staff the gallery, and handle the serious clients and artists. We had to give her unlimited signing authority and sixty percent of the profits. She's already put up a *New Management* sign to divert attention from you. The contract nullifies when you're released."

"Perfect."

He noticed Drew's hands trembling. "Something else bugging you?"

"Gillian said no to cutting out Nalin Crawford. Said the artist is too relevant to let go and that you'd understand."

Adam slammed his fist on the table.

That she-devil was up to something. Should have broken her spine in that hotel room when he had the chance.

Drew gathered his belongings and shrank away. "I have to go, Adam."

"Hey, man, it's not you. Hard to run a business when you're locked up. You and I are cool, Drew."

"Yeah, yeah. Of course. Take care of yourself. I'll see you soon."

Adam rattled the bars for the guard. "Tell Volinoff I want something stronger."

Good thing she'd agreed to up his dose. Even though business had doubled, Drew's subsequent visits gave rise to new irritants. Nalin's name popped up on every inventory and sales list. Gillian was making that traitor rich and famous. He bristled. It was the same with Dorian Conte. Under Adam's watchful eyes, Dorian had played by the rules and signed his own name to reproductions, but under Gillian?

Enough. He had to put a stop to this.

He phoned Drew. "Get an investigator on this. I don't want my name tainted."

The line went dead.

"Are you there?"

"Uh... yeah." Was Drew stifling a laugh? Adam could just imagine Drew's eyes and cheeks puffing out like a bullfrog.

He balled his fist. "It may sound weird to you, given where I am, but when it comes to the art business," said Adam, "I consider it sacred. 'Do no harm,' like a doctor's Hippocratic Oath. Not much I trust in this world, but art never lets you down."

Drew cleared his throat.

"You think I'm a murdering criminal, don't you?" Adam gritted his teeth. "Whatever I did to those goddamn people, they deserved it."

Uh oh. He held his breath.

"Those people," said Drew, "don't you mean her? Gladys? Who else did you kill?"

"Nobody. It just came out wrong. It's the meds." In fact, they were making his head mushy and his tongue loose. He'd begun to sound like Oliver.

"Anyway, back to business. You know the Kingsley name and collection are attached to major galleries around the world. Can't have Gillian messing that up."

"You're a Mansfield. There'd be no association with the Kingsley name. What's going on with you?"

Adam ignored the question and hung up. If his lawyer was trying to unlock his secrets, he'd never do it. And if Heather Holden did her job, he'd be out of this prison soon. Then he'd reinvent himself with the Kingsley name and disappear. No one would recognize him as a felon, at least not in the art circles he planned to hob-nob in. The only enemy of that crowd was boredom. Scandal, infamy, and salacious behaviour were acceptable indulgences to feed their passions.

That fortune was his. Adam deserved it after what his father and Gladys put him through. And he'd still be young enough to enjoy it with …? Hmm.

Chapter 31

Adam finished the last page of *Ulysses*, took a satisfying breath, and closed the book. He'd been up for hours. The grumblings in his stomach tolled the dawn.

Hope that good-for-nothing Jimmy shows up for a dose of revenge this week or I'll be reduced to reading comics.

Funny how he was at Jimmy's mercy, helping him survive in this sewer. Adam's GQ looks had made him a target. He had to keep one eye over his shoulder at all times. Good thing he had a private cell. Nice and peaceful. No one else snoring or getting up in the middle of the night. After proving his intellect to the prison population, he'd kept the vultures at bay by offering letter-writing and legal services in return for, well, just about anything, including protection. Yup. Even caged up, he could pull everyone's strings.

He heard the jingle of keys. "Bacon's ready. Come and get it."

About time.

From down the hall, someone yelled, "Hey, two trays for the Mansfield parlour. He has a visitor."

The guard approached and shoved a thin, middle-aged man to the side as he unlocked Adam's gate. "New roomie for you. Name's Denis Horvat."

"What do you mean, 'roomie'?" Adam bellowed. "No way. You've made a mistake. Take him down the hall. Those guys *like* company."

"This one's hand-picked for *you* by the warden. In you go, Horvat."

The beanpole, six foot six or more, shuffled in with shoulders stooped and head bent.

As if shrinking would hide him.

After removing the cuffs, the newbie lifted his chin, gave him a grin, and strolled over to his locker.

Creepy.

"Now play nice, you two."

Nothing Adam could do. At least the inmate looked clean. Crew-cut, no beard, no visible tattoos. Nerdy, as if he'd come from some military or Christian academy. But in prison, clean or not, no one could be trusted. Best to set this guy straight.

"Keep to your own side, man." Adam bit into a piece of bacon. "And I expect spotless from you, especially when it comes to those." He cocked both gun fingers and aimed them at the toilet and sink.

The man opened his palms. "Germ-phobic. No one cleaner than me."

"Hmm—we'll see."

Adam watched the giant arrange his belongings and stretch out on his cot, his feet extending over the end.

"Warden's going to hear about this. It's inhumane. Hope the food's better than this bed."

Adam laughed. "Sure. It's Michelin."

They both ate quietly for a moment, then set their plates down.

"So, what are you in for, Horvat? Who'd you kill?"

"Why, you scared of me?"

Adam puffed out his chest. "For the record, would I be in here if I was scared of anyone?"

Word travelled fast in this place. He'd find out soon enough.

"I've been hearing about overcrowding," continued Adam. "Never expected changes would start in this cell, though. Any idea why the warden stuck you in with me?"

"Don't know, don't care." His roommate reached for his eye glasses and lifted a book off his shelf. "Boss man let me bring in my own book. Seems prison's becoming a place of higher learning."

Adam tilted his head to peek at the title. *A Portrait of an Artist as a Young Man.* "Joyce fan, huh? Me too. Just finished *Ulysses*."

What do you know? A bookworm. Finally, someone interesting around here.

Maybe giving inmates something in common was the warden's new strategy. Even better if this guy played chess. The litmus test for intelligence.

Adam waited for his roommate to get up to relieve himself. "Hey man. Wouldn't mind taking a look at that book."

"Sure. You've got about ten seconds."

He flipped through the pages. "Cool. I have an art history and fine arts degree and an MBA. What about you?"

"Harvard grad."

"Impressive."

His cellmate gave him a half-smile. "Hard to believe, isn't it? Here we are. Both so damn educated and both behind bars."

"I don't plan to be here forever," Adam said with a wink. "I own an art gallery. Someone's taking care of business till I get out."

"*Touché.* Impressive."

Adam threw the book back.

Was this how true friendship started?

Three months had flown by, reading and discussing big ideas. Professor Kingsley would have been proud. Life in this cesspit wasn't half-bad. Nightly debates had gotten more and more intriguing. Adam couldn't wait to discuss the consequences of actions according to Kant's theories. Adam's life position had always been 'get it done' and 'screw morality'. Was Horvat's philosophy of life the same? Had to be—they were both in Max.

"Mail," yelled the guard.

Just as he jumped up and stepped forward, Denis lunged in front of him, knocking Adam back onto his bunk.

The guard grabbed his baton. "Hey, cut it out. Want me to use this?"

237

"Whoops. My mistake," said Denis. "A little too anxious, I guess." He raised his hands in apology. "Waiting for a letter."

"Yeah, yeah. No problem," said Adam.

"Good. Wouldn't want to write this up," threatened the guard.

Adam shot the guard an anemic smile. If there was ever a time to play by the rules, it was now and in this place. A stain on his record would hamper the appeal Heather was working on.

But ... why had his roommate suddenly become a bully? Sure, the guy had to have a violent streak to land him here, but there'd been no sign of it in three months. Denis Horvat had been a gentleman—refreshing after rubbing elbows with scumbags for the past year and a half. Maybe the guy was schizophrenic and simply forgot to take his meds.

Sure, that was it. Everyone was entitled to a bad mood.

Jesus. Was he making excuses for Denis or ... was he, *Adam Mansfield*, getting soft in the head?

Adam backed off and watched his roommate approach the bars, take the letter, and stuff it into his shirt pocket.

Weird. If it was so important, why hadn't he torn it open?

To hell with Horvat. The only thing he needed was to keep things under control in this cell.

The guard fanned the air with another envelope. "Mansfield, you want your letter or not? Smells like ... love."

Beanpole joined the guard's laughter.

Jerks.

Adam gritted his teeth and stepped up to the slot as the guard flung the letter through.

He caught it and strode back to his bunk. The scent wafted through the open flap. Probably one of Jimmy's pranks. He sighed. How ironic that Jimmy was the only person who ever wrote—even if it was to put the screws to him. With no return address or other markings on it, he couldn't really be certain of its origin.

He pulled out the note paper and unfolded it. Blank! Just an embossed border of tiny clusters of lilacs that had been sprayed with perfume.

Could it be Red? Did she miss him?

Denis chuckled as he swung his legs onto the bed and leaned back.

He gave his cellmate the finger, but the bastard continued to stare at him with a snide grin.

As adrenaline surged through Adam, his old urges surfaced. He wanted nothing more than to retaliate.

Old Volinoff's training flashed before him.

Close your eyes and breathe. Let the moment pass.

Chapter 32

Adam thrashed in his bed after lights out. A hand slammed across his mouth before he heard a whisper. "Got a message for you in my letter."

Was he dreaming?

"Pretty card ... same as yours. Want to smell it?" A subtle lilac scent drifted up his nose.

Adam opened his eyes as an arm swung across his chest.

"Lady didn't give her name," continued Denis in the faintest of voices. "Said to tell you it's over. She even sent a clipping from a trade periodical. It says, 'Gallery One's *Heat of the Night*, an early work by Dorian Conte, sold for eight hundred thousand dollars at auction last week'."

What? The good luck charm hanging in his gallery all these years? Sold?

Adam's heart twitched with anger and something he hadn't felt since childhood—*fear*. Gillian! How could Denis Horvat be linked to that bitch? Adam always knew that woman lived on the edge of danger. That's what had thrilled him about her, and she probably felt the same about him. He'd played her game well, but this move put her in a league of her own.

Using her money, power, and connections to set up a sting in his prison cell? With Denis Horvat—his friend? The guy had played him.

For the first time in his life, Adam knew what it felt like to be the target.

Arms, elbows, and knees pinned him down. "Got another message for you," purred Denis. Adam attempted to scream "Get off" and "Guard", but the words stuck in his throat as his mouth was stuffed with something fuzzy. A wool sock? Powerless, Adam's chest heaved. He inhaled through his nose, his eyes bulging as he stared into the darkness. A hand pinched his nostrils.

Air, air ... he needed air.

A slight reprieve as the sock was pulled out. He sucked in a breath. Something trickled down his throat.

No!

Denis pressed down on him like a block of cement. The room began to swim. Adam tried to buck, but nothing happened. He couldn't move—not his jaw, not a toe, not a finger. His tongue felt too big and too heavy for his mouth. He lay paralyzed like a tranquilized dog.

"I personally think this is a waste of a brilliant mind, but it's just a job," said Denis, his tone sounding falsely sympathetic. "And, although you're an elitist prig, I like you."

Denis Horvat, a cold-blooded killer? Of course, why else were they both here? Adam should never have let his guard down.

His heart fluttered. Tightness and sharp pain shot through his body.

Had his father felt the same way as he looked up at Adam with those pleading hazel eyes?

Adam's mind wandered back ... way back, before all those traitors ... Bill, Claire, Heather, Fayina, Nalin, Gillian, Jimmy, Marla, Oliver, Gladys, Donald ...

Wait! There she was! Momma—the red journal in her hand.

He began running.

"It's for you, my darling boy."

A peaceful stillness began to spread as emptiness filled the backs of his eyes.

A breath in Adam's ear sent ripples through him. "I know you can hear me. It'll all be over soon. I know heart attacks run in your family. I'll tell them that in the morning."

Soft flannel Cookie Monster pajamas warmed Adam's skin. It was good to be eight again. He stretched out his arms as his little legs scrambled to meet his mother.

Nothing else mattered.

Chapter 33

The scent of lilacs in full bloom at Clarence Creek permeated the air. Marla and the girls picked a few. "Your dad would have loved them," she said before linking arms with Sarah and Susan. How brave. They'd understood their dad's childhood trauma had caused a mess of his life. For all the good reasons, they'd never forget him.

The intimate gathering ... her parents, the Lams, and Drew Durban. Even Jimmy was there. "To make sure Adam was really six feet under," he'd said. Somehow, she sensed forgiveness in the voice of this sandy-haired man who'd stolen her heart as a young girl. She was so glad he'd found a new life, one he deserved.

Marla stared at the inscription on the headstone. Tears clouded her eyes.

Adam Mansfield
Artist and Scholar
Beloved son of Isabel Mansfield

Yes, those were the sentiments she wanted to remember.

Beloved Father of Sarah and Susan

That was also true.

For just a moment, Marla gave into warm, familiar thoughts and feelings. Adam had captured her heart after Jimmy. Theatre, music, romance. She could almost hear his voice as he recited from their favourite passages. 'Poetry in Motion'. Such beautiful memories to hold onto, and along with them, she had the comfort of her girls, precious Pepper, and her old piano.

The crunch of wheels broke the quiet of her heart. Marla glanced up to see a black, stretch limo meandering along the cemetery path. It came to a stop at a respectable distance. The backseat window had been lowered, but the faces of two figures, veiled in shadow, remained hidden.

Who else would be interested in Adam's burial? Most people connected to him were already present.

Her mother stared at the limo, took a few steps forward, and nodded twice.

A chill swept through her. "Mom?" she said. "Who ...?"

"They're in your past, Marla."

Lifting the lilacs to her nose, Marla drew in their scent and simply walked away.

Printed in the USA
CPSIA information can be obtained
at www.ICGtesting.com
LVHW041630040424
776439LV00004B/538